Hermann Broch was born in Vienna in 1886. He managed his father's textile firm and was almost forty before he studied philosophy and mathematics at Vienna University. He published the three parts of *The Sleepwalkers* trilogy (*The Romantic*, *The Anarchist* and *The Realist*) in 1931–2, and *The Unknown Quantity* in 1933. He was briefly imprisoned by the Nazis when they invaded Austria in 1938, but the help of friends such as James Joyce and Willa and Edwin Muir led to his emigration to America that year, where he remained until his death in 1951. *The Death of Virgil* was published to great acclaim in 1945, and *The Guiltless* in 1950. His last work, *The Spell*, an incomplete fragment, was published posthumously in 1953.

During his lifetime Broch's work brought him great praise as an innovative visionary writer, comparable to Joyce, Thomas Mann and Robert Musil. He was admired by Aldous Huxley, who wrote of *The Sleepwalkers*, 'We are haunted by the strange and disquieting feeling that we are at the very limits of the expressible ... Broch performs with an impeccable virtuosity.'

The Sleepwalkers is a trilogy whose component novels can be read completely independently of one another.

Each novel is set in a different year – *The Romantic* in 1888, *The Anarchist* in 1903 and *The Realist* in 1918.

HERMANN BROCH

The Anarchist

Translated by Willa and Edwin Muir

With a Biographical Note by John White

PENGUIN BOOKS

PENGUIN BOOKS

Published by the Penguin Group
Penguin Books Ltd, 27 Wrights Lane, London w8 5TZ, England
Penguin Putnam Inc., 375 Hudson Street, New York, New York 10014, USA
Penguin Books Australia Ltd, Ringwood, Victoria, Australia
Penguin Books Canada Ltd, 10 Alcorn Avenue, Toronto, Ontario, Canada M4V 3B2
Penguin Books (NZ) Ltd, Private Bag 102902, NSMC, Auckland, New Zealand

Penguin Books Ltd, Registered Offices: Harmondsworth, Middlesex, England

First published in German as *1903. Esch oder die Anarchie* 1931
This translation first published in the USA by Little, Brown, and Company, 1932

Published in Penguin Classics 2000
1 3 5 7 9 10 8 6 4 2

Copyright © The Estate of Hermann Broch
Biographical note copyright © John White 2000

Translation by Willa and Edwin Muir used by permission of Alfred A. Knopf, Inc.
All rights reserved

The moral right of the author of the biographical note
has been asserted

Printed in England by Clays Ltd, St Ives plc

Except in the United States of America, this book is sold subject
to the condition that it shall not, by way of trade or otherwise, be lent,
re-sold, hired out, or otherwise circulated without the publisher's
prior consent in any form of binding or cover other than that in
which it is published and without a similar condition including this
condition being imposed on the subsequent purchaser

Contents

The Anarchist 1

Biographical Note by John White 183

The Anarchist (1903)

I

THE 2nd of March 1903 was a bad day for August Esch, who was thirty years old and a clerk; he had had a row with his chief and found himself dismissed before he had time to think of giving notice. He was irritated, therefore, but less by the fact of his dismissal than by his own lack of resourcefulness. There were so many things that he could have flung in the man's face: a man who didn't know what was happening under his very nose, a man who believed the insinuations of a fellow like Nentwig and had no idea that the said Nentwig was pocketing commissions right and left—unless, indeed, he was shutting his eyes deliberately because Nentwig knew something shady about him. And what a fool Esch had been to let the pair of them catch him out like that: they had fallen foul of him over an alleged mistake in the books that wasn't a mistake at all, now that he came to think of it. But they had bullied him so insolently that it had simply turned into a shouting match, in the middle of which he suddenly found himself dismissed. At the time, of course, he hadn't been able to think of anything but guttersnipe abuse, whereas now he knew exactly how he could have scored. " Sir," yes, " Sir," he should have said, drawing himself up to his full height, and Esch now said " Sir " to himself in a sarcastic voice, " have you the slightest idea of the state your business is in . . . ? " yes, that's what he should have said, but now it was too late, and although he had gone and got drunk and slept with a girl he hadn't got rid of his irritation, and Esch swore to himself as he walked along beside the Rhine towards the town.

He heard steps behind him and, turning, caught sight of Martin, who was swinging along between his crutches with the foot of his game leg braced against one of them. If that wasn't the last straw! Esch would gladly have hurried on, at the risk of getting a wallop over the head from one of the crutches—serve him right too if he did get one over the head—but he felt it would be a low-down trick to play on a cripple, and so he stood waiting. Besides, he would have to look round for another job, and Martin, who knew everybody, might have heard of something. The cripple hobbled up, let his crooked leg swing free, and said bluntly: " Got the sack? " So he had heard of it already? Esch replied with bitterness: " Got the sack." " Have you any money left? " Esch shrugged his shoulders: " Enough for a day or two." Martin reflected: " I know of a job that might suit you." " No, you won't get me into your union." " I know, I know; you're too high and mighty for that. . . . Well, you'll join some day. Where shall we go? " Esch was going nowhere in particular, so they proceeded to Mother Hentjen's. In the Kastellgasse Martin stopped: " Have they given you a decent reference? " " I'll have to call for it to-day." " The Central Rhine people in Mannheim need a shipping clerk, or something in that line . . . if you don't mind leaving Cologne," and they went in. It was a fairly large, dingy room that had been a resort of the Rhine sailors probably for hundreds of years; though except for the vaulted roof, blackened with smoke, no sign now indicated its antiquity. The walls behind the tables were wainscoted in brown wood half-way up, to which was fixed a long bench that ran round the room. Upon the mantelpiece was an array of Munich quart-jugs, among which stood an Eiffel Tower in bronze. It was embellished with a red-and-black-and-white flag, and when one looked more closely the words " Table reserved " could be deciphered on it in faded gold-lettering. Between the two windows stood an orchestrion with its folding-doors open, showing its internal works and the roll of music. Actually the doors should have remained closed, and anyone who wished to enjoy the music should have inserted a coin in the slot. But Mother Hentjen did nothing shabbily, and so the customer had merely to thrust his hand into the machinery and pull the lever; all Mother Hentjen's customers knew how to work the apparatus. Facing the orchestrion the whole of the shorter back wall was taken up by the buffet, and behind the buffet was a huge mirror flanked on either side by two glass cabinets containing brightly hued liqueur bottles. When in the evening Mother Hentjen took her post behind the buffet, she had a habit of turning round to the mirror every now and then to pat her blond coiffure, which was perched on her round, heavy skull like a hard little sugar-loaf. On the counter itself stood rows of large wine and Schnapps bottles, for the gay liqueur bottles in the cabinet were seldom called for. And finally, between the buffet and the glass cabinet, a zinc washing-basin with a tap was discreetly let into the wall.

The room was unheated, and its coldness stank. The two men chafed their hands, and while Esch sat down dully on a bench Martin put his hand into the works of the orchestrion, which blared out *The March of the Gladiators* into the cold atmosphere of the room. In spite of the din they could presently hear a wooden stair creaking under someone's footsteps, and the swing door beside the buffet was flung open by Frau Hentjen. She was still in her morning working-garb, an ample blue-cotton apron was tied over her dress, and she had not yet donned her evening corset, so that her breasts lay like two sacks in her broad-checked dimity blouse. Her hair, however, was still as stiff and correct as ever, crowning like a sugar-loaf her pale, expressionless face, which gave no indication of her age. But everybody knew that Frau Gertrud Hentjen had thirty-six years to her credit, and that for a long, long time—they had reckoned a little while ago that it must certainly be fourteen years—she had been the relict of Herr Hentjen, whose photograph, yellow with age, gazed out over the Eiffel Tower between the restaurant licence and a moonlit landscape, all three in fine black frames with gold scroll-work. And although with his little goat's beard Herr Hentjen looked like a snippet of a tailor, his widow had remained faithful to him; at least nobody could say anything against her, and whenever anyone dared to approach her with an honourable proposal she would remark with disdain: " Yes, the business would suit him to a T, no doubt. No, I'd rather carry on alone, thank you."

" Morning, Herr Geyring. Morning, Herr Esch," she said. " You're early birds to-day." " We've been long enough on our legs, though, Mother Hentjen," replied Martin, " if one works one must eat," and he ordered wine and bread and cheese; Esch, whose mouth and stomach were still wry with the wine he had drunk yesterday, took Schnapps. Frau Hentjen sat down with the men and asked after their news. Esch was monosyllabic, and although he was not in the least ashamed of his dismissal, it annoyed him that Geyring should publish the fact so openly. " Yes, another victim of capitalism," the trade-union organizer concluded, " but now I must get to work again; of course the Duke here can spread himself at his ease now." He paid and insisted on settling for Esch's Schnapps at the same time—" One must support the unemployed "—grasped his crutches, which he had propped beside him, braced his left foot against the wood, and swung himself out through the door between his two supports with a great clatter.

After he had gone the two of them remained silent for a little; then

Esch jerked his chin towards the door: "An anarchist," he said. Frau Hentjen shrugged her plump shoulders: "And what if he is? He's a decent man." "He's a decent man, right enough," Esch corroborated, and Frau Hentjen went on: "but they'll lay him by the heels again sooner or later: he's done time for six months already . . ." then: "Well, it's all in his day's work." Once more they became silent. Esch was wondering whether Martin had been a cripple since his childhood; misbegotten, he thought to himself, and said: "He would like to land me among his socialist friends. But I'm not having any." "Why not?" asked Frau Hentjen without interest. "It doesn't suit my plans. I want to get to the top of the tree; law and order are necessary if you want to get to the top." Frau Hentjen could not but agree with that: "Yes, that's true, you must have law and order. But now I must go to the kitchen. Will you be having dinner with us to-day, Herr Esch?" Esch might as well dine here as anywhere else, and after all why should he wander about in the icy wind? "Strange that the snow hasn't come yet," he said, "the dust fairly blinds you." "Yes, it's dismal outside," said Frau Hentjen. "Then you'll just stay here?" She disappeared into the kitchen, the swing door vibrated for a little longer, and Esch dully followed its vibrations until it finally came to rest. Then he tried to sleep. But now the coldness of the room began to strike into him; he walked up and down with a heavy and rather unsteady tread and took up the newspaper that lay on the buffet; but he could not turn the pages with his stiff fingers; his eyes too were painful. So he resolved to seek out the warm kitchen; with the newspaper in his hand he walked in. "I suppose you've come to have a sniff at the saucepans?" said Frau Hentjen, suddenly remembering that it was cold in the eating-room, and as it was her custom not to put on a fire there until the afternoon she suffered him to bear her company. Esch watched her bustling about the hearth and had a longing to seize her beneath the breasts, but her reputation for inaccessibility checked his desire at once. When the kitchen-maid who helped Frau Hentjen with her work went out he said: "I can't understand your liking to live alone." "Aha!" she replied, "you're beginning that song too, are you?" "No," said Esch, "it isn't that. I was just wondering." Frau Hentjen's face had taken on a strangely frozen expression; it was as though she were disgusted at some thought, for she shook herself so violently that her breasts quivered, and then went about her work with the bored and empty face with which she always confronted her customers. Esch, sitting at the window, read his newspaper and afterwards looked out into the yard, where the wind was raising little cyclones of dust.

Later the two girls who acted as waitresses in the evening arrived, unwashed and unslept. Frau Hentjen, the two waitresses and the little kitchenmaid and Esch took their places round the kitchen table, stuck out their elbows, hunched themselves over their plates, and ate their dinner.

Esch had drawn up his application for the Mannheim post; he now needed only the reference to enclose with it. Actually he was glad that things had turned out as they had. It wasn't good for a man to vegetate all the time in one place. He felt he must get out of Cologne, and the farther the better. A fellow must keep his eyes open; as a matter of fact he had always done that.

In the afternoon he went to the office of Stemberg & Company, wholesale wine merchants, to get his reference. Nentwig kept him waiting at the counter, and sat at his desk, fat and slouching, totting up columns. Esch tapped impatiently with his strong finger-nails on the counter. Nentwig got up: "Patience, patience, Herr Esch," and he stepped to the barrier and said condescendingly: "Oh, about your reference?—that can't be so very urgent. Well? Date of birth? Date of employment here?" With his head averted Esch supplied this information and Nentwig took it down. Then Nentwig dictated to the stenographer and brought the reference. Esch read it through. "That isn't a reference," he said, handing the paper back. "Oh! Then what is it?" "You must certify to my ability as a book-keeper." "You—a book-keeper! You've shown us what you can do in that line." Now the moment of reckoning had come: "It's a very special kind of book-keeper that's needed for the inventories you draw up, I happen to know." Nentwig was taken aback: "What do you mean?" "I mean what I say." Nentwig changed his tune, became friendly: "You only harm yourself with your obstreperousness; here you had a good post, and you had to get into a row with the chief!" Esch tasted victory and began to roll it on his tongue: "I mean to have a talk with the chief later." "For all I care you can say what you like to the chief," Nentwig countered. "Well, what do you want me to put in your reference?" Esch decreed that he should be described as "conscientious, reliable and thoroughly versed in all matters relating to book-keeping." Nentwig wanted to be rid of him. "It isn't true, of course, but as far as I'm concerned——" He turned again to the stenographer to dictate the new version. Esch grew red in the face: "Oh, so it isn't true? ... then please add: 'We heartily recommend him to any employer who may be in need of his services.' Have you got that?" Nentwig bowed elaborately: "Delighted, I'm sure, Herr Esch." Esch read the new copy through and was appeased. "The chief's signature," he commanded. But this was too much for Nentwig, who shouted: "So mine isn't good enough for you?" "If the firm authorizes you I'll let that pass," was Esch's large and magnanimous reply, and Nentwig signed.

Esch stepped out into the street and made for the nearest pillar-box. He whistled to himself; he felt rehabilitated. He had his reference, good; it was in the envelope with his application to the Central Rhine Company. The fact that Nentwig had given in showed that he had a bad conscience. So the inventories were faked then, and the man should be handed over to the police. Yes, it was simply one's duty as a citizen to give him in charge straight away. The letter dropped into the post-box with a soft, muffled thud, and Esch, his fingers still in the aperture, considered whether he should go at once to the police headquarters. He wandered on irresolutely. It had been a mistake to send off the reference, he should have given it back to Nentwig; to force a reference out of a man and then give him in charge wasn't decent. But now it was done, and besides, without a reference he had little chance of getting a post with the Central Rhine Shipping Company—there would be absolutely nothing left for him but to go back to his old job in Stemberg's again. And he saw a vision of the chief discovering the fraud, and Nentwig languishing in prison. Yes, but what if the chief himself was involved in the swindle? Then of course the public interrogation would bring the whole concern toppling down. And then there would be another bankruptcy, but no post for a book-keeper. And in the newspapers people would read: "Revenge of a dismissed clerk." And finally he would be suspected of collusion. And then he would be left without a reference and without a job, for nobody would take him on. Esch congratulated himself on the shrewdness with which he drew all the consequences, but he was furious. "A fine bloody firm!" he swore under his breath. He stood in the Ring in front of the Opera House, cursing and swearing into the cold wind which blew the dust into his eyes, and could not come to any decision, but finally resolved to postpone the affair; if he didn't get the post with the Central Rhine there would still be time left to act the part of Nemesis. He went through the darkening evening, his hands buried in the pockets of his shabby overcoat, actually went, indeed, as a matter of form, as far as the police headquarters. There he stood looking at the policemen on guard, and when a police wagon drove up he waited until all the prisoners had got out, and felt disappointed when the policeman finally slammed to the door without Nentwig's having put in an appearance. He remained standing for a few moments, then he turned resolutely and made for the Alt Markt. The two faint vertical lines on his cheeks had deepened. " Wine faker," he muttered in a fury, " vinegar tout." And morose and disillusioned over his poisoned victory, he ended the day by getting drunk again and sleeping with another girl.

In her brown-silk dress, which she was accustomed usually to don only in the evening, Frau Hentjen had been spending the afternoon with a woman friend, and now, as always on her return, she was put into a bad temper by the sight of the house and the restaurant in which for so long she had been compelled to pass her life. Certainly the business allowed her to lay by a little now and then, and when she was praised and flattered by her women friends for her capability she experienced a faintly pleasant sensation which made up for a good deal. But why wasn't she the owner of a linen-draper's shop, or a ladies' hairdressing saloon, instead of having to deal every evening with a pack of drunken louts? If her corset had not prevented her she would have shaken herself with loathing when she caught sight of her restaurant; so intensely did she hate the men who frequented it, these men that she had to serve. Though perhaps she hated still more the women who were always such fools as to run after them. Not a single one of her women friends belonged to the kind that took up with men, that trafficked with these creatures and like animals lusted for their embraces. Yesterday she had caught the kitchenmaid in the yard with a young lad, and the hand which had dealt the buffet still tingled pleasantly; she felt she would like to have it out with the girl again. No, women were probably still worse than men. She could put up only with her waitresses and all the other prostitutes who despised men even though they had to go to bed with them; she liked to talk to these women, she encouraged them to tell her their stories in detail, and comforted and pampered them to indemnify them for their sufferings. And so a post in Mother Hentjen's restaurant was highly prized, and her girls looked upon it as well worth the best they could give in return and did all they could to retain it. And Mother Hentjen was delighted with such devotion and love.

Her best room was up on the first floor; really too big, with its three windows on the narrow street it took up the full breadth of the house above the restaurant; in the back wall, corresponding to the buffet downstairs, there was an alcove shut off by a light curtain which was always drawn. If one drew aside the curtain and let one's eyes get used to the darkness, one could make out the twin marriage-beds. But Frau Hentjen never used this room, and nobody knew whether it had ever been used. For a room of such a size was difficult to heat except at a considerable cost, and so Frau Hentjen could not be blamed for choosing the smaller room above the kitchen as her bed- and sitting-room, employing the chill and gloomy parlour only for storing food that might go bad. Also the walnuts which she was accustomed to buy in autumn were stored here and lay strewn in heaps about the floor, upon which two broad green strips of linoleum were laid crosswise.

Still feeling angry, Frau Hentjen went up to the parlour to fetch sausage for her customers' suppers, and as anger makes one careless she stumbled into some of the nuts, which rolled before her feet with an exasperatingly loud clatter. It exasperated her still more when one cracked beneath her foot, and while she picked up the nut so that it might not be altogether wasted, and carefully detached the kernel from the splintered pieces of shell, and stuck the white fragments with the bitter pale-brown skin into her mouth, she kept meanwhile screaming for the kitchenmaid; at last the brazen trollop heard her, came stumbling up the stairs, and was received with a torrent of incoherent abuse: of course a girl that flirted with half-grown louts would be stealing nuts too—the nuts had been stored beside the window and now they were just inside the door, and nuts didn't walk across a floor of their own accord—and Frau Hentjen was preparing to raise her fist, and the girl had ducked and put up her arm, when a piece of shell caught in her mistress's teeth, who contented herself with spitting it out contemptuously; then, followed by the sobbing maid, she descended to the kitchen.

When she entered the restaurant, where already a thick cloud of tobacco smoke was hanging, she was overcome again, as almost every evening, by that apprehensive torpor which was so incomprehensible to her and yet so difficult to overcome. She went up to the mirror and mechanically patted the blond sugar-loaf on her head and pulled her dress straight, and only when she had assured herself that her appearance was satisfactory did her composure return. Now she looked round and saw the familiar faces among her customers, and although there was more profit on the drinks than on the food, she prized the eaters among her customers above the drinkers, and she stepped out from behind the buffet and went from table to table asking whether the food was to their liking. And she summoned the waitress almost with elation when a customer demanded a second helping. Yes, Mother Hentjen's cooking had no need to fear examination.

Geyring was already there; his crutches were leaning beside him; he had cut the meat on his plate into small pieces and now ate mechanically while in his left hand he held one of his Socialist papers, a whole bundle of which were always sticking out of his pocket. Frau Hentjen liked him, partly because, being a cripple, he did not count as a man, partly because it was not to shout and drink and make up to the waitresses that he came, but simply because his post demanded that he should keep in touch with the sailors and dock workers; but above all she liked him because evening after evening he had his supper at her restaurant and praised up her food. She sat down at his table. " Has Esch been here yet? " asked Geyring. " He's got the job with the Central Rhine, starts work on Monday." " And it's you that got it for him, I'm sure, Herr Geyring," said Frau Hentjen. " No, Mother Hentjen, we haven't got the length yet of filling posts through the union . . . no, not by a long way . . . well, that'll come too in time. But I put Esch on the track of it. Why shouldn't one help a nice lad, even if he isn't one of ourselves? " Mother Hentjen showed little sympathy with this sentiment: " You just eat that up, Herr Geyring, and you'll have an extra titbit from myself as well," and she went over to the buffet and brought on a plate a moderate-sized slice of sausage which she had garnished with a sprig of parsley. Geyring's wrinkled face of a boy of fourteen smiled at her in gratitude, showing a mouthful of bad teeth, and he patted her white, plump hand, which she immediately drew back with a slight return of her frozen manner.

Later Esch arrived. Geyring looked up from his paper and said: " Congratulations, August." " Thanks," said Esch. " So you know already?—there was no difficulty, a reply by return engaging me. Well, I must thank you for putting me on to it." But his face beneath the short, dark, cropped hair had the wooden empty look of a disappointed man. " A pleasure," said Martin, then he shouted over to the buffet: " Here's our new paymaster." " Good luck, Herr Esch," replied Frau Hentjen dryly, yet she came forward after all and gave him her hand. Esch, who wished to show that all the credit was not due to Martin, pulled his reference out of his breast-pocket: " It wouldn't have gone so smoothly, I can tell you, if I hadn't made Stemberg's give me such a good reference." He heavily emphasized the " made," and then added: " A measly firm." Frau Hentjen read the reference absently: " A splendid reference." Geyring too read it and nodded: " Yes, the Central Rhine must be glad they've got hold of such a first-class fellow. . . . I'll really have to get the Chairman, Bertrand, to fork out a commission for my services."

" An excellent book-keeper, excellent, what? " Esch preened himself. " Well, it's nice when anyone can have such things said about him," Frau Hentjen agreed. " You may feel very proud of yourself, Herr Esch; you've every right to: do you want anything to eat? " Of course he did, and while Frau Hentjen looked on complacently to see that he enjoyed his food, he said that now he was going farther up the Rhine he hoped to get one of the travelling jobs; that would mean going as far as Kehl and Basel. Meanwhile several of his other acquaintances had come up, the new paymaster ordered wine for them all, and Frau Hentjen withdrew. With disgust she noticed that every time Hede, the waitress, passed the table, Esch could not help fondling her, and that finally he ordered her to sit down beside him, so that they might drink to each other. But the score was a high one, and when the gentlemen broke up after midnight, taking Hede with them, Frau Hentjen pushed a mark into her hand.

Nevertheless Esch could not feel elated over his new post. It was as though he had purchased it at the cost of his soul's welfare, or at least of his decency. Now that things had gone so far and he had already drawn an advance for his travelling expenses from the Cologne branch of the Central Rhine, he was overcome anew by the doubt whether he shouldn't give Nentwig in charge. Of course in that case he would have to be present at the official inquiry, could not therefore leave the town, and would almost certainly lose his new job. For a moment he thought of solving the problem by writing an anonymous letter to the police, but he rejected this plan: one couldn't wipe out one piece of rascality by committing another. And on top of it all he was beginning to resent his own twinges of conscience; after all he wasn't a child, he didn't give a damn for the parsons and their morality; he had read all sorts of books, and when Geyring had recently begged him yet again to join the Social Democratic Party he had replied: " No, I won't have anything to do with you anarchists, but I'll go with you this far: I'll turn Freethinker." The thankless fool had replied that that didn't matter a damn to him. That was what people were like: well, Esch wouldn't give a damn either.

Finally he did the most reasonable thing: he set off for Mannheim at the appointed time. But he felt violently uprooted, he had none of his accustomed pleasure in travelling, and as a safeguard he left part of his belongings in Cologne: he even left his bicycle behind. Nevertheless his travelling allowance put him in a generous mood. And standing with his beer-glass in his hand and his ticket stuck in his hat on Mainz platform, he thought of the people whom he had left, felt he wanted to show them a kindness, and, a newspaper man happening to push his barrow past at that moment, he bought two picture postcards. Martin in particular deserved a line from him; yet one did not send picture postcards to a man. So first he scribbled one to Hede: the second was destined for Frau Hentjen. Then he reflected that it might seem insulting to Frau Hentjen, who was a proud woman, to receive a postcard by the same post as one of her employees, and as he was in a reckless mood he tore up the first one and posted only the one to Frau Hentjen, containing his warmest greetings to her and all his kind friends and acquaintances and Fräulein Hede and Fräulein Thusnelda from the beautiful town of Mainz. After that he felt again a little lonely, drank a second glass of beer, and let the train carry him on to Mannheim.

He had been instructed to report to the head office. The Central Rhine Shipping Company Limited occupied a building of its own not far from the Mühlau Dock, a massive stone edifice with pillars in front of the door. The street in which it stood was asphalted, good for cycling; it was a new street. The heavy door of wrought-iron and glass—it would certainly swing smoothly and noiselessly on its hinges—stood ajar, and Esch entered. The marble vestibule pleased him; over the stair hung a glass sign-plate on whose transparent surface he read the words:

"Board Room" in gold letters. He made straight for it. When his foot was on the first stair he heard a voice behind him: "Where are you going, please?" He turned round and saw a commissionaire in grey livery; silver buttons glittered on it and the cap had a strip of silver braid. It was all very elegant, but Esch felt annoyed—what business was it of this fellow's?—and he said curtly: "I was asked to report here," and made to go on. The other did not weaken: "To see the Chairman?" "Why, who else, do you think?" replied Esch rudely. The stair led up to a large, gloomy waiting-room on the first floor. In the middle of it stood a great oaken table, round which were ranged a few upholstered chairs. It was certainly very splendid. Once more a man with silver buttons appeared and asked what he wanted. "The Chairman's office," said Esch. "The gentlemen are at a board meeting," said the attendant. "Is it important?" Driven to the wall, Esch had to tell his business; he drew out his papers, the letter engaging him, the receipt for his travelling allowance. "I've some references with me too," he said, and made to hand over Nentwig's reference. He was somewhat taken aback when the fellow did not even look at it: "You've no business with this up here ... ground floor, through the corridor, then the second stair—inquire down below."

Esch remained standing where he was for a moment; he grudged the attendant his triumph and asked once more: "So this isn't the place?" The attendant had already turned away indifferently: "No, this is the Chairman's waiting-room." Esch felt anger rising up in him; they made too much of a blow with their Chairman, their upholstered furnishings and their silver-buttoned attendants; Nentwig too would no doubt like to play this game; well, their fine Chairman was probably not so very different from Nentwig. But, willy-nilly, Esch had to go back the same road again. Down below the commissionaire was still at his post. Esch looked at him to see whether he was angry; but as the commissionaire merely gazed at him indifferently he said: "I want the engagement bureau," and asked to be shown the way. After taking a couple of steps he turned round, jerked his thumb towards the staircase, and asked: "What's the name of your boss up there, the Chairman?" "Herr von Bertrand," said the commissionaire, and there was almost a respectful ring in his voice. And Esch repeated, also somewhat respectfully: "Herr von Bertrand": he must have heard the name at some time or other.

In the engagement bureau he learned that he was to be employed as stores clerk in the docks. As he stepped out into the street again a carriage halted before the building. It was a cold day; the powdery snow, drifted by the wind, lay on the kerb and against the corners of the wall; the horse kept striking a hoof against the smooth asphalt. It was obviously impatient and with reason. "A carriage, no less, for the Chairman," Esch said to himself, "but as for us, we have to walk." Yet all the same he liked all this elegance, and he was glad that he belonged to it. After all, it was one in the eye for Nentwig.

In the warehouse of the Central Rhine Shipping Company the office was a glass-partitioned box at the end of a long line of sheds. His desk stood beside that of the customs officer, and at the back glowed a little iron stove. When one was bored with one's work, or felt lonely and forsaken, one could always watch the trucks being loaded and unloaded. The sailings were to begin in a few days, and on all the boats there was a great bustle. There were cranes which revolved and lowered their hooks as though to pick something or other cautiously out of the ships' entrails, and there were others which projected over the water like bridges that had been begun but never completed. Of course these sights were not new to Esch, for he had seen exactly the same in Cologne, but there he had been so used to the long row of storage sheds that he had never thought of them, and if he had forced himself to consider them, the buildings, the cranes and the landing-stages would have appeared almost meaningless, put there to serve human needs that were inexplicable. But now that he himself was concerned in these things they had grown into natural and purposive structures, and this gladdened him. While formerly he had at the most been surprised, occasionally indeed even irritated, that there should be so many export firms, and that the sheds, all alike, on the quays, should bear so many separate names, now the different businesses took on an individuality which one could recognize from the appearance of their stout or lean storekeepers, their gruff or pleasant stevedores. Also the insignia of His Majesty the Emperor of Germany's customs officers at the gates of the closed dock quarter flattered him: they made him vaguely conscious that here one lived and moved on foreign soil. It was both a constricted and a free life that one led in this sanctuary where wares could lie untaxed; it was frontier air that one breathed behind the iron gratings of the customs barriers. And even although he had no uniform to wear, and was, so to speak, only a private official, yet by virtue of his association with these customs and railway officials Esch had himself become almost an official figure, particularly as he carried in his pocket an official pass allowing him to wander at liberty through this exclusive province, and was already greeted with a welcoming salute by the watchman at the main gate. When he returned that salute he threw his cigarette away with a lordly sweep in obedience to the prohibition against smoking that was stuck up everywhere, and proceeded with long and important strides—a strict non-smoker himself, ready at any moment to come down upon any too familiar civilian for an infringement of the rule—to the office, where the storekeeper had already laid his list upon the desk. Then he drew on his grey-woollen mittens that left the finger-tips free, for without them his hands would have frozen in the musty coldness of the shed, looked over the lists, and checked the piled-up packing-cases and bales. Should a packing-case be in the wrong place he did not fail to throw the storekeeper, whose province it was to supervise the deliveries, a severe or at least an impatient look, so that he might give the docker responsible for it a proper talking-to. And when later the customs officer in his round stepped into the glass partition and said how warm it was in here, unfastening the collar of his tunic and pleasantly yawning in his chair, by that time the lists were checked and the contents copied into the books, and there was no difficulty about the rest; the two men sat at the table and lazily went over the papers. Then the customs officer, rapidly as ever, endorsed the lists with his blue pencil, took up the duplicates and locked them in his desk, and if there was nothing more to be done they proceeded together to the canteen.

Yes, Esch had made a good exchange, even if justice had suffered in the process. Still, he could not help wondering—and it was the only thing that disturbed his contentment—whether there mightn't be some way after all of duly giving Nentwig in charge; for only then would everything be in order.

Customs Inspector Balthasar Korn came from a very matter-of-fact part of Germany. He was born on the frontier-line between Bavaria and Saxony, and had received his earliest impressions from the hilly town of Hof. His mind was divided between a matter-of-fact desire for coarse amusements and a matter-of-fact parsimony, and after he had worked his way up to a sergeant's rank in active military service, he had seized the opportunity offered by a paternal Government to its faithful soldiers, and had obtained his transfer to the customs. A bachelor, he lived in Mannheim with his sister Erna, also unmarried, and as the empty best bedroom in his house was a standing offence in his eyes, he prevailed upon August Esch to give up his expensive room in the hotel and accept cheaper lodgings with him. And although he did not entirely approve of Esch, seeing that Esch as a Luxemburger could not boast of military service, yet he would not have been displeased to find in Esch a husband for his sister as well as an occupant for the spare bedroom; he was not sparing in unequivocal hints, and his sister, who was no longer young, accompanied them with bashful and tittering signs of protest. Indeed he actually went so far as to jeopardize his sister's good name, for he did not scruple to address Esch before the others in the canteen as " Herr Brother-in-Law," so that everybody must think that his friend already shared his sister's bed. Yet Korn did this not exclusively for the sake of having his joke; rather his intention was to compel Esch, partly by constantly accustoming him to the idea, partly through the pressure of public opinion, to transform into solid actuality the fictitious part which he was thus called on to play.

Esch had not been unwilling to move into Korn's house. Though he had knocked about so much he felt lonely. Perhaps the numbered streets of Mannheim were to blame, perhaps he missed the smells of Mother Hentjen's restaurant, perhaps it was that scoundrel Nentwig that still troubled him; at any rate he felt lonely and stayed on with the brother and sister, stayed on although he was quick to observe how the wind blew, stayed on although he had no intention of having anything to do with that elderly virgin; he was not impressed in the least by the great display of lingerie which Erna had gathered together in the course of the years, and which she showed him with considerable pride, nor did even the savings-bank book which she once let him see, showing a balance of over two thousand marks, attract him. But Korn's efforts to lure him into the trap were so amusing that they were worth taking some risk for; of course one had to be wary and not let oneself be caught. As for example: Korn would rarely let him pay for their drinks when they forgathered in the canteen before they went home together; and after they had heartily cursed the quality of the Mannheim beer Korn was not to be dissuaded from turning in for Munich beer at the Spatenbräu cellar. Then, if Herr Esch hastily put his hand into his pocket, Korn would again refuse to let him pay: "You'll have your revenge yet, Herr Brother-in-law." But when they were sauntering down Rheinstrasse the customs inspector would punctually halt before certain of the lighted shop-windows and clap Esch on the shoulder with his great paw: "My sister has been wanting an umbrella like that for a long time: I'll have to buy it for her birthday," or: "Every house should have a gas-iron like that," or: "If my sister had a wringer she would be happy." And when Esch made no reply to all these hints Korn would become as furiously angry as he had once been at recruits who refused to understand how to handle their rifles, and the more silent Esch was as they walked on, the more furious grew his burly companion's rage at the impudently knowing expression on Esch's face.

But it was by no means parsimony that made Esch dumb on those occasions. For although he was thrifty and fond of picking up small gains, yet the thorough and righteous book-keeping which in his soul he believed in did not allow him to accept goods without payment; service demanded counter-service, and goods must be paid for; nevertheless he thought it unnecessary to have a purchase forced on him in too great a hurry; indeed it would have seemed to him almost clumsy and inconsiderate to crown Korn's breezy demands with actual success. So for the time being he had hit upon a curious kind of revenge which allowed him to repay his obligations to Korn and at the same time show that he was in no hurry to marry; after dinner he would invite Korn out for a little evening's entertainment which took them to those beer-shops where there were barmaids, and unavoidably ended for them both in the so-called disreputable streets of the town. It sometimes cost a good deal of money to foot the bill for both of them—even if Korn could not get out of tipping his girl himself—yet the sight of Korn on the way home afterwards, walking along morosely, chewing at his black, bushy moustache, which was now limp and dejected, growling that this loose life Esch was leading him into must be put an end to: that was well worth all the expense. And besides, Korn was always in such a bad temper with his sister next morning that he went out of his way to wound her in her tenderest feelings, accusing her of never having been able to catch a man. And when thereupon she maintained hotly that she had had hosts of admirers, he would remind her contemptuously of her single estate.

One day Esch managed to wipe off his debt to a considerable extent. While he was on his way through the company's stores his vigilant eye was caught by the curiously shaped packing-cases and properties of a theatrical outfit, which were just being unloaded. A clean-shaven gentleman was standing by in great agitation, shouting that his valuable property, which represented untold wealth, was being handled as roughly as if it were firewood, and when Esch, who had been looking on gravely with the air of a connoisseur, threw a few pieces of superfluous advice to the labourers, and in this unmistakable fashion gave the gentleman to know that he was in the presence of a man of knowledge and authority, the formidable volubility of the stranger was turned upon him and they soon found themselves engaged in a friendly conversation, in the course of which the clean-shaven gentleman, raising his hat slightly, introduced himself as Herr Gernerth, the new lessee of the Thalia Theatre, who would be particularly flattered—in the meanwhile the work of unloading had been completed—if the Shipping Inspector and his esteemed family would attend the opening performance, and begged to present him with the necessary tickets at reduced prices. And when Esch agreed with alacrity, the manager put his hand in his pocket and actually wrote out three free tickets for him on the spot.

Now Esch was sitting with the Korns in the variety theatre at a table covered with a white cloth. The programme opened with a novel attraction, the moving pictures or, as they were called, the cinematograph. These pictures, however, did not meet with much applause from the audience, or indeed from the public in general at that time, not being regarded as serious and genuine entertainment, but merely as a prelude to it; nevertheless this modern art-form really held one's attention when a comedy was put on showing the comic effects of laxative pills, the critical moments being emphasized with a ruffle of drums. Korn roared with mirth and brought down the flat of his hand on the table; Fräulein Korn put her hand over her mouth and giggled, throwing stolen coquettish glances at Esch through her fingers, and Esch was as proud as though he himself were the inventor and producer of this highly successful entertainment. The smoke from their cigars ascended and melted into the cloud of tobacco smoke which very soon floated under the low roof of the hall traversed by the silvery beam of the limelight which lit up the screen. During the interval, which came after an act imitating the whistling of birds, Esch ordered three glasses of beer, though it cost considerably more here in the theatre than anywhere else, but he was relieved when it proved to be flat and stale and they decided to give no further orders, but to have a drink in the Spatenbräu after the performance. He felt once more in a generous mood, and while the prima donna was being passionate and despairing to the best of her ability he said significantly: " Ah, love, Fräulein Erna, love." But when, after the vociferous applause which greeted the singer from all sides, the curtain rose again, the whole stage glittered as with silver, and little nickel-plated tables stood about, and all the other glittering apparatus of a juggler. On the red-velvet cloths with which the various stands were either hung or completely draped stood balls and flasks, little flags and banners, and also a great pile of white plates. On a ladder running up to a point—it too shone with nickel-plating—hung some two dozen daggers whose long blades glittered no less brilliantly than all the shining metal round them. The juggler in his black dress-suit was supported by a female assistant, whom he brought on, it was clear, simply to display her striking beauty to the public, and also the spangled tights she wore must have been designed merely to that end, for all that she had to do was to hand the juggler the plates and the flags, or to fling them to him in the midst of his performance whenever, as a signal, he clapped his hands. She discharged this task with a gracious smile, and when she threw him the hammer she emitted a short cry in some foreign tongue, perhaps to draw the attention of her master to her, perhaps also to beg for a little affection, which her austere tyrant, however, sternly denied her. And although he must certainly have known that he ran the risk of losing the audience's sympathy by his hard-heartedness, he did not accord his beautiful helper even a single glance, and only when he had to acknowledge the applause with a bow did he indicate by a casual wave of his hand in her direction that he allowed her a certain percentage of it. But then he walked to the back of the stage, and quite amicably, as though the affront which he had just put upon her had never happened, they lifted up together a great black board which, noticed by nobody, had been waiting there all the time, brought it forward to the waiting array of shining paraphernalia, set it up on end, and fastened it securely to the ladder. Thereupon, mutually encouraging each other with short cries and smiles, they pushed the black board, now set up vertically, to the front of the stage, and secured it to the floor and the wings with cords which suddenly appeared from nowhere. After they had seen to this with profound solemnity, the beautiful assistant once more emitted her short cry and skipped over to the board, which was so high that, stretching her arms upwards, she could scarcely touch the top edge. And now one saw that two handles were fixed into the board near the top, and the assistant, who stood with her back against the board, seized hold of those handles, and this somewhat constrained and artificial posture gave her, as she stood sharply outlined in her glittering and flimsy attire against the black board, the look of someone being crucified. Yet all the same she still went on smiling her gracious smile, even when the man, after regarding her with sharp half-shut eyes, went up to her and altered her position, altered it so slightly as to be unnoticeable, it is true, yet in such a way that the spectators became aware that everything depended on that fraction of an inch. All this was done to the subdued strains of a waltz, which immediately broke off at a slight sign from the juggler. The theatre became quite still; an extraordinary isolation, divested even of music, lay on the stage up there, and the waiters did not dare to walk up to the tables with the beer and food they were carrying, but stood, themselves tense with excitement, by the yellow-lighted doors at the back; guests who were on the point of eating put back their forks, on which they had already spitted some morsel, on their plates, and only the limelight, which the operator had directed full on the crucified girl, went on whirring. But the juggler was already testing one of the long daggers in his murderous hand; he bent his body back and now it was he who sent out the discordant exotic cry, while the dagger flew whistling from his hand, whizzed straight across the stage, and quivered in the black wood with a dull impact beside the body of the crucified girl. And now, faster than one could follow him, he had both hands full of glittering daggers, and while his cries became more rapid and more brutal, indeed, veritably bestial, the daggers whizzed in more and more rapid succession through the quivering air, struck with ever more rapid impact on the wood, and framed the girl's face, which still smiled, numb and yet confident, appealing and yet challenging, brave and yet apprehensive. Esch could almost have wished that it was himself who was standing up there with his arms raised to heaven, that it was himself being crucified, could almost have wished to station himself in front of that gentle girl and receive in his own breast the menacing blades; and had the juggler, as often happened, asked whether any gentleman in the audience would deign to step on to the stage and place himself against the black board, in sober truth Esch would have accepted the offer. Indeed the thought of standing up there alone and forsaken, where the long blades might pin one against the board like a beetle, filled him with almost voluptuous pleasure; but in that case, he thought, correcting himself, he would have to stand with his face to the board, for a beetle was never spitted from the under side: and the thought of standing with his face to the darkness of the board, not knowing when the deadly daggers might fly, transfixing his heart and pinning it to the board, had so extraordinary and mysterious a fascination for him, grew into a desire so novel, so powerful and satisfying, that he started as out of a dream of bliss when with a flourish of drums and fanfares the orchestra greeted the juggler, who had triumphantly dispatched the last of the daggers, and the girl skipped out of her frame, which was now complete, and both of them with a graceful pirouette, holding hands and executing spacious gestures with their free arms, bowed to the audience, now released from its ordeal. It was the fanfare of the Last Judgment, when the guilty were to be trodden underfoot like worms; why shouldn't they be spitted like beetles? Why, instead of a sickle, shouldn't Death carry a long darning-needle, or at least a lance? One always lived in fear of being awakened to the Last Judgment, for even if one had once upon a time almost thought of joining the Freethinkers, yet one had a conscience. He heard Korn saying: " That was great," and it sounded like blasphemy: and when Fräulein Erna remarked that, if they asked her, she would take good care not to be set up there almost naked and have knives thrown at her before the whole audience, it was too much for Esch, and in the most ungentle manner he flung away her knee, which was leaning against his; one shouldn't take people like these to see a superior entertainment; interlopers without a conscience, that's what they were; and he was not in the least impressed by the fact that Fräulein Erna was always running to her confessor; indeed the life of his Cologne friends seemed to him by far more secure and respectable.

In the Spatenbräu Esch drank his dark beer in silence. He was still in the grip of an emotion that could only be called yearning. Especially when it took shape as a need to send a picture postcard to Mother Hentjen. It was of course only natural that Erna should add a line: " Kind regards from Erna Korn," but when Balthasar too insisted on contributing and beneath his, "Regards, Korn, Customs Inspector," scored in his firm hand a black definitively conclusive flourish, it was like a sort of homage to Frau Hentjen, and it softened Esch so much that he became unsure of himself: had he really quite fulfilled his obligation to give an honest return for the Korns' kindness? Actually, to round off the evening, he should steal across to Erna's door, and if he had not thrust her away so ungently just now the door would certainly have been left unbarred. Yes, properly regarded, that was the right and fitting conclusion to the evening, yet he did nothing to bring it about. A sort of paralysis had fallen on him; he paid no further attention to Erna, did not seek her knee with his, and nothing happened either on the way home or afterwards. For some reason or other his conscience was troubling him, but finally he decided in his mind that he had done enough after all, and that it might even lead to trouble if he showed too much attention to Fräulein Korn; he felt a fate hovering over his head with threateningly upraised lance ready to strike if he should go on behaving like a swine, and he felt that he must remain true to someone, even though he did not know who it was.

While Esch was still feeling the stab of conscience in his back so palpably that he declared he must have sat in a cold draught, and every night rubbed himself as far as he could reach with a pungent embrocation, Mother Hentjen was rejoicing over the two picture postcards which he had sent her, and stuck them, before they should go for final preservation into her picture-postcard album, in the mirror frame behind the buffet. Then in the evening she took them out and showed them to the regular customers. Perhaps she did this also lest anybody might say of her that she was carrying on a secret correspondence with a man; for if she let the postcards go the round of the restaurant then they were no longer directed merely to her, but to the establishment, which was only incidentally personified in her. For this reason too she was glad that Geyring undertook the task of replying; yet she would not hear of Herr Geyring going to any expense, so she herself procured next day a particularly beautiful panorama card, as it was called, three times the length of an ordinary postcard, showing the whole of Cologne stretching along the dark-blue banks of the Rhine, and leaving space for a great number of signatures. At the top she wrote: "Many thanks for the beautiful postcards from Mother Hentjen." Then Geyring gave the command: "Ladies first," and Hede and Thusnelda signed their names. And then followed the names of Wilhelm Lassmann, Bruno May, Hoelst, Wrobek, Hülsenschmitt, John, the English mechanic Andrew, the sailor Wingast, and finally, after several more, all of which were not decipherable, the name of Martin Geyring. Then Geyring wrote out the address: "Herr August Esch, Head Book-keeper, Shipping Depot, Central Rhine Shipping Company Limited, Mannheim," and handed the finished product to Frau Hentjen, who, after reading it through carefully, opened the cash drawer to take from the large wire basket in which the bank-notes lay the necessary postage stamp. To her now the enormous card, with the long list of signatures, seemed almost too marked an honour for Esch, who had not been after all among the best patrons of the restaurant. But as everything she did she liked to do thoroughly, and as on the huge card there still remained, in spite of all the names, enough empty space not only to offend her sense of proportion, but also to provide the desired chance of putting Esch in his place by filling it in with a name of more humble rank, Mother Hentjen bore the card to the kitchen for the maid to sign her name, doubly pleased that in this way she could give pleasure to the poor girl without its costing anything.

When she returned to the restaurant Martin was sitting at his usual place in the corner near the buffet, buried in one of the Socialist journals. Frau Hentjen sat down beside him and said jestingly, as she often did: "Herr Geyring, you'll get my restaurant a bad name yet if you use it all the time for reading your seditious papers." "I'm disgusted enough myself with these scribblers," was the answer, "fellows like us do all the work, and these chaps only scribble a lot of nonsense." Once more Frau Hentjen felt a little disappointed in Geyring, for she had never given up the hope that he would yet come out with something revolutionary and full of hatred on which she might feed her own resentment against the world. She had often glanced into the Socialist papers, but really what she found there had seemed to her pretty tame, and so she hoped that Geyring's living speech would have more to give her than the printed word. So to a certain extent she was pleased that Geyring too did not think much of the newspaper writers, for she was always pleased when anyone did not think much of anyone else; yet, on the other hand, he still continued to disappoint her expectations. No, these anarchists didn't get you very far, there wasn't much help in a man like Geyring who sat in his trade-union bureau just like a police sergeant in his office, and Frau Hentjen was once more firmly convinced that the whole structure of society was simply a put-up job among the men, who laid their heads together to injure and disappoint women. She made one more attempt: " What is it that you don't like in your papers, Herr Geyring? " " They write such stuff," growled Martin, " turn the people's heads with their revolutionary rant, and then we've got to pay for it." Frau Hentjen did not quite understand this; besides, she was no longer interested. Mainly out of politeness she sighed: " Yes, life isn't easy." Geyring turned over a page and said absently: " No, life isn't easy, Mother Hentjen." " And a man like you, always on the go, always at it from early morning till late at night. . . ." Geyring said almost with satisfaction: " There won't be any eight-hour day for men like me for a long time yet: everybody else will get it first. . . ." " And to think that they try to make it harder for you! " said Frau Hentjen in amazement, shaking her head and throwing a glance at her coiffure in the mirror behind the buffet. " Yes, they can make a fine noise in the Reichstag and the newspaper, our friends the Jews," said Geyring, " but when it comes to the real work of organization they turn tail." Frau Hentjen could understand this: she agreed indignantly: " They're everywhere, these Jews; they have all the money and no woman is safe from them, they're just like bulls." The old expression of petrified loathing overspread her face. Martin looked up from his paper and could not help smiling: " It isn't as bad as all that, surely, Mother Hentjen." " So now you're sticking up for the Jews next? " there was a hint of hysterical aggressiveness in her voice, " but you always stick up for one another, you men," and then quite unexpectedly: " a girl in every port." " That may be, Mother Hentjen," laughed Martin, " but you won't find such good cooking as Mother Hentjen's anywhere in a hurry." Frau Hentjen was appeased: " Not even in Mannheim, maybe," she said, handing Geyring the picture postcard that he was to send off to Esch.

Gernerth, the theatre manager, now belonged to Esch's intimate circle of friends. For Esch, an impetuous man, had bought another ticket the very day after the first performance, not merely because he wanted to see that brave girl again, but also that he might look up a somewhat astonished Gernerth after the performance and introduce himself as a paying client; while doing this he once more thanked the manager for a lovely evening's enjoyment, and Gernerth, who saw a request for more free tickets in the offing, and was already preparing to refuse them, could not but feel touched. And heartened by his cordial reception Esch simply remained sitting; thus achieving his second object, for he was presented to the juggler Herr Teltscher and also to his brave companion Ilona, who, it turned out, were both of them of Hungarian birth, at least Ilona was, and she had very little command over German, while Herr Teltscher, whose professional name was Teltini, and who employed English on the stage, came from Pressburg.

Herr Gernerth, on the other hand, was an Egerlander, and this was a matter for great joy to Korn, the first time that the two men met; for the towns of Eger and Hof were close neighbours, and Korn could not but regard it as an extraordinary coincidence that two men who were almost landsmen should meet in Mannheim of all places. Still his expressions of joy and surprise were more or less rhetorical, for in less desirable circumstances the fact that he was meeting almost a landsman would have left him quite indifferent. He invited Gernerth to visit his sister and himself, partly perhaps because he could not bear the idea of his presumptive brother in law having private acquaintanceships of his own, and Herr Teltscher too was presently invited to a repast of coffee and cakes.

So now on a dull Sunday afternoon they all sat at the round table, on which beside the bulging coffee-pot the cakes, contributed by Esch, were piled up artistically in a pyramid, while outside the rain poured down the window-panes. Herr Gernerth began, trying to set the conversation going: "You've a very nice place here, Herr Customs Inspector, roomy, lots of light. . . ." And he looked out through the window at the dreary suburban street, in which lay great puddles of rain. Fräulein Erna remarked that it was really too small for their circumstances, yet a fireside of one's own was the only thing that could make life sweet. Herr Gernerth became elegiac: no place like home, yes, she might well say that, but for an artist it was an unfulfillable dream; no, for him there could be no home; he had a flat, it was true, a pleasant and comfortable flat in Munich, where his wife lived with the children, but he was almost a stranger to his family by this time. Why didn't he take them with him? It was no life for children, on tour all the time. And besides—— No, his children would never be artists, *his* children wouldn't. He was obviously an affectionate father, and Esch as well as Fräulein Erna felt touched by his goodness of heart. And perhaps because he felt lonely Esch said: " I'm an orphan, I can scarcely remember my mother." " Poor fellow! " said Fräulein Erna. But Herr Teltscher, who did not seem to relish this lugubrious talk, now made a coffee-cup revolve on the tip of his finger so that they could not help laughing, all but Ilona who sat impassively on her chair, recuperating, it seemed, from the perpetual smiles with which she had to embellish her evenings. At close quarters she was by no means so lovely and fragile as she had been on the stage, but might even have been called plump; her face was slightly puffy, there were heavy pouches covered with freckles under her eyes, and Esch, now become mistrustful, began to suspect that her beautiful blond hair, too, might not be genuine, but only a wig; yet his suspicions faded whenever he looked at her body, for he could not help seeing the knives whizzing past it. Then he noticed that Korn's eyes too were caressing that body, and so he tried to attract Ilona's attention, asked her whether she liked Mannheim, whether she had seen the Rhine before, with similar geographical inquiries. Unfortunately his attempts were unsuccessful, for Ilona only replied now and then and at the wrong point. " Yes, very nice," and wished, it seemed, to have nothing to do either with him or with Korn; she drank her coffee heavily and seriously, and even when Teltscher spluttered something at her in their sibilant native idiom, obviously something disagreeable, she scarcely listened. Meanwhile Fräulein Erna was telling Gernerth that a happy family life was the most beautiful thing in the world, and she gave Esch a little nudge with her toe, either to encourage him to follow Gernerth's example, or perhaps merely to withdraw his attention from the Hungarian girl, whose beauty, however, she praised none the less; for the greedy longing with which her brother was regarding the girl had not escaped her vigilant glance, and she considered it preferable that the lovely charmer should fall to her brother rather than to Esch. So she stroked Ilona's hands and praised their whiteness, rolled up the girl's sleeve and said that she had a lovely fine skin, Balthasar should only look at it. Balthasar put out his hairy paw to feel it. Teltscher laughed and said that every Hungarian woman had a skin like silk, whereupon Erna, who also had a skin of her own, replied that it was all a matter of tending one's complexion, and that she washed her face every day in milk.

Certainly, said Gernerth, she had a marvellous, indeed an international, complexion, and Fräulein Erna's withered face parted in a smile, showing her yellow teeth and the gap where one tooth was missing in her left upper jaw, and blushed to the roots of the hair at her temples, which hung down thin and brown and a little faded, from her coiffure.

Twilight had fallen; Korn's fist grasped Ilona's hand more and more firmly, and Fräulein Erna was waiting until Esch, or Gernerth at least, should do the same with hers. She hesitated to light the lamp, chiefly because Balthasar would have radically disapproved of the disturbance, but at last she was forced to get up so as to fetch the blue carafe of home-brewed liqueur which stood ostentatiously on the sideboard. Proudly announcing that the recipe was her own secret she served out the brew, which tasted like flat beer, but was applauded as delicious by Gernerth; in his admiration he even kissed her hand. Esch remembered that Mother Hentjen did not like Schnapps drinkers, and it filled him with particular satisfaction to think that she would have had all sorts of hard things to say of Korn, for he was tossing down one glass after another, smacking his lips each time, and sucking the drops from his dark, bushy moustache. Korn poured out a glass for Ilona too, and it may have been her imperturbable indifference and impassivity that made her allow him to lift the glass to her mouth and raise no objection even when he took a sip from it himself, dipping his moustache into it, and declaring that it was a kiss. Evidently Ilona did not understand what he had said, but on the other hand Teltscher must know what was happening. Incomprehensible that he should look on so calmly. Perhaps he was suffering inwardly, and was simply too well-bred to create a scene. Esch had a strong desire to do it for him, but then he remembered the rough tone in which Teltscher had ordered the brave girl to hand him things on the stage; perhaps he was deliberately trying to humiliate her? Something or other should be done, somebody ought to shield Ilona! But Teltscher merely clapped him jovially on the shoulder, calling him colleague and brother, and when Esch looked at him questioningly pointed to the two couples and said: " We must stick together, we young bachelors." " I'll have to take pity on you, I see," said Fräulein Erna, changing places so that she sat now between Gernerth and Esch, but Herr Gernerth said in an offended tone: " That's how we poor artists are always being slighted . . . for these commercial fellows." Teltscher declared that Esch shouldn't allow this, for it was only in the commercial class that solidity and breadth of vision were still to be found. The theatrical industry itself might even be regarded as a branch of commerce, and indeed as the most difficult of the lot with all respect to Herr Gernerth, who was not only his manager, but in a sense his partner, besides being in his own way a very capable man of business, even if he didn't exploit possible avenues of success as he might. He, Teltscher-Teltini, could see that very well, for before he felt drawn to an artist's life he had been in commerce himself. " And what's been the end of it all? Here I sit, when I might have lots of first-class engagements in America.... And I ask you, is my turn a first-class one, or isn't it? " A vague memory rose up rebelliously in Esch; what reason had they to praise up the commercial classes so much? The precious solidity they talked of wasn't so solid as they thought. He said so frankly, and ended: " Of course there's a great difference, for instance, between Nentwig and von Bertrand, the Chairman of our company; they're both in commerce, but the one is a swine and the other . . . well, he's something different, something better." Korn growled contemptuously that Bertrand was a renegade officer, everybody knew that, he needn't give himself airs. Esch was not displeased to hear this; so the difference between them wasn't so very great after all! But that didn't alter matters: Bertrand was something better, and in any case these were speculations which he had no desire to pursue too far. Meanwhile Teltscher went on talking about America; over there one could soon come to the top, over there one didn't need to work oneself to skin and bone for nothing as one did here. And he quoted: " America, you lucky land." Gernerth sighed: yes, if he had only had enough of the commercial spirit things would be different now; he had been very rich once himself, but in spite of all his business acumen he had kept the childlike trustfulness of the artist and had been cheated out of all his capital, almost a million marks, by pure fraud. Yes, Herr Esch might well look at him, Gernerth had once been a rich man! *Tempi passati*. Well, he would make his pile again. He had the idea of a theatrical trust, a huge limited liability company for whose shares people would yet be falling over one another. One had simply to march with the times and get hold of capital. And once more kissing Fräulein Erna's hand he asked his glass to be filled again, and said with the air of a connoisseur: " Delicious," still clasping her hand, which remained willingly and contentedly surrendered to him. But Esch, overwhelmed by all that he had heard, and now sunk in thought, scarcely noticed that Fräulein Erna's shoe was pressing against his, and saw only as from a distance and in the darkness Korn's yellow hand which lay on Ilona's shoulder and made it easy to guess that Balthasar Korn had put his powerful arm round Ilona's neck.

But then finally the lamp had to be lit, and now the conversation became general, only Ilona remaining silent. And as it was time to leave for the theatre, and they did not want to break up, Gernerth invited his hosts to attend the performance. So they got ready and took a tram to the theatre. The two ladies went inside and the men smoked their cigars on the platform at the back. Cold drops of rain spattered now and then into their heated faces, refreshing them pleasantly.

The name of the tobacconist from whom August Esch usually bought his cheap cigars was Fritz Lohberg. He was a young man about the same age as Esch, and this may have been the reason why Esch, who was always in the company of people older than himself, treated him as if he were a fool. Nevertheless the fool must have had some slight importance for him, and really it should have given Esch himself matter for thought that just in this shop he should feel so much at home as to become a regular customer. True, the shop lay on the way to his work, yet that was no reason why he should feel at home in it so immediately. Certainly it was very spick-and-span, a pleasant place to dawdle in: the light, pure fragrance of tobacco that filled it gave one an agreeable titillation in the nose, and it was nice to run one's hand over the polished counter, at one end of which, beside the glittering nickel-plated automatic cash register, invariably stood several open sample boxes of light-brown cigars and a little stand containing matches. If one made a purchase one received a box of matches free, a stylishly ample one. Further, there was a huge cigar-cutter which Herr Lohberg always had at hand, and if one wanted to light one's cigar on the spot, then with a sharp little click he snipped off the end that one held out to him. It was a good place to spend one's time in, bright and sunny and hospitable behind its plate-glass windows, and during these cold days full of a sort of pleasant smooth warmth that lay on the white floor-tiles and was a welcome change from the dusty, overheated atmosphere of the glass cage in the warehouse. But while that was sufficient reason for liking to come here after one's work or during the lunch-hour, it had no further significance. At these times one was full of praise for neatness and order, and grumbled at the filth one had to slave among; yet one did not intend this quite seriously, for Esch knew quite well that the perfect orderliness which he kept in his books and his goods lists couldn't be imposed on piles of packing-cases and bales and barrels, no matter how good the foreman might be at his job. But here in this shop, on the other hand, a curiously satisfying sense of order, an almost feminine precision, ruled, and this seemed all the stranger to Esch because he could scarcely picture to himself, or only with discomfort, girls selling cigars; in spite of all its cleanliness it was a job for men, a thing suggesting good-fellowship; yes, this was what friendship between men should be like, and not careless and perfunctory like the casual helpfulness of a trade-union secretary. But these were things which Esch really did not bother his mind about; they occurred to him only by the way. On the other hand, it was both funny and curious that Lohberg shouldn't be content with a job that suited him so well and in which he might have been happy, and still funnier were the grounds that he offered for his dissatisfaction, and in advancing which he showed so clearly that he was a fool. For although he had hung over the automatic cash register a board with the inscription: " Smoking has never harmed anybody "; although his boxes of cigars were accompanied by neat cards which displayed not only his business address and the names of the different brands, but also a little couplet: " Smoke good and pure tobacco every day, And you will have no doctors' bills to pay," yet he himself did not believe in these sentiments; indeed he smoked his own cigarettes simply from a sense of duty and because his conscience pricked him, and, in perpetual dread of so-called smoker's cancer, constantly felt in his stomach, his heart, his throat, all the evil symptoms of nicotine-poisoning. He was a lank little man with a dark shadow of a moustache and lifeless eyes which showed a great deal of white, and his somewhat coy charm and bearing were just as incompatible with his general principles as the business which he carried on and had no thought of exchanging for another; for he was not content to regard tobacco as a popular poison undermining the national well-being, perpetually reiterating that the people must be saved from this virus; no, he was also an advocate of a spacious, natural, genuinely German way of life, and it was a great disappointment to him that he could not live in the open air, a deep-chested, blond giant. For this deprivation, however, he partly compensated himself by subscribing to anti-alcoholic and vegetarian associations, and so beside the cash register there was always lying a pile of pamphlets on such subjects, most of them sent to him from Switzerland. No doubt about it, he was a pure fool.

Now Esch, who smoked cigars and drank wine and treated himself to huge portions of meat whenever he had the chance, might not have been so deeply impressed by Herr Lohberg's arguments, in spite of the persuasive phrases about saving the people which always recurred in them, if he had not been struck by a curious parallelism between them and the principles of Mother Hentjen. Of course Mother Hentjen was a sensible woman, even an unusually sensible woman, and so her opinions had nothing in common with Lohberg's jargon. Yet when Lohberg, true to the Calvinistic convictions which reached him from Switzerland along with his pamphlets, inveighed like a priest against sensual indulgence and in the same breath pleaded like a Socialist orator addressing a Freethinking audience for a free and simple life in the bosom of nature; when in his own modest way he let it be understood that there was something amiss with the world, a glaring error in the books which could only be put right by a wonderful new entry, in all this confusion only one thing was absolutely clear, that Mother Hentjen's restaurant was in the same case as Lohberg's tobacconist shop: she had to depend for her living on the men who boozed at her tables, and she too hated her business and her customers. No doubt about it, it was a queer coincidence, and Esch half thought of writing to Frau Hentjen to tell her about it, it would interest her. But he dropped the idea when he reflected that Frau Hentjen might think it odd, perhaps even feel insulted, to be compared with a man who, in spite of all his virtues, was an idiot. So he saved it up until he should see her; in any case he would soon have to go to Cologne on business.

All the same the case of Lohberg was well worth mentioning; and one evening, while Esch was sitting at dinner with Korn and Fräulein Erna, he gave way to his desire to talk about it.

Of course the two Korns knew of Lohberg. Korn had already been in his shop several times, but he had observed none of the man's peculiarities. "One wouldn't think it to see him," he said, after an interval of silent thought, and agreed with Esch that the man was a fool. But Fräulein Erna seemed to be seized with a violent aversion to this spiritual double of Frau Hentjen, and inquired sharply whether Frau Hentjen perchance was Herr Esch's long and carefully concealed lady-love. She must be a very virtuous lady, no doubt, but Fräulein Erna thought all the same that she herself was just as good. And as for Herr Lohberg's virtuous scruples, of course it wasn't nice when a man made the curtains stink with his perpetual smoking as her brother did. Yet on the other hand one knew at least that there was a man about the house. " A man that does nothing but drink water ... " she searched for words, " would sicken me." And then she inquired, did Herr Lohberg even know what it was to have a woman? " He's still an innocent, I suppose, the fool," said Esch, and Korn, foreseeing that there was sport to be had out of him yet, exclaimed: " A pure Joseph! "

Whether for this purpose, or because he wished to keep an eye on his lodger, or simply by pure chance, Korn too now became a regular customer of Lohberg's, and Lohberg shrank every time that the Herr Customs Inspector noisily entered his shop. His fear was not without cause. A few evenings later the blow fell; shortly before closing time Korn appeared with Esch and commanded: " Make yourself ready, my lad; to-night you're going to lose your innocence." Lohberg rolled his eyes helplessly and pointed to a man in the uniform of the Salvation Army who was standing in the shop. " Fancy dress? " said Korn, and Lohberg stammeringly introduced the man: " A friend of mine." " We're friends too," replied Korn, holding out his paw to the Salvation Army soldier. He was a freckled, somewhat pimply, red-haired youth, who had learned that one must be friendly to every soul one meets; he smiled in Korn's face and rescued Lohberg: " Brother Lohberg has promised to testify in our ranks to-night. I've come to fetch him." " So, you're going out to testify? Then we'll come too." Korn was enthusiastic. " We're all friends." " Every friend is welcome," said the joyful Salvation Army man. Lohberg was not consulted; he had the look of a thief caught in the act, and closed up the shop with a guilty air. Esch had followed the proceedings with great amusement, yet as Korn's high-handedness annoyed him he clapped Lohberg jovially on the shoulder, reproducing the very gesture that Teltscher had often expended on him.

They made for the Neckar quarter. In Käfertalerstrasse they could already hear the beating of the drums and tambourines, and Korn's feet, as if remembering their time in the army, fell into step. When they came to the end of the street they saw the Salvation Army group standing at the corner of the park in the dying twilight. Watery sleet had fallen, and where the group was gathered the snow had melted into black slush which soaked through one's boots. The Lieutenant was standing on a wooden bench and cried into the falling darkness: "Come to us and be saved, poor wandering sinners, the Saviour is near!" But only a few had answered his call, and when his soldiers, with drums and tambourines beating, sang of the redeeming love and made their chorus resound: "Lord God of Sabaoth save, Oh, save our souls from Hell," hardly anybody in the crowd standing round joined in, and it was obvious that the majority were merely looking on out of curiosity. And although the honest soldiers sang on lustily, and the two girls struck their tambourines with all their might, the crowd grew thinner and thinner as the light faded, and soon they were left alone with their Lieutenant, their only audience now being Lohberg, Korn and Esch. Yet even now Lohberg was probably ready to join in the hymn, and indeed he would certainly have done so without feeling either embarrassed or intimidated by Esch and Korn if Korn had not kept on digging him in the ribs and saying: "Sing, Lohberg!" It wasn't a very pleasant situation for Lohberg, and he was glad when a policeman arrived and ordered them to move on. They all set out for the Thomasbräu cellar. And yet it was almost a pity that Lohberg hadn't joined in the singing, yes, then perhaps a minor miracle might have happened, for it wouldn't have taken much to make Esch too lift up his voice in praise of the Saviour and His redeeming love; indeed only a slight impetus would have been required, and perhaps the sound of Lohberg's voice would have provided it. But one can never be sure of those things afterwards.

Esch himself could not make out what had happened to him at the open-air meeting: the two girls had beaten their tambourines when the officer standing on the bench gave the signal, and that had reminded him strangely of the commands which Teltscher gave Ilona on the stage. Perhaps it was the sudden dead silence of the evening that had affected him, for there at the outskirts of the city the sounds of the evening broke off as abruptly as the music in the theatre; perhaps it was the motionlessness of the black trees that gazed up into the darkening sky; and then behind him in the square the arc-lamps had flared out. It was all incomprehensible. The biting coldness of the wet snow had pierced through his shoes; but that was not the only reason why Esch would have liked to be standing up there on the bench pointing out the way of salvation, for his old strange feeling of orphaned isolation had returned again, and suddenly it had become dreadfully clear to him that some time he would have to die in utter and complete loneliness. A vague and yet unforeseen hope had risen in him that things would go better, far better, with him if he could but stand up there on the bench; and he saw Ilona, Ilona in the Salvation Army uniform, gazing up at him and waiting for his redeeming signal to strike the tambourine and cry "Hallelujah!" But Korn was standing beside him, grinning out from between the great upturned collars of his damp customs cloak, and at the sight of him Esch's hopes had ignominiously melted away. Esch's mouth twisted wryly, his expression became contemptuous, and all at once he was almost glad to be orphaned and alone. In any case he too was relieved that the policeman had moved them on.

Lohberg was walking in front with the pimply Salvation Army man and one of the girls. Esch trudged behind. Yes, whether a girl like that beat a tambourine or threw plates, one only had to order her to do it, it was just the same, only the clothes were different. They sang about love in the Salvation Army as in the theatre. "Perfect redeeming love," Esch had to laugh, and he decided to sound the good Salvation Army girl on this question. When they were nearing the Thomasbräu cellar the girl stopped, planted her foot on a ledge projecting from the wall, bent down, and began to tie the laces of her wet, shapeless boots. As she stood there bent double, her black hat almost touching her knee, she looked lumpish and hardly human, a monstrosity, yet with a certain, as it were, mechanical effectiveness of structure, and Esch, who in other circumstances would have requited such a posture with a clap on the part most saliently exposed, was a little alarmed that no desire to do so awoke in him, and it almost seemed as though another bridge between him and his fellow-creatures had been broken, and he felt homesick for Cologne. That day in the kitchen he had wanted to take hold of Mother Hentjen under the breasts; yes, he would not have been put off had Mother Hentjen bent down and laced her shoes. But as all men have the same thoughts, Korn, who felt on good terms with all the world, now pointed to the girl: "Any chance with her, do you think?" Esch threw him a furious glance, but Korn did not stop: "Among themselves they're probably hot enough, the soldiers." Meanwhile they had reached the Thomasbräu cellar, and they walked into the bright, noisy room, which smelt pleasantly of roast beef, onions and beer.

Here, at any rate, Korn met with a disappointment. For the Salvation Army people were not to be prevailed upon to sit down at the same table; they said good-bye and gathered at one end of the room to distribute the *War Cry*. Esch too would have preferred not to be left alone with Korn; some remnant of hope still fluttered in his soul that these people might be able to bring back to him what he had felt under the darkening trees and yet had not been able to grasp. But it was a good thing, on the other hand, that they were now beyond the reach of Korn's raillery, and it would have been still better if they had taken Lohberg with them, for Korn was now anxious to get his own back and was beginning his joke at Lohberg's expense by trying to make the helpless fellow violate his principles with the aid of a portion of steak and onions and a great jug of beer. But the ninny stood his ground, merely saying in a quiet voice: " You shouldn't joke with a fellow's convictions," and touched neither the meat nor the beer, and Korn, once more disappointed, had to be content with morosely devouring them himself, so that they might not be wasted. Esch contemplated the dark residue of beer at the bottom of his jug; absurd to think that one's salvation could depend on whether one drank that up or not. All the same he felt almost grateful to the mild and obstinate fool. Lohberg sat there smiling meekly, and sometimes one almost expected tears to start to his great eyes with the exposed whites. Yet when the Salvation Army people in their round of the tables drew near again he stood up and it looked as though he were about to shout something to them. Against Esch's expectations he did not do so, but simply remained standing where he was. Then suddenly he uttered without warning or reason a single word, a word quite incomprehensible to everyone who heard it; he uttered loudly and distinctly the word " Redemption," and then sat down again. Korn looked at Esch and Esch looked at Korn. But when Korn put his finger to his brow and twirled it to indicate that Lohberg was weak in the head, the whole situation changed in the most extraordinary and terrifying manner, for it was as though the word of redemption, now set free, hovered over the table maintained in its detachment by an invisibly revolving mechanism, detached even from the mouth that had uttered it. And although Esch's contempt for Lohberg remained undiminished, yet it seemed now that the kingdom of salvation did exist, could exist, must exist, if only because Korn, that dead lump of flesh, was sitting on his broad hindquarters in the Thomasbräu cellar, quite incapable of sending his thoughts even as far as the next street corner, far less of losing them in the infinite spaces of freedom. And although, in spite of these ideas, Esch refused to act the prig, but instead rapped with his jug on the table and ordered another beer, yet he too became silent like Lohberg; and when on rising to leave Korn proposed that they should take the pure Joseph to visit the girls, Esch refused to second him, left a completely disappointed Balthasar Korn standing on the pavement, and escorted the tobacconist home, quite pleased that Korn should shout insults after them. It had stopped snowing, and in the warm wind that had risen Korn's rude words fluttered past like light spring blossoms.

Driven by that extraordinary oppression which falls on every human being when, childhood over, he begins to divine that he is fated to go on in isolation and unaided towards his own death; driven by this extraordinary oppression, which may with justice be called a fear of God, man looks round him for a companion hand in hand with whom he may tread the road to the dark portal, and if he has learned by experience how pleasurable it undoubtedly is to be with another fellow-creature in bed, then he is ready to believe that this extremely intimate association of two bodies may last until these bodies are coffined: and even if at the same time it has its disgusting aspects, because it takes place under coarse and badly aired sheets, or because he is convinced that all a girl cares for is to get a husband who will support her in later life, yet it must not be forgotten that every fellow-creature, even if she has a sallow complexion, sharp, thin features and an obviously missing tooth in her left upper jaw, yearns, in spite of her missing tooth, for that love which she thinks will for ever shield her from death, from that fear of death which sinks with the falling of every night upon the human being who sleeps alone, a fear that already licks her as with a tongue of flame when she begins to take off her clothes, as Fräulein Erna was doing now; she laid aside her faded red-velvet blouse and took off her dark-green skirt and her petticoat. Then she drew off her shoes; but her stockings, on the other hand, as well as her white, starched under-petticoat, she kept on; indeed she could not even summon the resolution to undo her corsets. She was afraid, but she concealed her fear behind a knowing smile, and by the light of the flickering candle-flame on the bedside-table she slipped, without undressing further, into bed.

Now it came to pass that she heard Esch walking several times through the lobby, in doing which he made a greater noise than the necessary arrangements he was engaged in should have required. Perhaps these arrangements themselves were not indeed altogether necessary, for what need could there be to fetch water to his room twice? And the water-jug was surely not so heavy that he had to set it down with a bang in the passage immediately outside Erna's door. But every time that Fräulein Erna heard anything she resolved not to be outdone and made a noise too; stretched herself till the bed creaked, even pushed deliberately with her toes against the foot of it and sighed an audible " This is nice," as if she were sleepy; also she coughed and cleared her throat in pursuit of her purpose. Now Esch was an impetuous man, and after they had telegraphed to each other in this way for a little while he walked resolutely into her room.

There lay Fräulein Erna in bed and smiled knowingly and slyly and yet a little invitingly at him with her missing tooth, and really she did not attract him very much. All the same he paid no attention to her protest: " But Herr Esch, you mustn't stay here," but remained calmly where he was; and he did this not merely because he was a man of coarse appetites, like most men, he did it not merely because two people of different sexes living on intimate terms in the same house can scarcely escape the automatic functioning of physical attraction, and with the reflection " Why not, after all," will eventually yield casually to it, he did it not only because he divined that her feelings were much the same as his and so discounted her words, he did it therefore not simply in obedience to a low impulse, even if we add jealousy to it, the jealousy which any man might feel on seeing a woman flirting with Herr Gernerth; no, Esch did it because he was a man for whom it was essential that this pleasure, which people imagine one seeks for its own sake, should serve also a higher purpose, a purpose which he could scarcely name and yet felt bound to obey, but which nevertheless was nothing but the compulsion to put an end to a tremendous fear that extended far beyond himself, even if sometimes it might seem to be merely the fear that befalls the commercial traveller when, far from his wife and children, he lies down in his lonely hotel bed; the fear and desire of the traveller who resorts to the plain and elderly chambermaid, sometimes heartbroken by the squalor of the affair, and generally filled with remorse of conscience. Of course when Esch banged down his water-jug hard on the floor he was no longer thinking of the loneliness which had descended upon him since he had left Cologne, nor was he thinking of the isolation that had lain on the stage before Teltscher let fly the whistling, glittering daggers. Yet now that he sat on the edge of Fräulein Erna's bed and bent over her in desire, he wanted more from her than is currently construed as the satisfaction of an average sensual man's lust, for behind the very palpable, indeed banal, immediate object of desire, yearning was hidden, the yearning of the captive soul for redemption from its loneliness, for a salvation which should embrace himself and her, yes, perhaps all mankind, and most certainly Ilona, a salvation which Erna could not vouchsafe him, because neither she nor he knew what he wanted. So the rage which seized him when she refused him the final favour and gently said: "When we're man and wife," was neither merely the rage of the thwarted male, nor simple fury at the discovery of the trick she had played him in only half-undressing; it was more, it was despair, even if the words with which, sobered now, he rudely replied, were by no means high-sounding: "Well, it's all off, then." And although her refusal seemed to him a sign from God warning him to be chaste, he left the house immediately and went to a more willing lady. And thus deeply wounded Erna.

From that evening there was open war between Esch and Fräulein Erna. She let no opportunity pass of provoking his desire, and he no less eagerly seized every pretext to renew his attempt and to lure the recalcitrant one into his bed without promise of marriage. The battle began in the morning when she brought his breakfast into his room before he was properly dressed, a lascivious kind of mothering that maddened him; and it ended in the evening in indifference, whether she had barred her door or let him in. Neither of them ever mentioned the word love, and the fact that open hatred did not break out between them, but was dissembled in spiteful jests, was due simply to the other fact that they had not yet possessed each other.

Often he thought that with Ilona things must be different and better, but strangely enough his thoughts did not dare to rise to her. She was something better, much in the same way as the Chairman of the company, Bertrand, was something better. And Esch did not even mind very much that one of Erna's tricks was to frustrate any chance of his meeting Ilona, indeed he was even glad of this, bitterly as he resented all her silly fuss and her tittering facetiousness. Meanwhile Ilona was about the place almost every day, and between her and Erna a sort of friendship had grown up, yet what they could find in each other was incomprehensible to Esch; if when he got home he smelt the cheap and powerful scent which Ilona used, and which always excited him, he was sure to find the two ladies in an extraordinary dumb dialogue; for Ilona knew scarcely a word of German and Fräulein Erna was forced to fall back on fondling her friend, stationing her before the mirror and admiringly patting and rearranging her coiffure and her dress. But generally Esch found himself excluded. For Erna now set herself to conceal from him even the presence of her friend in the house. So one evening he happened to be sitting quite innocently in his room when the door-bell rang. He heard Erna opening the door and would not have thought anything further about the matter if he had not suddenly heard the key of his door being turned. Esch made a spring for the door; he was locked in! The trollop had locked him in! And although he should simply have ignored the stupid joke, it was too much for him, and he began to bawl and bang on the door, until at last Fräulein Erna opened it and slipped into the room with a giggle. "Well," she said, "now I can attend to you ... we have a visitor, I may say, but Balthasar is looking after her all right." Esch rushed out of the house in a rage.

When he returned late at night the lobby again reeked of Ilona's perfume. So she must have come back again, or rather she must still be here, for now he saw her hat hanging on the hat-rack. But where could she be? The parlour was dark. Korn was snoring next door. She simply couldn't have gone away without her hat! Esch listened at Erna's door; the agitating and oppressive thought came into his mind that the two women were lying in there side by side. He cautiously tried the door-handle; the door did not yield, it was barred as always when Fräulein Erna really wanted to sleep. Esch shrugged his shoulders and walked noisily to his room. But he could not rest in bed; he peered out into the passage; the perfume still hung in the air and the hat was still there. Something wasn't in order, one could feel that, and Esch stole through the house. It seemed to him that he could hear whispering in Korn's room; Korn wasn't the man to speak in a whisper, and Esch listened more intently: then suddenly Korn groaned, unmistakably he groaned, and Esch, a fellow who had no occasion to fear a man like Korn, fled back to his room in his bare feet as though something dreadful were pursuing him. He even felt he wanted to put his hands to his ears.

Next morning Erna awakened him out of a leaden sleep, and before he could bring out his question she said: "Hsh! I've a surprise for you. Get up at once!" He hastily put on his clothes, and when he walked into the kitchen, where Erna was busy, she took him by the hand and led him on tiptoe to her room, opened the door slightly and asked him to look in. There he saw Ilona; her round white arm, which still did not show any dagger wounds, was hanging over the edge of the bed, the heavy pouches under her eyes showed distinctly on her somewhat puffy face, and she was asleep.

Now Ilona frequently arrived at a late hour at the flat, and this lasted for a comparatively long time before Esch grasped the fact that she spent the night with Balthasar Korn and that Erna was shielding her brother's love affair, in a sense, with her own body.

Martin called on him at his work. It was extraordinary, the ease with which this pariah, whom every gate-keeper had orders to keep out, always managed to get himself admitted everywhere quite openly and swung at his ease on his crutches through places of business, nobody stopping him, many saluting him affectionately, partly no doubt because one was shy of appearing unkind to a cripple. Esch was not particularly pleased to receive a visit from a trade-union secretary at his work; Martin could just as well have waited for him outside, but on the other hand one could rely on his discretion; he knew the right time to come and the right time to go; he was a decent fellow. " 'Morning, August," he said. " I just wanted to see how you were getting on. You've a nice job here, made a good exchange." Did the cripple want to remind him that he had him to thank for being in this accursed Mannheim? All the same Martin could not be held responsible for the affair between Ilona and Korn, and so Esch simply replied in a morose voice: "Yes, a good exchange." And somehow it rang true. For now that Martin reminded him of his former job and Nentwig, Esch was jolly glad that he had nothing more to do with Cologne. Like a thief he still kept Nentwig's misdemeanour concealed, and the fact that one might come across the man's ugly mug at any street corner in Cologne took away all pleasure at the thought of returning there. Cologne or Mannheim, there was nothing to choose between them. Was there really any place where one could be rid of all this rottenness? Nevertheless he asked how things were in Cologne. "Later," said Martin, "I haven't time just now; where are you having your dinner?" And as soon as Esch told him he swung himself hastily away.

By now Esch really felt glad at meeting Martin again, and as he was an impatient fellow he could scarcely wait for the dinner-hour to come. Spring had arrived overnight, and Esch left his greatcoat in the office; the flagstones between the sheds were bright with the cool sunshine, and in the corners of the buildings young tender grass had suddenly appeared between the cobbles. As he passed the unloading stage he laid his hand on the iron bands with which the clumsy grey wooden erection was clamped together, and the iron too felt warm. If he shouldn't be transferred to Cologne he must arrange to have his bicycle sent on soon. He breathed in the air deeply and easily, and the food had quite a different taste; perhaps because the windows of the restaurant were open. Martin related that he had come to Mannheim on strike business; otherwise he would have taken his time. But something was happening in the South German and Alsatian factories, and such things soon spread: "For all I care they can strike as much as they like, only we can't afford any nonsense just now. A strike of the transport workers would be pure madness at the moment . . . we're a poor union and there's no money to be had from the central office . . . it would be a complete wash-out. Of course it's no use talking to a docker: if a donkey like that makes up his mind to go on strike nothing will stop him. But sooner or later they'll have my blood yet." He said all this indulgently, without bitterness. "Now they're raising the cry again that I'm being paid by the shipping companies." "By Bertrand?" asked Esch with interest. Geyring nodded: "By Bertrand too, of course." "A proper swine," Esch could not help saying. Martin laughed. "Bertrand? He's a very decent fellow." "Oho, so he's a decent fellow? Is it true that he's a renegade officer?" "Yes, he's supposed to have quit the service—but that only speaks in the man's favour." Oho, that spoke in the man's favour, did it? Nothing was clear and simple, thought Esch in anger, nothing was clear and simple, even on a lovely spring day like this: "All I would like to know is why you stick to this job of yours." "Everybody must stay where God has put him," said Martin, and his old-young face took on a pious look. Then he told Esch that Mother Hentjen sent her greetings and that everybody was looking forward to seeing him soon.

After dinner they went along to Lohberg's shop. They were in no hurry, and so Martin rested in the massive oaken chair that stood beside the counter and was as bright and solid as everything else in the shop. Accustomed to pick up anything in print that came within his reach, Martin glanced through the anti-alcoholic and vegetarian journals from Switzerland. " Dear, dear! " he said, " here's almost a comrade of mine." Lohberg felt flattered, but Esch spoilt his pleasure for him: " Oh, he's one of the teetotal wash-outs," and to crush him completely he added: " Geyring has a big meeting to-night, but a real one—not a meeting of the Salvation Army! " " Unfortunately," said Martin. Lohberg, who had a great weakness for public demonstrations and oratorical performances, proposed immediately to go. " I advise you not to," said Martin. " Esch at least mustn't go, it might go badly with him if he were seen there. Besides, there's bound to be trouble." Esch really had no anxiety about endangering his post, yet strangely enough to attend the meeting seemed to him an act of treachery towards Bertrand. Lohberg, on the other hand, said boldly: " I'll go in any case," and Esch felt shamed by the teetotal ninny; no, it would never do to leave a friend in the lurch; if he did he would never dare to face Mother Hentjen again. But meanwhile he said nothing about his decision. Martin explained: " I fancy that the shipping companies will send an *agent provocateur* or two; it's all to their interest that the strike should be as violent as possible." And although Nentwig was not a shipper, but only the greasy head clerk in a firm of wine merchants, to Esch it seemed that the rascal had his greasy fingers in this piece of perfidy too.

The meeting took place, as was usual in such cases, in the public room of a small tavern. A few policemen were standing before the entrance keeping an eye on those who went in, who on their side pretended not to notice the policemen. Esch arrived late; as he was about to enter someone tapped him on the shoulder, and when he turned round he saw it was the inspector of the dock police squad: " Why, what takes you here, Herr Esch? " Esch thought quickly. Actually simple curiosity; he had learned that Geyring, the trade-union secretary, whom he had known in Cologne, was to speak, and as in a way he was connected with shipping he felt interested in the whole business. " I advise you against it, Herr Esch," said the inspector, " and just because you're in a shipping firm; it will look fishy, and it can't do you any good." " I'll just look in for a minute," Esch decided, and went in.

The low room, adorned with portraits of the Kaiser, the Grand Duke of Baden, and the King of Württemberg, was crammed full. On the raised platform stood a table covered with a white cloth, behind which four men were sitting; Martin was one of them. Esch, at first a little envious because he too was not sitting in such a prominent position, was surprised next moment that he had noticed the table at all, so great was the uproar and disorder in the room. Indeed it was some time before he noticed that a man had mounted on a chair in the middle of the hall and was shouting out an incomprehensible rigmarole, emphasizing every word—he seemed to love particularly the word " demagogue "— with a sweeping gesture, as though to fling it at the table on the platform. It was a sort of unequal dialogue, for the only reply from the table was the thin tinkle of a bell which did not pierce the din; yet it finally had the last say when Martin, supporting himself on his crutches and the back of his chair, got up, and the noise ebbed. True, it wasn't very easy to grasp what Martin, with the somewhat weary and ironical fluency of a practised speaker, was saying, but that he was worth twice all these people bawling at him Esch could see. It almost looked as though Martin had no wish to get a hearing, for with a faint smile he stopped and let the shouts of " Capitalist pimp! " " Twister! " and " Kaiser's Socialist! " pass over him, until suddenly, amid the whistling and cat-calls, a sharper whistle was heard. In the sudden silence a police officer appeared on the platform and said curtly: " In the name of the law I declare this meeting closed; the hall must be cleared." And while Esch was being borne through the door by the crush he had time to see the police officer turning to Martin.

As if by arrangement the most of the audience had made for the side-door of the tavern. But that did not help them much, for meanwhile the whole place had been encircled by the police, and every one of them had either to explain his presence or go to the police station. At the front entrance the crush was not so great; Esch had the good luck to encounter the dock inspector again and said hastily: " You were right, never again," and so he escaped interrogation. But the affair was not yet ended. The crowd now stood before the place quite quietly, contenting themselves with swearing softly at the committee, the union and Geyring. But all at once the rumour flew round that Geyring and the committee were arrested and that the police were only waiting for the crowd to disperse to lead them away. Then suddenly the feeling of the crowd swung round; whistles and cat-calls rose again, and the crowd made ready to rush the police. The friendly police inspector gave Esch a push: " You'd better disappear now, Herr Esch," and Esch, who saw that there was nothing else he could do, withdrew to the nearest street corner, hoping at least to run up against Lohberg.

Before the hall the noise still went on for a good while. Then six mounted police arrived at a sharp trot, and because horses, who although docile are yet somewhat insane creatures, exert on many human beings a sort of magical influence, this little equestrian reinforcement was decisive. Esch looked on while a number of workers in handcuffs were led away amid the terrified silence of their comrades, and then the street emptied. Wherever the police, now become rough and impatient, saw two men standing together, they drove them harshly away, and Esch, considering with good reason that he would be handled just as ruthlessly, vacated the field.

He went to Lohberg's house. Lohberg had not yet returned, and Esch remained waiting before his door in the warm spring night. He hoped that they hadn't led Lohberg away too in handcuffs. Although really that would have been a good joke. Lord! what would Erna say if she saw this paragon of virtue before her in handcuffs? Just when Esch was about to give up his watch Lohberg arrived in a terribly excited state, and almost weeping. Bit by bit, and very disconnectedly, Esch managed to discover that at first the meeting had proceeded quite quietly, even if the audience had shouted all sorts of abuse at Herr Geyring, who had spoken very well. But then a man had got up, obviously one of those *agents provocateurs* whom Herr Geyring himself had mentioned at dinner-time, and had made a furious speech against the rich classes, the State and even the Kaiser himself, until the police officer threatened to close the meeting if anything else of that nature was said. Quite incomprehensibly Herr Geyring, who must have known quite well what sort of a bird he had to deal with, had not unmasked the man as an *agent provocateur*, but had actually come to his assistance and demanded freedom of speech for him. Well, after that it grew worse and worse, and finally the meeting was broken up. The committee and Herr Geyring were under arrest; he could vouch for that, for he had been among the last to leave the hall.

Esch felt upset, indeed more upset than he would admit. All that he knew was that he must have some wine if he was to bring order into the world again; Martin, who was against the strike, was arrested by police who were in with the shipping companies and a renegade officer, police who, in the most infamous manner, had seized an innocent man —perhaps because Esch himself had not handed Nentwig over to them! Yet the inspector had acted in a very friendly way towards him, actually had shielded him. Sudden anger at Lohberg overcame him; the confounded fool was probably so taken aback simply because he had expected harmless and uplifting twaddle about brotherhood and did not understand that things could turn to deadly earnest. Suddenly all this brotherhood twaddle seemed disgusting to Esch; what was the use of all these brotherhoods and associations? They only made the confusion greater and probably they were the cause of it; he brutally let fly at Lohberg: " For God's sake put away that cursed lemonade of yours, or I'll sweep it off the table . . . if only you drank honest wine you would be able at least to give a sensible answer to a plain question." But Lohberg only looked at him with his great uncomprehending eyes, in whose whites little red veins now appeared, and was in no state to resolve Esch's doubts, doubts which next day became much worse when he heard that as a protest against the arrest of their union secretary the transport and dock workers had gone on strike. Meanwhile Geyring was sentenced to await his trial for the crime of sedition.

During the performance Esch sat with Gernerth in the so-called manager's office, which always reminded him of his glass cage in the bonded warehouse. On the stage Teltscher and Ilona were going through their act, and he heard the whizzing knives striking against the black board. Above the writing-table was fixed a little white box marked with a red cross, supposed to contain bandages. For a long time it had certainly contained none, and for decades nobody had even opened it, yet Esch was convinced that at any moment Ilona might be carried in to have her bleeding wounds bound. But instead Teltscher appeared, slightly perspiring and slightly proud of himself, and wiping his hands on his handkerchief said: " Real work, good honest work . . . must be paid for." Gernerth made some calculations in his notebook: " theatre rent, 22 marks; tax, 16 marks; lighting, 4 marks; salaries . . ." " Oh, stow that! " said Teltscher. " I know it all by heart already. I've put four thousand crowns into this business and I'll never see them again . . . I'll just have to grin and bear it. . . . Herr Esch, don't you know anybody who would buy me out? He can have a twenty-per-cent rebate, and I'll give you ten-per-cent commission over and above." Esch had already heard these outbursts and these offers and no longer paid any attention to them, although he would gladly have bought out Teltscher to get rid both of him and Ilona.

Esch was in an ill humour. Since Martin's imprisonment life had become radically darker: the fact that his skirmishing with Erna had grown burdensome and intolerable was really secondary; but that Bertrand had bribed the police, and that the police had behaved abominably, was more than exasperating, and Ilona's relations with Korn, no longer concealed either by them or by Erna, were repulsive in his sight. It was disgusting. The very thought of it repelled him: Ilona, after all, was something superior. Yes, better that he should know nothing about her, and that she should disappear out of his life for ever. And Bertrand as well, along with his Central Rhine Shipping Company. This became quite clear to Esch for the first time now that Ilona came in in her outdoor clothes and silently and seriously sat down without being accorded a glance by the two men. Korn would presently appear to take her away; lately he had been going in and out here quite at his ease.

Ilona had been overcome by a genuine passion for Balthasar Korn, perhaps because he reminded her of some sergeant whom she had loved in her youth, perhaps simply because he was such a complete contrast to the adroit, sickly, blasé Teltscher, who in spite of his sickliness was so essentially brutal. Frankly, Esch did not waste any thought on such things; enough that a woman whom he himself had renounced, because she was destined for a better fate, was now being degraded by a man like Korn. But Teltscher's attitude was quite inexplicable. The fellow was clearly a pimp, and yet that wasn't a thing to trouble one's head about. Besides, the whole business could not bring him in very much; Korn certainly was generous enough, and in the new clothes which he had given her Ilona really looked superb, so superb that Fräulein Erna no longer regarded her brother's expensive love affair with by any means the same favour as at first; but in spite of all this Ilona would accept no money from Korn, and he had literally to force his presents on her; so deeply did she love him.

Korn appeared at the door and Ilona flung herself on his uniformed breast with Eastern words of endearment. No, it was past endurance! Teltscher laughed: "See that you enjoy yourself," and as they went out together he shouted after her in Hungarian a few words, obviously spiteful, which earned him not only a glance full of hatred from Ilona, but also a half-joking, half-serious threat from Korn that he would give the Jewish knife-thrower a beating yet. Teltscher paid no attention to this, but returned to his beloved business speculations: "We must provide something that isn't too expensive and that will draw the crowd." "Oh, what an epoch-making discovery, Herr Teltscher-Teltini," said Gernerth, making calculations in his notebook again. Then he looked up: "What do you say to wrestling matches for women?" Teltscher whistled reflectively through his teeth: "Might be considered: of course that can't be done either without money." Gernerth scribbled in his notebook. "We'll need some money, but not so very much; women don't cost much. Then tights ... we'll have to get someone interested in it." "I'm willing to teach them," said Teltscher, "and I can be the referee too. But here in Mannheim?" he made a contemptuous gesture, "there's no closing one's eyes to the fact that business is bad here. What do you say, Esch?" Esch had formed no definite opinion, but the hope rose within him that with a change of scene Ilona might be saved from Korn's clutches. And as it lay nearest to his heart, he replied that Cologne seemed to him a splendid place for staging wrestling matches; in the previous year wrestling matches had been given there in the circus, serious ones of course, and the place had been packed. "Ours will be serious too," Teltscher decided. They talked it over from all sides for a while longer, and finally Esch was empowered to discuss the matter, on his approaching visit to Cologne, with the theatrical agent, Oppenheimer, whom Gernerth would have written to in the interval. And if Esch should succeed in hunting up some money for the undertaking, it would not only be a friendly service, but he might get a percentage on it himself.

Esch knew at the moment of nobody likely to invest money. But in secret he thought of Lohberg, who might almost be regarded as a rich man. But would a pure Joseph have any interest in wrestling matches for women?

The arrests that had been made in advance of the strike had deprived the dock labourers of all their leaders, yet after ten days the strike was still lingering on. There were indeed some blacklegs, but they were too few to handle the railway freights, and since shipping in any case was partially paralysed, they were employed only on the most urgent work. In the bonded warehouses a Sabbath quiet reigned. Esch was annoyed, because it was unlikely that he could get away until the strike was over, and he lounged idly round the sheds, leaned against the door-posts, and finally sat down to write to Mother Hentjen. He gave her the details of Martin's arrest and told her about Lohberg, but he did not even mention Erna and Korn, for the mere thought of doing so disgusted him. Then he procured a fresh batch of picture postcards and addressed them to all the girls he had slept with in recent years, and whose names he could remember. Outside in the shadow the foremen and stevedores stood in a group, and behind the half-open sliding doors of an empty goods truck some men were playing cards. Esch wondered whom he should write to next, and tried to count in his head all the women he had ever had. He could not be sure of the total, and it was as if a column in his books would not balance properly, so to get it right he began to make a list of the names on a piece of paper, entering the month and year after each. Then he added them up and was satisfied, more especially as Korn came in boasting, as usual, what a fine woman Ilona was, and what a fiery Hungarian. Esch pocketed his list and let Korn go on talking; he would not be able to talk like that for much longer. Only let the strike once come to an end, and the Herr Customs Inspector would have to run all the way to Cologne for his Ilona, perhaps even farther still, to the end of the world. And he was almost sorry for the man because he did not know what was in store for him. Balthasar Korn went on boasting happily of his conquest, and when he had said his say about Ilona he drew out a pack of cards. In brotherly amity they sought out a third man and settled down to play for the rest of the day.

In the evening Esch looked in on Lohberg, who was sitting in his shop with a cigarette in his mouth before a pile of vegetarian journals. He laid these aside when Esch came in and began to talk about Martin. "The world," he said, "is poisoned, not only with nicotine and alcohol and animal food, but with a still worse poison that we can hardly even recognize . . . it's just like boils breaking out." His eyes were moist and looked feverish; he gave one an unhealthy impression; it seemed possible that there really was some poison working within him. Esch stood, lean and robust, in front of him, but his head was empty after so much card-playing and he did not catch the sense of these idiotic remarks, he hardly realized that they referred to Martin's imprisonment; everything was wrapped in a fog of idiocy, and his only definite wish was to have the affair of the theatre partnership cleared up once and for all. Esch didn't like hole-and-corner methods: "Will you go shares in Gernerth's theatre?" The question took Lohberg quite by surprise, and opening his eyes wide he merely said: "Eh?" "I'm asking you, are you willing to go shares in the theatre business?" "But I have a tobacco business." "You've been lamenting all this time that you don't like it, and so I thought you might want a change." Lohberg shook his head: "So long as my mother's alive I'll have to keep on the shop; the half of it's hers." "Pity," said Esch, "Teltscher thinks that putting on women wrestlers would bring in a hundred-per-cent profit." Lohberg did not even ask what the theatre had to do with wrestling, but merely said in his turn: "Pity." Esch went on: "I'm as tired of my trade as you are of yours. They're on strike now and there's nothing to do but sit about, it's enough to make one sick." "What do you want to do, then? Are you going into the theatre business too?" Esch thought it over; that meant simply being tied to a stool in some dusty manager's office beside Gernerth and Teltscher. The artists didn't appeal to him now that he had been behind the scenes; they weren't much better than Hede or Thusnelda. He had really no idea what he wanted to do; the day had been so stale. He said: "Clear out, to America." In an illustrated journal he had seen pictures of New York; these now came into his head; there had been also a photograph of an American boxing match and that brought him back to the wrestling. "If I could make enough money out of it to pay my fare I'd go to America." He was himself astonished to find that he meant it seriously, and now began seriously counting up his resources: he had nearly three hundred marks; if he put them into the wrestling business he could certainly increase them, and why shouldn't he, a strong, capable man with book-keeping experience, try his luck in America as well as here? At the very least he would have seen a bit of the world. Perhaps Teltscher and Ilona might actually come to New York on that engagement Teltscher was always talking about. Lohberg interrupted his train of thought: "You have some knowledge of languages, but I haven't, unfortunately." Esch nodded complacently; yes, with his French he could manage somehow, and English couldn't be so very much of a mystery; but Lohberg didn't need to know languages in order to go shares in promoting wrestling bouts. "No, not for that, but for going to America," Lohberg replied. And although to Lohberg it was almost inconceivable that any man, let alone himself, should live in any town but Mannheim, both Esch and he felt almost like fellow-travellers as they discussed the cost of the voyage and how the money could be raised. This discussion brought them back, by a natural concatenation of thought, to the chances of making money through women wrestlers, and after much hesitation Lohberg came to the conclusion that he could quite well abstract a thousand marks from his business and invest them with Gernerth. Of course that wouldn't be enough to buy out Teltscher, but it was quite good for a start, especially when Esch's three hundred were counted in.

The day had ended better than it began. As he went home Esch brooded over the problem of raising the rest of the money, and Fräulein Erna came into his mind.

Strong as was Erna's temptation to bind Esch to her by financial obligations, she remained firm even here to her principle of parting with nothing except to her affianced husband. When she archly intimated this resolve Esch was indignant: what kind of a man did she think he was? Did she imagine he wanted the money for himself? But even as he said this he felt that it was beside the point; that it was not really the money that was in question, and that Fräulein Erna was much more in the wrong than she could ever be made to understand; of course the money was only a means of ransoming Ilona, of shielding defenceless girls from ever having knives hurled at them again; of course he didn't want it for himself. But even that was by no means all, for over and above that he wanted nothing from Ilona herself—not he, not at the cost of other people's money—and he was quite glad, too, to be in that position; he didn't give a fig for Ilona, he was thinking of more important things, and he had every right to be angry when Erna supposed him to be self-seeking, every right to tell her rudely: well, she could keep her money, then. Erna, however, took his rudeness as an admission of guilt, exulted in having unmasked him, and giggled that she knew all about that, thinking meanwhile of a commercial traveller in Hof, who had not only enjoyed her favours, but had involved her in the more serious loss of fifty marks.

It was altogether a good day for Fräulein Erna. Esch had asked her for something which she could refuse him, and besides she was wearing a pair of new shoes that made her feel gay and looked well on her feet. She was ensconced on the sofa, and as a saucy and slightly mocking gesture she let her feet peep from under her skirt, and swung them to and fro; she liked the faint creaking of the leather and the pleasant tension across her instep. She had no desire to abandon this delightful conversation, and in spite of the rude end that Esch had put to it she asked again what he wanted so much money for. Esch once more remarked that she could keep it; Lohberg had been glad enough to get a share in the business. " Oh, Herr Lohberg," said Fräulein Erna, " he has plenty, he can afford it." And with that waywardness which characterizes many phases of love, and in virtue of which Fräulein Erna would have given herself to any chance comer rather than to Herr Esch, who was to be granted nothing except in wedlock, she was very eager now to infuriate him by giving the money to Lohberg instead of to him. She swung her feet to and fro. " Oh, well, in partnership with Herr Lohberg, that's a different story. He's a good business man." " He's an idiot! " said Esch, partly from conviction and partly from jealousy, a jealousy that pleased Fräulein Erna, for she had reckoned on it. She turned the knife in the wound: " I wouldn't give it to *you*." But her remark was strangely ineffective. What did it matter to him? He had given up Ilona, and it was really Korn's business to redeem her from those knives. Esch looked at Erna's swinging feet. She would open her eyes if she were told that her money was really to be applied in helping her brother's affair. Of course even that wouldn't do what was needed. Perhaps it was really Nentwig who should be made to pay. For if the world was to be redeemed one must attack the virus at its source, as Lohberg said; but that source was Nentwig, or perhaps even something hiding behind Nentwig, something greater—perhaps as great and as securely hidden in his inaccessibility as the chairman of a company —something one knew nothing about. It was enough to make a man angry, and Esch, who was a strong fellow and not in the least afflicted with nerves, felt inclined to stamp on Fräulein Erna's swinging feet to make her quiet. She said: " Do you like my shoes? " " No," retorted

Esch. Fräulein Erna was taken aback. " Herr Lohberg would like them
... when are you going to bring him here? You've simply been hiding
him ... out of jealousy, I suppose, Herr Esch?" Oh, he could bring the
man round at once if she was so anxious to see him, remarked Esch,
hoping privately that they would come to an understanding about the
theatre business. " No need for him to come at once," said Fräulein Erna,
" but why not this evening for coffee? " All right, he'd arrange that, said
Esch, and took himself off.

Lohberg came. He held his coffee-cup with one hand and stirred in it
mechanically with the other. He left his spoon in the cup even while he
was drinking, so that it hit him on the nose. Esch spread himself insolently,
asking if Balthasar and Ilona were coming, and making all kinds of tact-
less remarks. Fräulein Erna took no notice of him. She regarded with
interest Herr Lohberg's rachitic head and his large white eyeballs;
truly, he looked as if it would not take much to make him cry. And she
wondered if, in the heat and ardour of love, he would be moved to tears;
it annoyed her to think that her brother had pushed her into an unsatis-
factory relation with Esch, a brute of a man who upset her, while only
two or three houses farther away there was a well-established tradesman
who blushed whenever she looked at him. Had he ever had a woman,
she wondered, and to satisfy these speculations and to provoke Esch she
skilfully piloted the conversation towards the subject of love. " Are you
another of these born bachelors, Herr Lohberg? You'll repent it when
you're old and done and have nobody to look after you."

Lohberg blushed. " I'm only waiting for the right girl, Fräulein
Korn."

" And she hasn't turned up yet? " Fräulein Korn smiled encouragingly
and pointed her toe under the hem of her skirt. Lohberg set down his
cup and looked helpless.

Esch said tartly: " He hasn't tried yet, that's all."

Lohberg's convictions came to his support: " One can only love once,
Fräulein Korn."

" Oh! " said Fräulein Korn.

That was clear and unambiguous. Esch was almost ashamed of his
unchaste life, and it seemed to him not improbable that this great and
unique love was what Frau Hentjen had felt for her husband, and perhaps
that was why she now expected chastity and restraint from her customers.
All the same it must be dreadful for Frau Hentjen to have to pay for her

brief wedded bliss by renouncing love for ever afterwards, and so he said: " Well, but what about widows, then? At that rate, a widow shouldn't go on living . . . especially if she has no children . . ." and because he was observant of what he read in the illustrated papers he added: " Widows ought in that case really to be burned, so that . . . so that they might be redeemed, in a manner of speaking."

" You're a brute, Herr Esch," said Fräulein Erna. " Herr Lohberg would never say such things."

" Redemption is in God's hands," said Herr Lohberg, " if He grants anyone the great gift of love it will last for all eternity."

" You're a clever man, Herr Lohberg, and lots of people would be the better of taking your words to heart," said Fräulein Erna, " the very idea of letting oneself be burned for any man! The impudence . . ."

Esch said: " If the world was as it should be it could be redeemed without any of your silly organizations . . . yes, you can both look incredulous," he almost shouted, " but there would be no need for a Salvation Army if the police locked up all the people who deserved to be locked up . . . instead of the ones that are innocent."

" I wouldn't marry any man unless he had a pension, or could leave something for his widow, some kind of security," said Fräulein Erna, " that's only what one is entitled to expect from a good man."

Esch despised her. Mother Hentjen would never think of talking in such a way. But Lohberg said: " It's a bad provider who doesn't set his house in order."

" You'll make your wife a happy woman," said Fräulein Erna.

Lohberg went on: " If God blesses me with a wife, I hope I can say with confidence that we shall live in true Christian unity. We shall renounce the world and live for each other."

Esch jeered: " Just like Balthasar and Ilona . . . and every evening she gets knives chucked at her."

Lohberg was indignant: " A man who drinks cheap spirits can't appreciate crystal-clear water, Fräulein Korn. A passion of that kind isn't love."

Fräulein Erna took the crystalline purity as a reference to herself and was flattered: " That dress he gave her cost thirty-eight marks. I found that out in the shop. To fleece a man like that . . . I could never bring myself to do it."

Esch said: " Things need to be set right. An innocent man sits in jail, and another runs around as he pleases; one ought either to do *him* in or do oneself in."

Lohberg soothed him down: " Human life isn't to be lightly taken."

" No," said Fräulein Erna, " if anyone should be done in it's a woman who has no feelings where men are concerned . . . as for me, when I have a man to look after I'm a woman of feeling."

Lohberg said: " A genuine Christian love is founded on mutual respect."

" And you would respect your wife even if she weren't as educated as yourself . . . but more a creature of feeling, as a woman should be."

" Only a person of feeling is capable of receiving the redeeming grace and ready for it."

Fräulein Erna said: " I'm sure you're a good son, Herr Lohberg, one that is capable of feeling gratitude for all his mother has done for him."

That made Esch angry, angrier than he knew: " Good son or no . . . I don't give *that* for gratitude; as long as people look on while injustice is being done there's no grace in the world . . . why has Martin sacrificed himself and been put in jail? "

Lohberg answered: " Herr Geyring is a victim of the poison that's destroying the world. Only when they get back to nature will people stop hurting each other."

Fräulein Erna said that she too was a lover of nature and often went for long walks.

Lohberg went on: " Only in God's good air, that lifts our hearts up, are men's nobler feelings awakened."

Esch said: " That kind of thing has never got a single man out of jail yet."

Fräulein Erna remarked: " That's what you say . . . but I say, a man with no feelings is no man at all. A man as faithless as you are, Herr Esch, has no right to put in his word. . . . And men are all the same."

" How can you think so badly of the world, Fräulein Korn? "

She sighed: " The disappointments of life, Herr Lohberg."

" But hope keeps our hearts up, Fräulein Korn."

Fräulein Erna gazed thoughtfully into space: " Yes, if it weren't for hope . . ." then she shook her head: " Men have no feelings, and too much brains is just as bad."

Esch wondered if Frau Hentjen and her husband had spoken in that strain when they got engaged. But Lohberg said: " In God and in God's divine Nature is hope for all of us."

Erna did not want to be outdone: " I go regularly to church and confession, thank God . . ." and with triumph she added: " Our holy Catholic faith has more feeling in a way than the Protestant religion—if I were a man I would never marry a Protestant."

Lohberg was too polite to contradict her:

" All ways to God are equally worthy of respect. And those whom God has joined will learn from Him to live peaceably together . . . all that is needed is good will."

Lohberg's virtue once more disgusted Esch, although he had often compared him with Mother Hentjen because of that same virtue. He burst out: " Any idiot can talk."

Fräulein Erna said with disdain: " Herr Esch, of course, would take anybody he came across, he doesn't bother about such things as feelings or religion; all he asks is that she should have money."

He simply couldn't believe that, said Herr Lohberg.

" Oh, you can take my word for it, I know him, he has no feelings, and he never thinks about anything . . . the kind of thoughts you have, Herr Lohberg, aren't to be found in everybody."

But if that were so he was sorry for Herr Esch, remarked Lohberg, for that meant he would never find happiness in this world.

Esch shrugged his shoulders. What did this fellow know about the new world? He said contemptuously: " First set the world right."

But Fräulein Erna had found the solution: " If two people worked together, if your wife, for instance, were to help you in your business, then everything else would be all right, even if the man was a Protestant and the wife a Catholic."

" Of course," said Lohberg.

" Or if two people should have something in common, a common interest, as they say . . . then they must stand by each other, mustn't they? "

" Of course," said Lohberg.

Fräulein Erna's lizard eye glanced at Esch as she said: " Would you have any objections, Herr Lohberg, if I joined you in the theatre business that Herr Esch was speaking of? Now that my brother has lost his senses I at least must try to bring in some money."

How could Herr Lohberg have any objection! And when Fräulein

Erna said that she would invest the half of her savings, say about a thousand marks, he cried, and she was delighted to hear it: " Oh! Then we'll be partners."

In spite of this Esch was dissatisfied. The fact that he had got his own way had all at once ceased to matter, maybe because in any case he had renounced Ilona, maybe because there were more important aims at stake, but perhaps only because—and this was the sole reason of which he was conscious—he suddenly had serious misgivings.

"Talk it over first with Gernerth, the manager of the theatre. I've only told you about it, I don't accept any responsibility."

"Oh yes," said Fräulein Erna, she knew well enough that he was an irresponsible man, and he didn't need to be afraid that he would be called to account. He wasn't much of a Christian, and she thought more of Herr Lohberg's little finger than of Herr Esch's whole body. And wouldn't Herr Lohberg come in now and then for a cup of coffee? Yes? And since it was getting late, and they had already got to their feet, she took Lohberg by the arm. The lamp above them shed a mild light upon their heads, and they stood before Esch like a newly engaged couple.

Esch had taken off his coat and hung it on the stand. Then he began to brush and beat it and examined its worn collar. Again he was conscious of some discrepancy in his calculations. He had given up Ilona, yet he was supposed to look on while Erna turned away from him and set her cap at that idiot. It was against all the laws of book-keeping, which demanded that every debit entry should be balanced by a credit one. Of course—and he shook the coat speculatively—if he chose he could keep a Lohberg from getting the better of *him*; he was easily a match for the man; no, August Esch was far from being such an ugly monstrosity, and he actually took a step or two towards the door, but paused before he opened it; tut, he didn't choose to, that was all. The creature across the passage might think he had come crawling to her out of gratitude for her measly thousand marks. He turned and sat down on his bed, where he unlaced his shoes. The balance was all right, so far. And the fact that he was at bottom resentful because he couldn't sleep with Erna, that was all right, too. One cut one's losses. Yet there was an obscure miscalculation somewhere that he couldn't put his finger on: granted that he wasn't going across the passage to that woman, granted that he was giving up his bit of fun, what was his real reason for doing so? Was it perhaps to escape marriage? Was he making the smaller sacrifice to escape the greater, to avoid paying in person? Esch said: "I'm a swine." Yes, he was a swine, not a whit better than Nentwig, who also shuffled off responsibility. His accounts were in a disorder which it would take the devil and all to clear up.

But disorderly accounts meant a disorderly world, and a disorderly world meant that Ilona would go on being a target for knives, that Nentwig would continue with brazen hypocrisy to evade punishment, and that Martin would sit in jail for ever. He thought it all over, and as he slipped off his drawers the answer came spontaneously: the others had given their money for the wrestling business, and so he, who had no money, must give himself, not in marriage, certainly, but in personal service, to the new undertaking. And since that, unfortunately, did not fit in with his job in Mannheim, he must simply give notice. That was the way he could pay his debt. And as if in corroboration of this conclusion, he suddenly realized that he ought not to remain any longer with a company that had been the means of putting Martin in jail. No one could accuse him of disloyalty; even the Herr Chairman would have to admit that Esch was a decent fellow. This new idea drove Erna out of his head, and he lay down in bed relieved and comforted. Going back to Cologne and to Mother Hentjen's would, of course, be pleasant, and that diminished his sacrifice a little, but so little that it hardly counted; after all, Mother Hentjen hadn't even answered his letter. And there were restaurants a-plenty in Mannheim. No, the return to Cologne, that unjust town, was a very negligible offset to his sacrifice; it was at most an entry in the petty-cash account, and a man could always credit himself with petty cash. His eagerness to report his success drove him to see Gernerth early next morning: it was no small feat to have raised two thousand marks so quickly! Gernerth clapped him on the shoulder and called him the devil of a fellow. That did Esch good. Yet his decision to give up his job and take service in the theatre astounded Gernerth; he could not, however, produce any valid objection. "We'll manage it somehow, Herr Esch," he said, and Esch went off to the head office of the Central Rhine Shipping Company.

In the upper floors of the head office buildings there were long, hushed corridors laid with brown linoleum. On the doors were stylish plates bearing the names of the occupants, and at one end of each corridor, behind a table lit by a standard lamp, sat a man in uniform who asked what one wanted and wrote down one's name and business on a duplicate block. Esch traversed one of the corridors, and since it was for the last time he took good note of everything. He read every name on the doors, and when to his surprise he came on a woman's name, he paused and tried to imagine what she would be like: was she an ordinary clerk casting up accounts at a sloping desk with black cuffs over her sleeves, and would she be cool and offhand with visitors like all the others? He felt a sudden desire for the unknown woman behind the door, and there arose in him the conception of a new kind of love, a simple, one might almost say a business-like and official kind of love, a love that would run as smoothly, as calmly, and yet as spaciously and neverendingly, as these corridors with their polished linoleum. But then he saw the long series of doors with men's names, and he could not help thinking that a lone woman in that masculine environment must be as disgusted with it as Mother Hentjen was with her business. A hatred of commercial methods stirred again within him, hatred of an organization that, behind its apparent orderliness, its smooth corridors, its smooth and flawless book-keeping, concealed all manner of infamies. And that was called respectability! Whether head clerk or chairman of a company, there was nothing to choose between one man of business and another. And if for a moment Esch had regretted that he was no longer a unit in the smoothly running organization, no longer privileged to go out and in without being stopped or questioned or announced, his regret now vanished, and he saw only a row of Nentwigs sitting behind these doors, all of them pledged and concerned to keep Martin languishing in confinement. He would have liked to go straight down to the counting-house and tell the blind fools there that they too should break out of their prison of hypocritical ciphers and columns and like him set themselves free; yes, that was what they should do, even at the risk of having to join him in emigrating to America.

"But it's a pretty short star turn you've given us here," the staff manager said when he gave in his notice and asked for a testimonial, and Esch felt tempted to divulge the real reasons for his departure from such a despicable firm. But he had to leave them unsaid, for the friendly staff manager immediately bent his attention to other matters, although he repeated once or twice: "A short star turn . . . a short star turn," in an unctuous voice, as if he liked the phrase and as if he were hinting that theatrical life wasn't so very different from or even superior to the business that Esch was relinquishing. What could the staff manager know about it? Was he really reproaching Esch with disloyalty and planning to catch him unawares? To trip him up in his new job? Esch followed his movements with a suspicious eye and with a suspicious eye ran over the document that was handed to him, although he knew very well that in his new profession nobody would ask to see a testimonial. And since the thought of his work in the theatre obsessed him, even as he was striding over the brown linoleum of the corridor towards the staircase he no longer remarked the quiet orderliness of the building, nor speculated about the woman's name on the door he passed by, nor saw even the notice-board marked " Counting House "; the very pomp of the board-room and the Chairman's private office in the front part of the main building meant nothing to him. Only when he was out in the street did he cast a glance back, a farewell glance, as he said to himself, and was vaguely disappointed because there was no equipage waiting at the main entrance. He would really have liked to set eyes on Bertrand for once. Of course, like Nentwig, the man kept himself well out of the way. And of course it would be better not to see him, not to set eyes on him at all, or on Mannheim for that matter and all that it stood for. Good-bye for ever, said Esch; yet he was incapable of departing so quickly and found himself lingering and blinking in the midday sunlight that streamed evenly over the asphalt of the new street, lingering and waiting for the glass doors to turn noiselessly on their hinges, perhaps, and let the Chairman out. But even though in the shimmering light it looked as if the two wings of the door were trembling, so that one was reminded of the swing doors behind Mother Hentjen's buffet, yet that was only a so-called optical illusion and the two halves of the door were immobile in their marble framework. They did not open and no one came out. Esch felt insulted: there he had to stand in the glaring sun simply because the Central Rhine Shipping Company had established itself in a flashy new asphalt road instead of a cool and cellar-like street; he turned round, crossed the street with long, rather awkward strides, rounded the next corner, and as he swung himself on to the footboard of a tram that rattled past, he had finally decided to leave Mannheim the very next day and go to Cologne to start negotiations with Oppenheimer, the theatrical agent.

II

It was natural that Esch should be annoyed because Mother Hentjen had never answered his letter, since even business letters were always answered within a certain time, and a private letter deserved more consideration, not being a mere matter of business routine. Still, Mother Hentjen's silence was in keeping with her character. It was common knowledge that a man needed only snatch at her hand, or try to pinch her on the more protuberant parts of her body, to make her stiffen into that rigidity of disgust with which she silently checked the importunate; perhaps Esch's letter had provoked a similar reaction in her. After all, a letter is something the writer's fingers have dirtied, not unlike dirty body-linen, and Mother Hentjen might be depended on to see it in that light. She was quite different from other women; she was not the woman to walk into a man's room early in the morning before it had been tidied without showing embarrassment even if he was washing himself. She was no Erna: she would never have asked Esch to think of her sometimes and to write her nice, sentimental letters. Nor was she the woman to have an affair with a man like Korn, although she was a more earthly creature than Ilona. Of course, like Ilona, Mother Hentjen was something superior, only it seemed to Esch that on the earthly plane she had to maintain by artifice what Ilona had by nature. And if she was disgusted by his letter he could understand and approve her attitude; he had almost a yearning to be scolded by her: it seemed as if she were bound to know what he had been up to, and he could feel again the cold look with which she had always reproached him whenever he slept with Hede; not even that had she been willing to tolerate, and yet the girl was a member of her own establishment.

When he arrived in Cologne, however, and made it his first business to call on Mother Hentjen, Esch was received neither with the friendliness he had hoped for nor the reproach he had feared. She merely said: "Oh, there you are again, Herr Esch. I hope you're staying for some time," and he felt like an outsider, felt actually as if he were doomed for all eternity to vegetate forgotten in the Korn household. When Frau Hentjen did come to his table later she wounded him even more deeply by speaking only of Martin: "Yes, he's got what he was asking for, Herr Geyring"—she had warned him often enough. Esch answered in monosyllables; he had told her all he knew when he wrote. " Oh! I must thank you for your letter, too," said Frau Hentjen, and that was all. In spite of his disappointment he pulled out a parcel: " I've brought you a souvenir from Mannheim." It was a replica of the Schiller Memorial outside the Mannheim theatre, and Esch indicated the shelf from which the Eiffel Tower looked down with its black-white-and-red flag; it would perhaps go all right up there. And although he merely handed the thing over without further ado, Frau Hentjen accepted it with unexpected and genuine delight, for this was something she could show to her friends. " Oh no, I won't let anybody so much as look at it down here; it's too lovely for that; it's going upstairs into my parlour . . . but it isn't right of you, Herr Esch, to go to such expense for me." Her warmth put him in a good mood again, and he began to tell her about his life in Mannheim, not omitting to express certain edifying sentiments which, though really emanating from that fool Lohberg, would, he assumed, be acceptable to Mother Hentjen. With many interruptions, for she was often called to the buffet, he extolled to her the beauties of nature, especially of the Rhine, and said he was surprised that she stuck so closely to Cologne and never made an excursion to places so easily within her reach. " All very well for sweethearting couples," said Mother Hentjen contemptuously, and Esch answered respectfully that she could quite well go alone or with a woman friend. That sounded plausible and reassuring to Frau Hentjen, and she said that she might consider it some day. " Anyhow," she remarked, dismissing it for the present, " I knew the Rhine well enough when I was a girl." Hardly had she said this than she stiffened and stared over his head. Esch was not surprised, for he knew Mother Hentjen's sudden withdrawals. But there was a particular reason for her reserve on this occasion, a reason that Esch could not have surmised: it was the first time that Frau Hentjen had ever mentioned her private life to a customer, and she was so upset by the realization that she fled to the buffet to look in the glass and finger her sugar-loaf coiffure. She was angry with Esch because he had drawn confidences from her, and she did not return to his table although the Schiller Memorial was still standing there. She felt like telling him to take it away, especially as one or two of his friends had sat down beside him and were running it over with masculine eyes and masculine fingers. She fled still farther, into the kitchen, and Esch knew that he had unwittingly committed some blunder or other. But when she finally reappeared he rose and took the statuette to the buffet. She polished it clean with one of the glass-cloths. Esch, who remained standing because he did not know how to extricate himself, told her that in the theatre opposite the memorial the *première* —that was a word he had learned from Gernerth—the *première* of one of Schiller's plays had taken place. He himself had now various connections with the theatre, and if everything went well he would soon be able to get tickets for her. Really? He had connections with the theatre? Oh, well, he had always been something of a wastrel. For Mother Hentjen connections with the theatre simply meant relations with the vulgar actresses, and she remarked, contemptuously and indifferently, that she could not bear the theatre, for there was nothing in it but love, love, and that bored her. Esch did not venture to contradict her, but while Frau Hentjen carried her present into safety upstairs he began talking to Hede, who had barely looked at him, being obviously offended because he had not thought it worth his while to send her a postcard too. Hede seemed thoroughly ill-humoured, and ill-humour seemed to pervade the whole restaurant, in which the automatic instrument, set a-going by a reckless client, was now grinding out its tunes. Hede rushed to the instrument to turn it off, since music at such a late hour was against the public regulations, and all the men laughed at the success of the prank. Through the half open window a stray night breeze wandered in, and Esch, who had got a whiff of it, slipped outside into the mild freshness of the night, quickly, before Hede could return, quickly, before he could encounter Frau Hentjen again; for she might get out of him that he had thrown up his job with the Central Rhine Shipping: and she certainly wouldn't be talked into believing that the promotion of wrestling matches was a respectable occupation; she wouldn't believe in its prospects, but would be sure to make adverse malicious comments— perhaps with justice. Still, he had had enough for one night, and so he took himself off.

In the black, cellar-like streets there was a chill stench, as always in summer. Esch was vaguely content. The air and the dark walls were familiar and comforting; a man did not feel lonely. He almost wished that he might meet Nentwig. He would have enjoyed giving the man a good hiding. And it exhilarated Esch to feel that life often provided quite simple solutions. Yet it was a lottery in which winning numbers were rare, and so he would just have to stick to the scheme for promoting wrestling matches.

Oppenheimer, the theatrical agent, possessed neither an antechamber with cushioned chairs, nor a reception clerk with forms for visitors to fill up. That was only to be expected. But nobody likes an exchange for the worse, and Esch had nursed a vague hope of finding an establishment not unlike that of the Central Rhine Shipping translated into theatrical terms. Well, it wasn't like that at all. After he had climbed a narrow dark staircase to the mezzanine floor, found a door marked " Oppenheimer's Agency," and knocked at it without getting any response, he was forced simply to walk in unannounced. He found himself in a room where an iron washstand was standing filled with dirty water and pigeonholes of all kinds were cluttered up with waste-paper. On one wall hung a large calendar issued by an insurance company, on the other wall, framed and glazed, was a picture of a ship of the Hamburg-Amerika line, the *Kaiserin Augusta Viktoria*, painted in gay colours with a swarm of smaller craft around her, as she left the harbour and clove the foaming blue waves of the North Sea. Esch did not give himself time to inspect the ship closely, for he had come on business, and since shyness was not one of his characteristics he pushed, although with some hesitation, into a second room. There he found a writing-desk that, in contrast to the disorder prevailing elsewhere, had nothing whatever upon it, not even any trace of writing materials, but was splotched with ink, its brown wood scored and nicked with old grey notches and new yellow ones, and its green-baize cloth torn in many places. There was no other door. In this room too, however, there were notable wall-decorations fastened to the wallpaper with drawing-pins, a collection of photographs that kindled Esch's interest, for there were many ladies in tights or spangles, in seductive and alluring poses, and he gave a glance round to see if Ilona was amongst them. But he thought it more proper to withdraw and inquire of somebody where Herr Oppenheimer might be found. There was no house porter, and so he rang at several doors until he was told, with a contempt that included himself, that Oppenheimer's office hours were highly irregular. " You can wait about for him if you've nothing better to do," said a woman.

So that was that. It was unpleasant to be treated in that way, and if his new profession were to expose him to such contempt it was hardly encouraging. Still, it couldn't be helped, he had taken it on for Ilona's sake (and the thought gave him a thrill of warmth about the heart); it was in any case his new profession, and so Esch waited. Fine office habits this Herr Oppenheimer had contracted! Esch had to laugh; no, this was not a job in which testimonials were likely to be asked for. He stood before the house door gazing down the street, until at length an insignificant, small, fair-haired, rosy man came towards the house and went up the stairs. Esch followed him. It was Herr Oppenheimer. When Esch explained his business Herr Oppenheimer said: " Women wrestlers? I'll fix it up, I'll fix it up all right. But what does Gernerth need you for? " Yes, what did Gernerth need him for? Why was he here? What had brought him here at all? Now that he had given up his post in the Central Rhine Shipping Company his visit to Cologne was by no means the official journey he had projected. Why had he come to Cologne, then? Surely not because Cologne was a stage nearer the sea?

When an honest man emigrates to America his relations and friends stand on the quay and wave their handkerchiefs to him. The ship's band plays, *Must I then, must I then, leave my native Town*, and although one might regard this, in view of the frequency with which ships make the voyage, as a show of hypocrisy on the part of the bandmaster, yet many of the listeners are moved. When the rope is once made fast to the tiny tug, when the ocean giant floats out on the dark, buoyant mirror of the sea, then fitful and forlorn over the water come faint gusts of more cheerful melodies with which the kindly bandmaster is trying to enliven the departing passengers. Then it becomes clear to many a man how dispersedly his fellows are scattered over the face of the sea and the earth, and how frail are the threads that bind them one to another. Thus, gliding out of the harbour into clearer waters, where the current of the river is no longer discernible and the tides of the sea actually seem to be setting backwards into the harbour, the great liner often swims in a cloud of invisible but tense anguish, so that many a spectator feels prompted to stop her. On she goes, past the ships that lie along the smoking, littered shores, rattling their cranes to and fro as they load and unload vague cargoes for vague destinations, past the littered shores that take on a dusty greenness towards the river-mouth and come to an end in scanty herbage, finally past the sand-dunes where the lighthouse comes into sight, on she goes, fettered like an outcast to her tiny escort, and on the ships and along the shores stand men who watch her go, raise their arms as if to stop her, yet summon up merely a half-hearted and awkward wave of the hand. Once she is out in the open sea and her hull is almost sunk below the horizon, so that her three funnels are barely visible, many a man peering out to sea from the coast asks himself if this ship is making for the harbour or forging her way into a loneliness that the longshoreman can never comprehend. And if he finds that she is heading for the land he is comforted, as though she were bringing home his sweetheart, or at least a long-expected letter that he had not known he was waiting for. Often in the light haze of that distant frontier two ships meet, and one can see them gliding past each other. There is a moment in which both the delicate silhouettes merge together and become one, a moment of subtle exaltation, until they softly separate again with a motion as quiet and soft as the distant haze in which they pair, and each one goes alone her own way. Sweet, never-to-be-fulfilled hope!

But the passenger out yonder on board the ship does not know that we have been anxious for him. He scarcely notices the undulating ribbon of the coast, and only when he vaguely divines the yellow ray of the lighthouse is he aware that there are those on land who are anxious for him and think of his danger. He does not understand the danger that in fact encompasses him, he is not conscious that a great mountain of water separates him from the sea-bottom that is the earth. Only the man who has an aim fears danger, for he is afraid of failure. But the passenger who walks on the smooth planks that run round the deck like a racing-track, and that are smoother than any path he has yet trod, the passenger on board ship has no aim, and can never complete his destiny; he is closed within himself. All his potentialities lie asleep. One who loves him can love him only for what he promises to be, for all that lies within him, not for what he will achieve or has achieved; he will never achieve it. So men on shore know nothing about love and mistake their fears for love. The sea-passenger, however, soon comes to this knowledge, and the threads that were spun from him to those on shore are broken before the coastline sinks out of sight. It is almost superfluous for the bandmaster to try enlivening melodies upon him, for the passenger is content to let his hand slide over the smooth brown polish of the railing and its glittering brass rings. The shining sea lies stretched before him; he is at peace. Mighty engines drive him on, and their humming shapes a path that leads nowhere. The eye of the passenger at sea is a different eye: it is the eye of an orphaned man that recognizes us no longer. He has forgotten what was once his daily task; he believes no longer in the correctness of addition sums, and if his way should take him past the telegraph operator's cabin and he should hear the ticking of the apparatus, he marvels maybe at the mechanism, but cannot convince himself that the operator is receiving messages from the land and sending messages to the land; indeed, if he were not a sober-minded man he might think that the operator was speaking to the cosmos. He loves the whales and the dolphins that play round the ship, and he has no fear of the icebergs. But if a distant coastline should come into sight he refuses to look at it and perhaps takes refuge in the belly of the ship until it has vanished again, for he knows that it is not love that awaits him there, not loose-footed freedom, but taut anxiety and the straight walls of his aim. For he who seeks love seeks the sea; he may perhaps speak of the land that lies beyond the sea, but he does not mean what he says, for he thinks of the voyage as endless, the voyage that nourishes in his lonely soul the hope of expanding and opening itself to receive that other who emerges free as air from the light haze and enters into him, that other whom he rightly recognizes as a potential, unborn immortal.

It is undeniable that none of these reflections occurred to Esch, although he remained obsessed by the thought of emigrating to America and taking the book-keepers of the Central Rhine Shipping Company as fellow-passengers. But whenever he came into Herr Oppenheimer's office he studied long and minutely the *Kaiserin Augusta Viktoria* as she clove the waves.

He had resumed his former life, occupied his old room, and often took his midday meal at Mother Hentjen's. He used his bicycle with zeal, but his daily routine took him now to Herr Oppenheimer's instead of to Stemberg & Company. Frau Hentjen had acknowledged the change in his vocation with a look that, in spite of her detachment, showed a blend of something like contempt, dissatisfaction, and perhaps even a hint of scorn, and although Esch had to admit that her concern was justified—indeed, maybe because of it—he exerted himself in painting to her in rosy colours the prospects and advantages of his new profession. He partly succeeded. Though she turned a deaf ear to his bold accounts of the greatness on the threshold of which he was now standing, and which would spread not only to America but over all the continents of the world, yet the compound of glittering riches, artistic success and joyous travel with which he tried to dazzle her, this destiny which another was to achieve and not herself, this far-flung greatness aroused the envy of the woman who had loathed for fifteen years the sordid narrowness of her fate. She was filled, one might say, with a kind of malicious admiration, for while on the one hand she maintained obstinately that his ambitions were hollow and unattainable, on the other she surpassed him in fantastic invention, gave him high-sounding advice, and encouraged him to think that he might rise to become the Chief or, as he said, the Chairman, of the whole gang of artists, performers and managers. "First of all they must be brought under severe order and discipline," he used to reply, " that's what they need most." Yes, he was convinced of that, and this profound contempt for artists was founded not merely on his distaste for Gernerth's greasy notebook and Oppenheimer's chaotic office, but coincided so closely with Mother Hentjen's principles that in one such moment of admiring assent—a world-embracing principle often debouches into a domestic triviality—Frau Hentjen granted his request to entrust her bills and accounts to his proficient supervision: she granted it with a condescending smile, as if fully persuaded that her simple books were kept in the most sensible and model manner. But scarcely had Esch bent himself over the columns when Mother Hentjen cried that he needn't put on such a superior air; she wasn't by any means impressed by his smattering of book-keeping; he had much better turn his attention to the theatrical business, which needed looking after much more than hers. And she snatched the books from him.

Yes, the theatrical business! With the casualness of his profession Oppenheimer was accustomed to accept lightly the accidents of chance, and although the persistence of Esch left him defenceless, he laughed over this man who came every day on his bicycle and behaved as if he were a partner in the firm; but he put up with it on learning that Esch was bringing new capital into the wrestling scheme, and even swallowed the insults that Esch daily flung at the disorder in his office. They had jointly bargained with the proprietor of the Alhambra Theatre for its lease during June and July, and since Esch's zeal for work had to be appeased, he was empowered to recruit the lady wrestlers.

Esch, experienced as he was in drinking dens, brothels and girls, was the very man for this job. He combed out all the establishments, and whenever he found likely girls who were willing to enter the lists, he wrote down their names and qualifications in a notebook which he had himself ruled and spaced, and in which he did not omit to enter after each name, in a special column headed by the business-like word "Observations," his judgment on the capabilities of the candidates according to a rough-and-ready classification. He was especially partial to girls with foreign-sounding names and of foreign race, for it was to be an international wrestling tournament, and the only ones he excepted were the Hungarians. It was often good enough fun trying the girls' muscles, and sometimes even their stalwart charms seduced him. None the less he did not really enjoy his task, and when he spoke of it to Mother Hentjen in a disparaging and casual manner he was quite sincere: he could no longer regard such an occupation as compatible with his dignity, and he much preferred to sit at Oppenheimer's vacant desk or to inspect the Alhambra.

He often betook himself there, traversing the empty grey auditorium in which one's steps echoed on the floor-boards, and crossing the teetering planks laid over the well of the orchestra up to the stage, whose gigantic, naked grey walls were almost too overpowering for the flimsy screens of the wings that would soon cover them. When he measured the stage with long strides it was as if in triumph because no more knives were to be hurled across it, and when he peeped into the managerial office it was to wonder whether he couldn't already install himself there. He reflected, too, that he must show Frau Hentjen round his new kingdom. The air was oddly grey and cool, although the beer-garden outside was glowing in the heat of the bright sun, and this self-contained kingdom of dusty strangeness was like a remote island of the unknown within a world of familiar things, it was a promise and an indication of all the strange potentialities that lay in wait across the great grey sea. In the evening, too, he often repaired to the Alhambra. But then the beer-garden was illuminated, and a band played on the wooden platform under the trees. The theatre lurked dark and almost unnoticed behind the lights, filled to the very roof with darkness, and one could not imagine how spacious and well arranged it was. Esch liked coming at such a late hour, for he found it pleasant to think that it was reserved for him and for no other to reawaken the life within that dark building.

When Esch visited the Alhambra again on one of the following mornings he found the proprietor playing cards with friends at the bar. He joined them and they played until late in the afternoon. By that time Esch felt his face vacant and wooden, and was aware that the life he was leading exactly resembled that in the Mannheim warehouses during the strike. It only needed Korn to come along and boast about Ilona's lovemaking. What was the sense of his having given up his job in the Central Rhine Shipping? Here he was frittering away his time in idleness, using up his money, and he had not even avenged Martin. If he had stayed in Mannheim he could at least have visited Martin in jail.

At supper he accused himself of having deserted Martin shamefully, but when Frau Hentjen replied that every man must look out for himself, and that Herr Geyring, who had been warned often enough by her, could not expect a friend of his to stay in Mannheim for his sake and give up a brilliant career, he flew into a rage and abused her so vehemently that she took refuge behind the buffet and fingered at her hair. He paid his bill on the spot and left the restaurant, infuriated because she had extolled his idleness as a brilliant career. He did not, however, admit to himself that that was the cause of his anger, but merely denounced her for cold heartlessness towards Martin, and he spent the whole night in brooding over ways and means of helping Martin.

Early in the morning he betook himself to Oppenheimer's office. He had procured writing materials for himself and spent the whole morning in composing a savage article in which he made it clear that that deserving union secretary, Martin Geyring, had fallen a victim to a diabolical intrigue between the Central Rhine Shipping Company and the Mannheim police. This article he carried forthwith to the editorial office of the Social Democratic *People's Guardian*.

The building in which *The People's Guardian* had its headquarters was no palace of journalism. Not a single marble vestibule or wrought-iron gate. In general it was not unlike Oppenheimer's office, only that it was much busier; but on Sundays, when the newspaper world was on holiday, it would be the exact double of his. The black iron railings of the staircase were sticky to the touch, the peeling, shabby walls bore the traces of frequent pictorial activity, and from a window one looked out on a small courtyard in which stood a dray loaded with rolls of paper. Printing machines were at work somewhere with asthmatic rattlings. One entered the editorial office through a door that had once been white and banged ruthlessly because its lock did not fit. Instead of an insurance calendar there was a timetable on the wall, instead of dancers' portraits a photograph of Karl Marx. Nothing else was different, and his incursion here seemed all at once so wholly superfluous that even his article, which had sounded powerful and sinister, suddenly appeared lame and superfluous too. The same crew everywhere, thought Esch with fury. The same crew of demagogues, living everywhere in the same disorder. It was a waste of time to put a weapon into the hand of any of them. In their hands it would droop ineffectually, for not one of them knew the ins and outs of anything.

He was directed to a second room. Behind a table that might have once been covered with cloth sat a man in a brown-velvet jacket. Esch gave him the manuscript. The editor skimmed it over hastily, folded it, and laid it in a basket beside him. " But you haven't read it," said Esch sharply. " Oh yes, I know what it's about . . . the Mannheim strike; we'll see if we can use it." Esch was amazed at the man's lack of curiosity about the article, and at his assumption that he knew all about it already. " Excuse me, these are facts that put the strike in an entirely new light," he insisted. The editor picked up the manuscript, but laid it down again immediately. " What facts? I saw nothing new in it." Esch felt that the other was trying to display his omniscience. " But I was an eyewitness; I was at the meeting!" " Well, our confidential agents were there too." " Have you made it public, then?" " As far as I know there was nothing special to make public." Esch was so astounded that he simply sat down on a chair, although he had not been asked to do so. " My dear comrade," the editor went on, " after all you can't expect us to wait until you choose to pitch in your report." " Yes, but," Esch was completely bewildered, " but why haven't you done something, then? Why do you let Martin," he corrected himself, " why do you let Geyring sit in jail though he's innocent?" " Oh, that's it? . . . all honour to your sense of justice," the editor glanced at the manuscript which bore Esch's name, " Herr Esch, . . . but do you really think we could get him out as easily as that?" He laughed. Esch was not to be put off with laughter: " It's the other side that should be in the lock-up . . . that was more than evident to anyone who was there!" " So you think that we should have the directors of the Central Rhine Shipping jailed instead of Geyring?" What a nasty laugh, thought Esch, and remained silent. Have Bertrand locked up? Why not Bertrand as well as Nentwig? After all, in the sober light of day there wasn't such an enormous difference between the chairman of a company and a Nentwig, except that the Mannheim chairman was something better than Nentwig, and the lock-up wouldn't be good enough for him. Absently he repeated:

"Have Bertrand locked up." The editor laughed more than ever. "That would just about put the lid on it." "And why?" asked Esch with irritation. "He's a decent chap, friendly and sociable," explained the editor amiably, "a first-class man of business, the kind of man one can get on with." "So you can get on with a man who's hand in glove with the police?" "Heavens above, of course the employers work with the police; if we were on top we'd do exactly the same." "And you call that justice?" said Esch indignantly. The editor raised his hands in amused resignation. "How can we help it? That's how justice is organized in the Capitalist State. Meanwhile a man who takes the trouble to keep his concerns going is of more use to us than one who simply shuts up shop. If you got your way and all the employers who are against us were put in jail we'd have an industrial crisis, and we'd get a lot of credit for that, wouldn't we?" Esch repeated with obstinate anger: "All the same, he should be locked up." The editor's mirth became more and more irritating. "Ah, now I see what you're getting at: you mean because he's a sodomite? ... " Esch pricked up his ears, the editor became still more genial, "that bothers you, does it? Well, I can set your mind at rest on that point: he only does it down in Italy. And anyhow a gentleman like him isn't so easily nabbed as a Social Democrat." So that was it: cushioned chairs, silver lackeys, equipages, and a sodomite, and Nentwig could run about and do what he liked! Esch stared the mirthful editor in the face: "But Martin's locked up!" The editor had laid down his pencil and opened his arms a little: "My dear friend and comrade, neither of us can alter events. The strike in Mannheim was sheer stupidity, and the only thing we could do was to let things take their course and pocket our discomfiture. We can only be glad that Geyring's three months is good propaganda material for us. Many thanks for your article, my dear fellow, and if you ever have something else for us bring it sooner next time." He shook Esch by the hand, and Esch, in spite of his resentment, achieved an awkward bow.

June was approaching. Esch did Oppenheimer's errands to the printers and the poster-designers; everything was ready, and bold advertisements on pillars and hoardings informed the town that the strongest women of all the nations would be assembled in Cologne to try their strength; and the list of names appended would have convinced any sceptic: there was Tatiana Leonoff, the Russian champion, Maud Ferguson, winner of the New York Championship, Mirzl Oberleitner, holder of the Viennese Cup, to say nothing of the German representative, Irmentraud Kroff. The names for the most part were fanciful inventions of Oppenheimer, who found the girls' real names too tame and insipid. Esch had vainly striven against this piece of deception; had he taken all the trouble to find genuinely international girls simply for a Jew to mess about with their names? He took it as a fresh symptom of the anarchical condition of the world, in which no one seemed to know whether he was on the right or on the left, in the van or in the rear, and where it was ultimately of no importance whether Herr Oppenheimer called a person by this name or that; one had even to be thankful that Oppenheimer hadn't thought of a Hungarian name. Hungary had no business to exist, anyway, and it was equally unseemly for Oppenheimer to have included Italy in the list of competing nations. Was it so certain that there were women there at all? Italy seemed to be a haunt of sodomites. Still, he was not displeased as he regarded the placard with all its international names: the different countries stood shoulder to shoulder, and that whole world was in a sense his own creation, an earnest and a promise for his future career. He brought one of his posters into Mother Hentjen's and without asking permission pinned it up on the wooden panelling beneath the Eiffel Tower.

Frau Hentjen, however, was still resentful of the way he had abused her on Geyring's account, and she called out from the buffet that he would kindly stick up his posters only where he was asked to; it was for her to decide that kind of thing. Esch, who had long forgotten the incident, and was only reminded of it whenever he saw her angry face, made as if to obey her order. This submissiveness disarmed Mother Hentjen; she came from behind the buffet, still scolding, to have a look at the poster. As she deciphered the list of names she was overcome by sympathy and disgust: these females deserved the degradation of exposing themselves before the eyes of objectionable men, but she was at the same time sorry for them. Esch, who had engineered the whole thing, stood revealed as a pasha in the middle of a harem, and this seemed a situation of such surpassing wickedness, of such deep debauchery, that by comparison with the rest of her customers who sat around with their contemptible little lusts and vices Esch was raised to a different plane, even a higher one. His short, stiff hair, his dark head, his tanned, ruddy skin, pah! he gave her the creeps; no, she did not understand why she put up with the man and his posters, and she started when he grasped her by the wrist. Did it not look as if he meant to overpower her and have her at his mercy and add her name to the list on the poster? She was almost disappointed when nothing happened, except that Esch guided her obediently outstretched finger from one name to the other: " Russia, Germany, United States of America, Belgium, Italy, Austria, Bohemia," he read out aloud, and because it sounded grand, and not at all dangerous, Frau Hentjen recovered her composure. She said: " But there's some missed out; for instance, Luxemburg and Switzerland." None the less she presently turned away from the poster with the list of feminine names as though it had an evil smell: " How can you mix yourself up with all these women ! " Esch replied by quoting Martin, that every man must stay where God had put him, adding that anyhow it was Teltscher's business, not his, to deal with the women; he was concerned only with the administrative side.

Teltscher came to Cologne and inspected Esch's recruits in Oppenheimer's office. He sat the whole morning in judgment, dismissed some of them outright, and appointed the others to meet him in the Alhambra for a first lesson and a trial of their abilities.

It turned out to be a jolly entertainment. Teltscher had brought the tights with him, and after Esch had called the roll from his notebook Herr Teltini invited the ladies to enter the dressing-room and get into their tights. Most of them refused to go until they had seen the others first in that unusual costume. When the pioneers, stripped and highly embarrassed, emerged from the dressing-room, there was a general outburst of laughter. The doors leading into the beer-garden were wide open; the green trees looked gaily in, and sudden wafts of air brought the warmth of the morning sun into the theatre. At the doors stood the proprietor and all the cooks from the restaurant, and Teltscher climbed up on the stage to give a demonstration, on the soft brown mat that was laid out, of the rules governing the Græco-Roman style of wrestling. Then he ordered up a couple to try it, but none of the girls would come; they giggled and nudged each other, pushing forward now one, now another, who resisted stoutly and took refuge in the crowd.

At long last two of them made up their minds to it; but when Teltscher proceeded to show them the preliminary holds they only laughed and let their arms hang and did not venture to touch each other. Teltscher ordered up a third girl, but when the same thing happened he made

Esch call the roll again and attempted by jocose observations on each name to create a bold and enterprising atmosphere. A French name he hailed with praise of Gallic courage, and invited the "Pride of France" to step up; then he announced the "Polish Giantess"; in brief, he rehearsed all the honourable and inspiring titles with which he intended to introduce the wrestlers to the public. Some of the girls now appeared on the stage, but others with shrieks of mirth called back that they weren't having any and that they wanted to put on their clothes, which Teltscher countered with expressions of regret and a pantomime of comic despair. The whole thing was not to go off without an upset, however. When Esch called out the name of Ruzena Hrushka and Teltscher added: "Up with you, O Lioness of Bohemia," a plump, soft creature, still dressed in her own clothes, pushed forward to the footlights and with the hard sing-song cadence of her race screamed that no one would laugh at her for dirty money. "I have throw away good money already because I not let no one laugh over me," she screamed at Teltscher, and while he was still trying to think of a joke that would save the situation she lifted up her parasol as if to fling it at him. But then she fell silent, her soft round shoulders began to heave, and it could be seen that she was crying. When she turned round and went out between the silent ranks of startled girls her eye fell on Esch, who was sitting at a table with his lists. She bent over to him and spat out: "You, you are bad friend, bring me here to shame me." Then she went out sobbing. Meanwhile Teltscher had got the situation in hand again, and the incident was not without its good effect; the girls, as if ashamed of their previous frivolity, showed themselves now ready for serious work. Teltscher heartened them with praise, and soon they had all forgotten the wild Czech woman. Even Esch dismissed her reproaches from his mind, although he could not but admit that he was a bad friend; yet in a little he would have Martin out of confinement. Such were his thoughts as he went home.

Frau Hentjen carefully blew her nose and regarded the result in her handkerchief. Perhaps from a feeling of guilt Esch had told her of the incident with the recalcitrant Czech woman, and Frau Hentjen had rated him, saying that it would have served him right if the poor, abused woman had scratched his eyes out. That was what came of degrading himself to the level of such women. Didn't he have any proper pride?

The trollop should have been glad he had given her a chance to earn a little money. Yes, that was all the thanks he got. But the Czech woman was quite right all the same; that's how men should be treated. They deserved nothing better. To enjoy seeing a few poor drabs rolling over each other on the stage in tights! The poor things were ten times better than these men who took advantage of them. And she said cuttingly: "Put that cigar away for goodness' sake." Esch listened to all this respectfully, not merely because of the abundant dinner she gave him at a ridiculously low price, but also because he conceded her the right to show up his sinful way of life as it deserved. His affairs were in a bad state: of the three hundred marks that had been put aside for the wrestling project all he possessed now was a bare two hundred and fifty, and although his profits would begin to accumulate from the very first day's takings, yet he did not know where he was heading for. He must have a settled source of livelihood if the sacrifice which he had taken on himself for Ilona's sake, and which he had actually almost lost sight of by now, was not to come a cropper; he would have liked to talk the matter over but his vanity prevented him, for Mother Hentjen wasn't in a mood to see that even the most splendid careers must grow out of humble beginnings. So he simply said: " Better wrestling matches than knife-throwing." Frau Hentjen regarded the knife in Esch's hand; she did not really understand what he meant, but she felt uncomfortable, so she replied briefly: " Perhaps." " Nice meat," said Esch, bending over his plate, and she replied with the dignity of the expert: " Sirloin." "The grub poor Martin is getting now . . ." Frau Hentjen said: " Meat only on Sundays," and she added with a hint of satisfaction, " and the rest of the time turnips mostly, I reckon." For whose sake was Martin doomed to eat turnips? For whom was he sacrificing himself? Did Martin himself know? Martin was a martyr and yet regarded his martyrdom simply as an occupation, partly pleasant, partly disagreeable; all the same he was a decent fellow. Frau Hentjen said: " If you won't be led you must be driven." Esch did not reply. Perhaps Martin was keeping something to himself which nobody else knew of; a martyr had always to suffer for some conviction, for an inward certainty that determined all his actions. Martyrs were decent people. Frau Hentjen declared: "That's what comes of these anarchist papers." Esch agreed. "Yes, they're a set of swine, now they've left him in the lurch." Martin himself, of course, had sneered at the Socialist papers, although one would have thought that it was their duty to represent the Socialist point of view and advance it. Had Martin really any Socialist convictions, or had he none at all? Esch was annoyed at the thought that Martin had kept something from him. A man who possessed the truth could redeem his fellowmen; that was what the Christian martyrs had done. And because he felt proud of his education he said: " In the times of the Romans there were wrestling matches too, but with lions. Blood all over the place. Over in Trier there's a Roman circus still." Frau Hentjen said with interest: " Well? " But when no answer came she continued: " And I suppose you want to introduce that next, eh? " Esch silently shook his head. If Martin sacrificed himself and lived on turnips neither for his convictions, nor for his better knowledge, nor for anything else, then he probably just did it for the sake of the sacrifice itself. Perhaps one had to sacrifice oneself first, so that—how had that idiot in Mannheim put it?—so that one might feel the power of redeeming grace. But in that case perhaps Ilona too needed the daggers for her act of sacrifice; who could make head or tail of it? And so Esch said: " I don't want to do anything. Maybe all this wrestling business is pure idiocy." Yes, said Mother Hentjen, that it was. And again he felt a sort of respectful esteem for Mother Hentjen which gave him a sense of security.

The room smelt of food and tobacco smoke and the sweetish odour of wine. Mother Hentjen was right: the women didn't want things to be different. That was why Ilona had taken up with Korn. And if the wily cripple really did possess higher knowledge he didn't give it away, allowed nobody else to share in it. He ran about, quite happy, like a dog on three legs, then whipped suddenly round a corner into prison, and prison made as little impression on him as a beating did on a dog. " Perhaps it even amuses them to be beaten and to sacrifice themselves," he said absently. " Who? " asked Mother Hentjen with interest, " the women? " Esch reflected: " Yes, the lot of them. . . ." Mother Hentjen was pleased: " Shall I get you another slice? " She went to the kitchen. Esch was sorry for the Czech woman; she had cried so softly. But there too Mother Hentjen was probably right; the Hrushka woman herself did not want things to be different. And when Frau Hentjen returned with Esch's plate he suddenly said: " No doubt she's looking for a knife-thrower too, the Czech woman." " Well! " said Mother Hentjen. " Poor devil," continued Esch, and he himself did not know whether he meant Martin or the Czech woman. Mother Hentjen, however, took him to mean the Czech woman and retorted sarcastically: " Well, you can easily comfort her, seeing you're so sorry for her ... you'd better run away to her now."

He made no reply: he had eaten well, and so he silently took up his newspaper and began to study the advertisement column, which had become to him the most important part of the paper since the announcement of the wrestling performances was to be found there. Yet the upright book-keeping of his soul demanded that for Frau Hentjen too an account should be opened; had she any less right to it, after all, than Ilona, who absolutely despised one's efforts to do her good? His eye was arrested by an announcement of a wine auction at Saint-Goar, and he asked Mother Hentjen where she bought her wine. She mentioned a wine-dealer in Cologne. Esch looked disdainful: " So you throw away your money on them! Why have you never asked me about it? I don't say that every firm is as bad as the set of swindlers our fine Herr Nentwig works for, but I bet you pay pretty well through the nose." She assumed a martyred expression: a weak woman fending for herself had to put up with lots of things. He suggested that he should go to Saint-Goar himself and buy wine for her. " Yes, and what about the expense? " she said. Esch became eager; the expense could easily be recouped in the price she charged, and if the quality was up to the mark the wine could be adulterated with a cheaper sort; he knew all about that. And besides he wasn't thinking of the expense; an excursion up the Rhine—Lohberg's idiotic twaddle about the joys of nature came into his mind—was always a pleasure, and she needn't refund him his expenses until she found she had made a profit on the transaction. " And I suppose you're going to take your Czech woman with you? " said Mother Hentjen suspiciously. The idea seemed to him not an unattractive one; yet he disavowed it loudly and indignantly; Mother Hentjen could see for herself by coming with him, why, she had said not so very long ago that she would like a day in the country—well, she could get both at the same time if she came with him, he added impatiently. She looked into his face, regarded his light-brown complexion, stiffened, and started back. " And who would look after the restaurant ... ? No, it would never do."

Well, he wasn't so keen on it as all that himself; besides, his finances wouldn't stand a trip for two at present, so Esch said nothing further about it, and Mother Hentjen regained her confidence. She took up the newspaper, saw with reassurance that the auction was not to take place for a fortnight still, and said that she would think it over. Yes, she could think it over, said Esch dryly, getting up. He must go to the Alhambra, where Teltscher was having a rehearsal. He chose the route past the restaurant where the Czech woman was employed. But he trod on the pedal of his bicycle and rode past.

Gernerth had now arrived in Cologne, and Esch went down daily to the docks to inquire after the stage properties, which had been sent by boat down the Rhine, his expert knowledge of shipping affairs fitting him for this duty and his need for something to do making him zealous. And though perhaps he really went there to gaze at the sheds and nurse his regret at having given notice so prematurely to the Central Rhine Shipping Company, and to let the sight of the bonded wine-stores remind him that Nentwig was still a bitter thorn in his flesh, yet he saw and experienced all this not without satisfaction, for it proved to him visibly that his sacrifice could stand comparison with Martin's. Also the fact that Ilona had not come to Cologne, but had remained with Korn, fitted into the scheme and gave it a sort of higher significance. Yet it must not be imagined that Esch had become a man glorying in his sufferings. Not at all! To himself he did not scruple to call Ilona a whore and even a filthy whore, and Teltscher a pimp and a scoundrel. And if he had met that rascal Nentwig between the piled-up rows of wine-barrels he would just have let fly at him. Yet whenever in passing the long row of warehouses belonging to the Central Rhine Company he caught sight of that hated sign bearing the firm's name, then high above all the swarm of petty scoundrels rose the splendid form of a man greater than life-size, the figure of a man of such high standing, a man so remote and lofty that he was almost more than human, and yet it was the figure of an arch-scoundrel; unimaginable and menacing rose that image of Bertrand, the rascally Chairman of this company, the sodomite who had got Martin thrown into prison. And that magnified figure, in essence unimaginable, appeared to subsume those of the two lesser scoundrels, and sometimes it seemed to Esch as though one had only to strike down this Antichrist to destroy as well all the pettier rascals in the world.

Of course it was stupid to bother one's head over such matters, for one had worse troubles; it was bad enough, in all conscience, to be loafing about these docks without pay. A man without a proper means of livelihood deserved to be exterminated. Mother Hentjen herself would agree with that, and it was curiously pleasant to picture this eventuality to oneself. Yes, the best solution perhaps would be for a super-murderer like that to come along and just do one in. And as Esch strolled along the quay and encountered once more the sign of the Central Rhine Shipping Company Limited he said loudly and distinctly: "Either him or me."

Esch was looking down into the barge that had brought up the theatrical properties, and supervising the unloading of its cargo. He saw Teltscher approaching with his rosy-cheeked friend, Oppenheimer: they advanced, so to speak, by stages, for every now and then they stopped, sometimes one seizing the other in his eagerness by the lapel of his coat, and Esch asked himself what they could have found to discuss so urgently. When they were near enough he heard Teltscher: "And I tell you, Oppenheimer, this is no job for me—you wait, I'll send for Ilona yet, and if in half-a-year's time I don't put on my turn in New York you can cut off my head." Hoho, so Teltscher hadn't given up his claims on Ilona even yet? Well, he would sing a different tune when things had been put in order. And Esch no longer found any pleasure in the thought of death. He snarled at the two of them: what did they want here? did they fancy, perhaps, that he had never seen to a job like this in his life before? or maybe they thought that he wanted to pinch something? or perhaps the gentleman wished to supervise his work? Well, he regretted bitterly that he had ever got other people to put their money into this business, not to mention his own. Here he had been slaving for nothing almost a whole month for this risky affair, and had put his last cent into it, and why? because a certain Herr Teltscher, who was apparently now intending to bolt, had wheedled him into it. Full of rage he began unskilfully to mimic Herr Oppenheimer's Jewish intonations. "Why, he's an Anti-Semite!" said Herr Oppenheimer, and Teltscher prophesied that after the first report from the box-office the day after next the Transport Director's spirits would rise considerably. And because he himself felt in a good humour and wanted to tease Esch he walked round the conveyance on which the properties were being loaded and checked them carefully, then went up to the horses and offered them a few lumps of sugar from his pocket. Esch, angry and offended, had turned away from the Jews and was checking the packing-cases, but he regarded the two men with the tail of his eye and was astonished at

Teltscher's amiability; yet he did not want to admit that it was genuine, and half expected that the horses would decline the gift with a shake of the head. But the horses, just like horses, took into their soft and friendly lips the sugar-lumps lying on Teltscher's flat palm, and Esch was annoyed; surely he himself might have thought of offering them a scrap of bread at least! But now that the work of loading was finished nothing remained for him but to give both the horses a sober clap on the crupper. Esch did so, and then, sitting on the packing-cases piled on the lorry, they all three drove into the town. Oppenheimer said good-bye at the Rhine Bridge; Teltscher and Esch drove on and got down at Mother Hentjen's.

Teltscher had been a few times in the restaurant and already put on the airs of an old and regular customer. Esch felt guilty at bringing such riff-raff to Mother Hentjen's place, instead of something better. He would have liked to fling the fellow off the lorry. A Judas like that to sit down in Martin's place, a lout who had no idea that there were better, more refined, more highly respectable men in the world; who had no idea that Martin had been struck down by the hand of a man who would think it beneath him even to spit on a mere knife-thrower! And this juggler, this pimp, gave himself the airs of a conqueror, as if Martin's seat belonged by rights to him, 'anymore' tricks, more juggling with dead things, sterile labour full of lies and trickery.

They had arrived at Mother Hentjen's. Teltscher clambered down first from the lorry. Esch shouted after him: " Here! Who's to unload this stuff? Supervising and spying round, that suits you all right, but when it comes to real work you make yourself scarce." " I'm hungry," Teltscher retorted simply and pushed open the restaurant door. No use arguing with a Jew; Esch shrugged his shoulders and followed him. And to disclaim any responsibility for this sort of customer he said jestingly: " I've brought you a fine customer this time, Mother Hentjen, well, I couldn't find anything better at the moment." But suddenly everything seemed not to matter: Teltscher might sit in Martin's place, and Martin in Nentwig's; one could not make head or tail of it, and yet somewhere it was all as it should be. Somewhere it was not a matter merely involving human beings, for human beings were all the same and nothing was changed if one of them melted into another, or one of them sat in another's place—no, the world was not ordered according to good and evil men, but according to good and evil forces of some kind.

He looked furiously at Teltscher, who was performing conjuring tricks with his knife and fork, and now announced that he would extract a knife from Mother Hentjen's bodice. She started back with a shriek, but already Teltscher was holding up the knife between his thumb and first finger: "Mother Hentjen, Mother Hentjen, fancy you carrying things like that about in your bodice!" Then he proposed to hypnotize her and she became petrified at the mere suggestion. That was past the limit, and Esch let fly at Teltscher: "You should be locked up." "That's a new trick," said Teltscher. Esch growled: "Hypnotism is against the law." "An interesting chap," said Teltscher, jerking his chin towards Esch, and by this gesture inviting Frau Hentjen also to find the interesting chap a source of amusement; but she was still petrified with fear and mechanically fingered her coiffure. Esch silently digested the success of his intervention to rescue Mother Hentjen, and was satisfied. Yes, he had let one of them go, that man Nentwig, but it wouldn't happen a second time; even if it wasn't a matter of the individual, and even if people melted into one another, so that one fellow couldn't be told from the next; the wrong done existed apart from the doer, and it was the wrong alone that had to be expiated.

When later he accompanied Teltscher to the Alhambra he felt lighthearted. He had acquired a new kind of knowledge. And he almost felt sorry for Teltscher. And also for Bertrand. And even for Nentwig.

He had now managed at last to extort from Gernerth a guarantee of a hundred marks a month from the receipts in consideration of his collaboration—what would he have had to live on otherwise?—but the very first evening brought him in no less than seven marks. If that continued his revenue for the month would be doubled. Frau Hentjen had steadfastly refused to attend the opening performance, and next day at lunch-time Esch told her excitedly of its success. When he reached the most interesting, one might almost say the crucial, point of his narrative, and told how Teltscher had ripped up one of the girls' tights and only loosely tacked it together again, so that during the wrestling it could not help bursting at a certain prominent protuberance, and went on to say that this incident would be repeated evening after evening; while at the very memory of it he still found himself so overcome by laughter that repeatedly he had to help out his words with dumb show, suddenly Frau Hentjen got up and said she had had enough. It was scandalous that a man whom she had taken to be a decent fellow, a man who once had followed a respectable occupation, should sink so low. She withdrew into the kitchen.

Quite taken aback, Esch remained where he was and dried his eyes, still wet with laughter. In one corner of his heart he had a feeling of guilt, and in that corner he admitted that Mother Hentjen was right; the bursting tights on the stage were vaguely akin to the knives which no longer ought to be thrown there; yet Mother Hentjen certainly did not have the faintest suspicion of this, and her anger was really incomprehensible. He had a feeling of respect for her, he had no wish to swear at her as he did at that fool Lohberg, yet she would certainly have got on better with Lohberg, for as a matter of fact he wasn't so refined as Lohberg. He contemplated the portrait of Herr Hentjen over the mantelpiece to see whether it had any resemblance to Lohberg, and when he had looked long enough at the features of the late restaurant-keeper they did actually melt into those of the Mannheim tobacconist. Yes, wherever one looked it seemed that one figure melted into another and that one could not even distinguish the living from the dead. Nobody was what he thought he was; a man imagined he was a chap with his feet planted firmly on the earth, pocketing his seven marks a night and going wherever he pleased; and in reality he was just sometimes in one place, and sometimes in another, and even when he made a sacrifice it was not himself who made it. An irresistible desire overcame him to produce some proof that this was not so and that it could not be so, and even if it was impossible to prove it to anybody else he was resolved to show that woman in there that he wasn't to be confused either with Herr Lohberg or with Herr Hentjen. Without further ado he went through to the kitchen and said to Frau Hentjen that she mustn't forget the wine auction at Saint-Goar next Friday. "You'll get plenty to keep you company without me," responded Frau Hentjen from the hearth. Her opposition exasperated him. What did this woman want from him? Must he only say things to her that she herself prescribed and wanted to hear? He could not help thinking of the orchestrion, which anybody could set going. And yet she couldn't stand the orchestrion. If the kitchenmaid hadn't been there, for two pins he would simply have fallen on her as she stood there by the hearth, to convince her of his existence. So he simply said: "I've arranged everything; we take the train to Bacharach, then the steamer to Saint-Goar. We'll arrive there about eleven o'clock. in time for the auction.

In the afternoon we can walk up to the Lorelei." She stiffened a little under the firmness of his decision, yet she tried to give her reply a mocking inflection: " Great plans, Herr Esch." Esch was now sure of himself. " Only a beginning, Mother Hentjen: by the end of next week I expect to have made a hundred marks." Whistling to himself he left the kitchen.

In the restaurant he looked again through the newspapers he had brought with him and marked in red pencil the notices of the opening performance. When he found no word of it in *The People's Guardian* he felt irritated. Yes, they could let a comrade and friend of theirs who had sacrificed himself lie in prison. But they couldn't put in a measly little report of the wrestling performance. Here, too, things must be set in order. He felt within him the strength required for it and the faith that he would succeed in mastering and resolving the chaos in which everything was so painfully entangled, in which friend and foe, sullen and yet resigned, were so inextricably involved.

As he was walking through the theatre during the interval he suddenly caught sight of Nentwig, and he started so violently that it brought to his mind a phrase, " struck to the heart." Nentwig was sitting with four other men at a table, and one of the wrestlers, a bath-robe flung over her tights, was sitting with them. The bath-robe gaped and Nentwig was occupied in widening the opening by adroit movements of his pudgy hands. Esch walked past with his head averted, but the girl called out to him, so that he had to turn round. " Hallo, Herr Esch, what are you doing here? " he heard Nentwig's voice. Esch hesitated: then he said briefly: " 'Evening." Nentwig did not feel the rebuff, but lifted his glass to him, while the girl said: " You can have my chair, Herr Esch. I must go back to the stage now." Nentwig, who had been drinking, held Esch's hand firmly clasped, and while he poured out a glass of wine for him looked up at him with a sentimental, vinous gaze. " No, fancy meeting like this, it's quite an unexpected pleasure." Esch said that he too was needed on the stage, and Nentwig, still holding his hand, gurgled with laughter: " Aha! going to see the ladies behind the scenes. I'll come too, I'll come too." Esch tried to make Nentwig understand that he was here on business. At last Nentwig grasped it: " Oh? So you're employed here? A good post? " Esch's vanity would not allow him to admit this. No, he wasn't employed here; he was a partner in the concern. " Think of that, think of that," said Nentwig in astonishment; " a good business, a nice little business, obviously a nice little business "—he looked round at the well-packed hall—" and he forgets his good old friend Nentwig, who would always be glad to share in a thing like that." He became quite alert: " Who caters for the wine, Esch? " Esch explained that he had nothing to do with the catering; the proprietor looked after that. " Hm, but all the rest "—Nentwig made a grand comprehensive gesture embracing the hall and the stage—" you're concerned in all that? Come, drink a glass of wine anyway," and Esch could not avoid clinking glasses with Nentwig, and must shake hands with Nentwig's companions too, and drink to them. In spite of the cunning with which Nentwig had cornered him he could not summon up the hate he ought to have felt against Nentwig. He tried to bring to his mind again the sins of the head clerk; he did not succeed; there had been something fishy in the balance sheet, something very fishy, and Esch sat up a little straighter so as to keep his eye on the one policeman in the hall. But Nentwig's guilt had grown so strangely shadowy and contourless that Esch became aware at once of the senselessness of his intentions, and somewhat awkwardly and a little ashamed of himself he put out his hand for his wine-glass. Meanwhile Nentwig gazed with swimming eyes at his good old book-keeper, and it seemed to Esch as if along with those swimming eyes the whole plump form of Nentwig was dissolving into indeterminacy. This vinegar faker had treacherously accused him of erroneous book-keeping, had tried to deprive him of his livelihood and his existence, and would always go on conspiring against him. Yet one could hardly feel angry with him now. From the inextricable coil of happenings an arm projected, an arm with a threatening dagger in its hand, but if one were to discover that it was Nentwig's arm the whole thing would turn into a stupid and almost sordid episode. Death dealt by the hand of a Nentwig could scarcely even be called murder, and a sentence pronounced over Nentwig would be nothing but the shabbiest form of revenge for a mistake in book-keeping that was not a mistake at all. No, there was little point in handing over a head clerk to justice, for it was not a matter of striking down a hand, even if that hand held the threatening dagger, it was a matter of striking a blow at the whole thing, or at least at the head of the offence. Something inside Esch told him: " A man who sacrifices himself must be decent," and he decided to take no further notice of Nentwig. The fat little man had again sunk back into his drunken doze, and when the strains of *The Gladiators' March* began, to which the wrestlers, under Teltscher's direction, now came marching on to the stage, Nentwig did not notice that Esch had disappeared.

When Esch walked into the manager's office Gernerth was sitting with a glass of beer before him and lamenting: " A fine life this, a fine life! . . . " Oppenheimer was toddling up and down wagging his head, indeed his whole body wagged: " Can't see what there is to upset you so much." Gernerth's notebook was lying before him: " The taxes simply eat everything up. Why are we toiling and slaving here? To pay the taxes! " They could hear the resounding smack of sweating women's bodies coming to grips on the stage, and Esch felt indignant that this man sitting here should talk of toiling and slaving, merely because he was making calculations in a notebook. Gernerth went on with his lament: " The children must go away for a holiday; that costs money . . . where am I to get it? " Herr Oppenheimer evinced sympathy: " Children are a blessing and children are a trial; don't you worry too much, it'll come all right." Esch felt sorry for Gernerth, a good fellow, Gernerth; all the same the affairs of the world became confused again when you reflected that out there on the stage a pair of tights must presently burst so that Gernerth's children might go away for a holiday. Somewhere or other there was cause for Mother Hentjen's disgust at the whole business, though not where she imagined it to be. Esch himself could not tell where it lay; perhaps it was simply the muddle and confusion that filled him with disgust and rage. He went out; in the wings some of the wrestlers were standing about, their bodies smelling of sweat; to clear a passage for himself Esch seized them from behind by the thick arms or by the breasts, hugging them tightly, until one or two began to laugh wantonly. Then he stepped on to the stage and took his place as clerk at the so-called jury bench. Teltscher, the referee's whistle between his teeth, was lying on the floor peering sharply under the arched body of one girl, who was resisting the efforts of another to flatten her out, efforts ostensibly great, but only ostensibly, of course, for the girl underneath was the German representative who was bound to free herself forthwith by a patriotic upward heave from ignominious captivity. And although Esch knew by heart this prearranged farce he experienced a feeling of relief when the almost beaten wrestler got on to her feet again: and yet he was filled with indignant pity for her opponent when Irmentraud Kroff now sprang upon her and, amid the patriotic acclamations of the audience, pressed the shoulders of the enemy against the mat.

When Frau Hentjen got up the dawn was just breaking. She opened the window to see how the day promised. The sky arched clear and cloudless over the dark, grey yard, which lay below her in motionless silence, a little rectangle within dark walls. The clean washtubs from last washing day were still standing down there. A cool wind, imprisoned between the walls, smelt of the city. She trailed up to the kitchenmaid's room and knocked at the door; she didn't intend to leave without her breakfast; on the top of everything else that would be the last straw. Then she carefully began her toilet and drew on the brown-silk dress. When Esch called for her she was sitting morosely at her morning coffee in the restaurant. She said morosely: " Let's go," but at the house door it occurred to her that Esch too might want some coffee; it was got for him hastily in the kitchen, and he drank it standing. The sun was already up, but the bright strips of sunshine that lay on the cobbles between the long shadows of the house walls did not improve the temper of either. Esch merely announced curtly and abruptly: " I'll get the tickets," and then: " Platform five." In the carriage they sat side by side in silence, but when they reached Bonn he leaned out inquired whether there were any fresh rolls to be had, and bought her one. She ate it morosely and resentfully. After Coblenz, when the passengers as usual crowded to the window to admire the Rhineland scenery, Frau Hentjen too felt moved to follow their example. But Esch did not budge from his place; he knew the neighbourhood so well that he was sick of it, and besides he had not proposed to indicate the beauties of nature to Frau Hentjen until they were on the steamer. Now he felt annoyed at her for anticipating this pleasure and for listening to the edifying explanations of the other people in the compartment. So every tunnel that interrupted the view was a salve to his ill humour, and his irritation mounted so high that at Ober-Wesel he peremptorily called her away from the window: " I had a job myself once in Ober-Wesel." Frau Hentjen looked out; there was nothing of interest to be seen in the station. She replied politely: " Yes, you've been in lots of places." Esch was not yet finished: " A wretched job it was, I stuck it out all the same for a few months on account of a girl in the place ... Hulda, her name was." Then he could just get out and look for her, was Frau

Hentjen's furious rejoinder, he needn't trouble himself on her account. But presently they arrived at Bacharach, and for the first time in his life Esch experienced the helpless feeling which descends on the pleasure-tripper who, standing in a railway station, has a vacant hour in front of him. According to his programme they should have had a lunch on the boat, but simply to cover his embarrassment he now suggested that they should go to a restaurant that he knew. But as they were walking through the narrow streets of the town which lay so quiet and peaceful in the clear morning light, suddenly in front of one of the timbered houses Mother Hentjen exclaimed: "That's where I would like to live, that would be my ideal." Perhaps it was the flowers in the window-boxes that touched her, perhaps it was simply the feeling of release that often comes over people when they are on unfamiliar ground, or perhaps her bad temper had simply exhausted itself—in any case the world had become brighter; at peace with each other they gazed at everything, climbed up as far as the ruins of the church, of which they could not make very much, hurried too soon to the landing-stage for fear of missing the boat, and did not mind in the least when they found that they must wait for half-an-hour.

On the boat, it is true, they quarrelled more than once, for Frau Hentjen's pride could not endure for long that Esch alone should know the neighbourhood. She racked her memory for names of well-known places, began in her turn to make conjectures and to provide information, and was deeply insulted when he scrupulously refused to let any error pass. Yet even this could not cloud their good humour, and, arrived at Saint-Goar, they were sorry they had to leave the boat, indeed for a moment they could not think why they were landing at all. The business aspect of their journey had become in some way indifferent, and when at the auction-rooms they learned that the sale of the cheap wines was already finished it did not disturb them, but was almost like a deliverance from an obligation, for it seemed far more important to them that they should be in time for the next journey of the ferry-boat, which with outstretched sail was making for the sunny and alluring shores of Goarshausen on the other bank. And when Esch, aping the precision of a methodical business man, noted the prices the wines had reached at the auction "for future reference," as he said, this affectation of commercial zeal was a sham and gave him a queer kind of bad conscience which made him diligently ignore the more favourable prices, and yet on the other hand depressed him so acutely that when he was sitting in the ferry-boat he suddenly entered the missing prices in his list from memory, meanwhile regarding Frau Hentjen with a hostile glare.

Frau Hentjen sat on the sun-steeped wooden seat of the ferry-boat and contentedly dipped one finger into the water, very carefully, however, so as not to wet her cream-coloured lace mittens, and if she could have had her will she would simply have gone on sailing from one bank of the Rhine to the other, for the curiously light feeling of dizziness induced by the sight of water obliquely streaming past her was a pleasant one. But the day was already too far advanced, and it was pleasant enough under the trees in the inn garden on the bank of the river. They ate fish and drank wine, and smoking his cigar Esch revolved the question of establishing closer relations, earnestly considering whether Mother Hentjen, who sat there stout and magnificent, might not even expect it. Certainly she wasn't like other women, and so he began very cautiously to speak about Lohberg, who had really moved him to take this lovely trip, and he began to praise Lohberg, so that from this exordium he might in decorous terms lead up to an exposition of the vegetarian view of true love; but Frau Hentjen, who saw with anxiety where he was heading, broke off the conversation, and although she herself felt tired, and would rather have rested in peace, she referred him to his programme, according to which they must now climb up to the Lorelei. Esch felt indignant; he had done his best to speak like Lohberg and without effect. Evidently he was not yet refined enough for her.

He got up and paid the bill. While they were passing through the inn garden he noticed the summer visitors; among them were pretty young women and girls; and suddenly Esch could not understand why he was attached to this elderly woman, stately as was her appearance in the brown-silk dress. The girls were in light, gay, summer dresses, and Mother Hentjen's brown silk had become somewhat dusty and draggled on the roads. Nevertheless there seemed to be a certain amount of justice in it; one had a conscience, after all, and if one thought of Martin pining for the sun in his cell, after sacrificing himself for a base, ungrateful crowd, then one's own lot, all things considered, was still a long way too fortunate! And while he ploughed through the dust of the main road with Frau Hentjen, instead of lying in the grass with one of those pretty girls, it actually seemed to him quite fair that this woman should not feel any gratitude for his sacrifice. A man who sacrificed himself must be decent. He considered whether he could inform her with propriety that it was a sacrifice, but then he remembered Lohberg and refrained: a man of refinement suffered in silence. Some time or other, perhaps when it was too late, she would be bound to realize it. A painful agitation overcame him, and walking in front he took off first his coat and then his waistcoat. Mother Hentjen regarded with repulsion the two large wet patches where his shirt stuck to his shoulder-blades, and when after turning into a wood-path he remained standing and she caught up on him, she suddenly smelt the warm odour of his body and started back in alarm. Esch said good-humouredly: " Well, what is it, Mother Hentjen? " " Put on your jacket," she said severely, but she added in a maternal tone: " It's cold here, quite cold, you'll get a chill." " It's quite warm when you're walking," he replied, " you should let out a hook or two at the neck of your dress." She shook her head with the old-fashioned little hat perched on it; no, she wouldn't think of doing that, a fine sight she would be! " Well, there's nobody to see us here," said Esch, and this sudden open declaration that they were alone and together, in a seclusion in which they need not be ashamed before each other because nobody could see them, confused her. All at once she found it understandable that, as if in confidence, he should reveal his sweat to her; and if she still felt disgust she felt it no longer on the surface; it was dulled and muffled, as it were, hidden away; and even her fear of his strong white teeth now left her, and she accepted it as part of this strangely permitted and shameless freedom when he bared them laughingly again: " Forward, Mother Hentjen; it's no use saying you're tired." She felt offended that he should openly doubt whether she could keep up with him, and, a little short of breath, and supported on her fragile pink parasol, she again set herself in motion. Esch now remained by her side and at the steeper places attempted to assist her. She regarded him suspiciously at first, fearing a brazen approach to familiarity, and only after some hesitation finally took his arm, to relinquish this support immediately, however, indeed to push it away, as soon as she saw another traveller, or even a child, approaching.

They climbed slowly, and when with panting lungs they made a halt, gradually they became aware of the things round about them: the whitish clay of the wood-path cracked with the heat, the faded green plants sticking out of the dry soil, the roots which with their dusty fibres wandered over the narrow footpath, the dry, withered odour of the woods almost breathless under the heat, the shrubs among whose foliage hung black, lifeless berries, ready to shrivel at the touch of autumn. They took all this in, yet could not have described it, but presently they reached the first seat commanding a view and beheld the valley outspread before them, and although they were still a long way from the top of the Lorelei Rock it seemed to them, as they sank upon the seat, that they were already at their goal, from which they could drink in the scenery; and Frau Hentjen carefully smoothed out her dress so that her weight might not crease it. The air was so still that the sound of voices at the landing-stage and in the beer-gardens of Saint-Goar came over to them, as well as the drowsy, dull thud of the ferry-boat against the pier; and the unusualness of these impressions made them both a little uncomfortable. Frau Hentjen regarded the hearts and initials cut all over the bench and in a strained voice asked Esch whether he too had immortalized himself here with his Hulda from Ober-Wesel. When he jestingly began to look for his initials she told him he needn't bother: for whether in visible form or not, a man would always find his filthy past wherever he went. But Esch, who did not want to give up his jest, replied that maybe he might find her name too enclosed within a heart, and this made her really angry; what would he read next into people's words? thank God her past was pure and she could stand her ground with any young girl. Of course a man who all his life had been constantly running after loose women wouldn't understand that. And Esch, stricken to the heart by this accusation, felt common and despicable at having prized her less highly than the young girls in the inn garden, most of whom were probably unworthy to lace Mother Hentjen's shoes. And it did him good to know that here was a human being whose character was decided and unequivocal, a human being who knew her right hand from her left, who knew virtue from vice. For a moment he had the feeling that here was the longed-for rock, rising clear and steadfast out of the universal confusion, to which one might cling in security; but then the memory of Herr Hentjen and his portrait in the restaurant came to disturb him, and he could not get rid of the thought that somewhere a heart must be engraved that contained her initials and Herr Hentjen's lovingly interlaced. He did not trust himself to touch on this, however, but merely asked where her home had been originally. She replied curtly that she came from Westphalia; besides, that was nobody's business but her own. And as she could not reach her coiffure she patted her hat instead. No, and she couldn't stand people who stuck their noses into other people's affairs either, and it was only men like Esch, who were incapable of imagining that some people mightn't have a shady past, who would do that kind of thing. Wastrels, who when they couldn't have a woman for themselves did their best to fasten a past love affair on to her. In her indignation she shifted a little farther away from him, and Esch, whose thoughts were still circling round Herr Hentjen, was now certain that she must have been very unhappy. His face took on an expression of bitter sorrow. Quite possible that she had been driven into her marriage with kicks and blows. So he said that he hadn't intended his question to be offensive. And, accustomed to comfort by physical caresses women who cried or otherwise gave signs of being unhappy, he took her hand and fondled it. Perhaps it was the extraordinary stillness of everything round her, perhaps however it was only her exhaustion, but she offered no resistance. She had expressed her point of view, but her last words had fallen from her lips like a succession of meaningless sounds which she herself scarcely recognized, and now she felt quite empty, incapable even of feeling repulsion or disgust. She looked at the outspread valley without seeing it, and knew no longer where she was. All those mechanical years in which her life had been passed between the buffet in the restaurant and a few familiar streets shrank to a tiny point, and it seemed to her that she had sat here for ever in this unfamiliar place. The world was so unfamiliar that it was impossible to grasp it, and nothing now connected her with it, nothing but the thin twig with the pointed leaves which hung over the back of the seat and which the fingers of her left hand occasionally touched. Esch asked himself whether he should kiss her, but he felt no desire to do so, and he reflected also that it would not be refined.

So they sat on in silence. The sun was declining in the west and shone on their faces, but Mother Hentjen did not feel its heat on her face, nor the smarting of her stiff, reddened, dust-covered skin. And it almost seemed as if this dreamlike, semi-conscious state were about to enclose Esch too and clasp him in its embrace, for although he saw the lengthening and broadening mountain shadows in the valley as an alluring promise of coolness he felt reluctant to move, and only with hesitation did he at last take up his waistcoat, one of whose pockets contained his great silver watch. It was time to go, and Frau Hentjen, now quite will-less, obeyed his command. While descending she rested heavily on his arm, and he carried the flimsy pink parasol over his shoulder; his waistcoat and jacket dangled from it. To ease the exertion of walking for her he undid two hooks on her high-necked dress, and Mother Hentjen submitted to it, nor did she push him away when other pedestrians approached; she did not see them. The skirt of her brown-silk dress trailed in the dust of the main road, and when in the station Esch deposited her on a seat while he went to quench his thirst she sat there helpless and will-less, waiting for him to return. He brought a glass of beer for her too, and she drank it at his bidding. In the dark compartment of the train he made a pillow for her head on his shoulder. He did not know whether she was asleep or awake, and she herself scarcely knew it. Her head rolled to and fro awkwardly on his hard shoulder. To his attempts to draw her to him her thick-set body in its casing of whalebone put up a stiff resistance, and the hatpins on her nodding head threatened his face. Impatient now, he pushed her hat back, which, sliding downwards along with her coiffure, gave her a drunken look. Her silk dress smelt of dust and heat; only now and then was one aware of the delicate lavender scent that still remained in the folds. Then he kissed her on the cheek as it slid past his mouth, and finally he took her round, heavy head in his hands and drew it to him. She responded to his kiss with dry, thick lips, somewhat like an animal which presses its muzzle against a window pane.

Not until she was standing in the entrance hall did she find herself back in her world again. She gave Esch a push on the chest and with uncertain steps made her way to her place behind the buffet. There she sat down and stared out into the restaurant, which seemed to lie before her in a mist. At last she recognized Wrobek sitting at the nearest table and said: " Good-evening, Herr Wrobek." But she did not see that Esch had followed her into the restaurant, nor did she notice that he was among the last to leave. When he shouted good-night to her she replied noncommittally: " Good-evening, gentlemen." Nevertheless as he stepped out of the restaurant Esch felt a strange and almost proud sensation: that of being Mother Hentjen's lover.

III

When a man has once kissed a woman the train of consequences follows inevitably and unalterably. One can hasten or delay it, but one cannot escape a law of nature. Esch knew that. Yet his imagination balked at picturing the course of his relationship to Mother Hentjen, and so he was relieved to have Teltscher beside him when he entered the restaurant next day at noon; that made it easier for him to meet Mother Hentjen, and simplified everything.

Teltscher had hit upon a new idea; they should get hold of a negress for the wrestling; that would make the final rounds peculiarly attractive; she could be called the " Black Star of Africa," and after two indecisive rounds would finally be beaten by the German. Esch was rather apprehensive that Teltscher would hold forth about this African scheme to Mother Hentjen, and he was not mistaken, for hardly was he inside the door before Teltscher paraded his new idea. "Frau Hentjen, our Esch is going to find a negress for us." She did not at first understand, not even when Esch truthfully declared that he didn't know where he was to get hold of a negress. No, Mother Hentjen simply refused to listen, taking refuge in biting sarcasm: " One woman more or less, that makes no difference to him." Teltscher jovially smacked him on the knee: " Of course, a man like him has so many women running after him, there's nobody that can put his nose out of joint." Esch glanced up at Herr Hentjen's portrait; there was a man who had put his nose out of joint. " Yes, that's the kind of fellow Esch is," repeated Teltscher. To Frau Hentjen this was a confirmation of her own judgment, and she sought to strengthen her alliance with Teltscher; she regarded the short bristles of Esch's hair, which were like a stiff dark brush above the yellowish skin of his head, and she felt that to-day she needed an ally. Turning her back on Esch she praised up Teltscher: it was only to be expected that a man who thought something of himself should avoid meddling with these women and should rather hand the job over to a man like Esch. Esch retorted huffily that most men would fall over each other to get jobs of that kind, but very few could handle them. And he despised Teltscher, who had not even managed to keep Ilona for himself. Still, she would soon be beyond anybody's reach. " Well, Herr Esch," said Frau Hentjen, " why don't you get on with it? Your negress is waiting;

away you go." Very well, he would go, he returned, and as soon as he had eaten his dinner he got up and left the somewhat disconcerted Frau Hentjen to Teltscher's society.

He dawdled about for a while. He had nothing to do. It annoyed him that he had left Frau Hentjen alone with Teltscher, and finally he was driven to return. It was hardly likely that Teltscher was still there, but he wanted to make sure. The restaurant was empty, nor could he find anybody in the kitchen. So Teltscher had gone, and there was nothing to hinder him from also taking himself off; but he knew that at this hour Frau Hentjen usually stayed in her own room, and suddenly he realized that that was why he had come back. He hesitated a moment and then quietly mounted the wooden stairs. Without knocking he entered the room. Mother Hentjen was sitting by the window darning stockings; when she caught sight of him she uttered a faint shriek and stood petrified. He went straight up to her, pressed her down into her chair again and kissed her on the mouth. She twisted and turned her heavy body in her efforts to evade him, and gasped hoarsely: "Go away ... you've no business here." More keenly than his violence she resented the fact that he had come into her room, he, fresh from the arms of a Czech or a negress, into her room that no man had yet entered. She was fighting for her room. But he held her firmly, and at length with thick, dry lips she began to return his kisses, perhaps only as a concession to persuade him to go, for between the kisses she kept repeating with set teeth: "You've no business here." Finally she implored merely: "Not here." Esch, weary of the grim struggle, remembered that this was a woman to be treated with consideration and respect. If she wanted to change the scene of action, why not? He let her go, and she urged him to the door. When they were in the lobby he said gruffly: "Where, then?" She did not understand, for she believed that he would go now. Esch, with his face close to hers, again asked: "Where, then?" And since she made no move and gave no answer he grasped her again to push her back into the room. She was aware only that she must defend that room. Helplessly she gazed round, saw the door leading into the parlour, had a sudden hope that the primness of the parlour would bring him back to his senses and to decent behaviour, and indicated the door with her eyes; he made way for her, but followed with his hand on her shoulder as if she were a captive.

When they were inside she said uncertainly: "There, now perhaps you'll be sensible, Herr Esch," and strained towards the window to fling back the shutters. But he had seized her from behind, and Frau Hentjen could not move from the spot. She tried to wrest herself free, but they swayed and stumbled among the nuts, so that they almost fell. The nuts cracked under their feet, and as Frau Hentjen, anxious to save her stores, struggled backwards towards the alcove in search of firm footing and something she could get a purchase on, she had a momentary flash of dreamlike awareness, as if she were walking in her sleep: was it not her own doing that the man was being enticed into that corner? But that thought only made her angrier, and she hissed: " Go to your negress . . . you can get round these sluts, but you won't get round me." She clawed at the corner of the alcove, but instead caught hold of the curtain; the wooden rings on the curtain-pole rattled slightly, and being afraid of damaging the good curtain she let go, so that Esch was able to force her into the dark corner where the twin beds stood. He was still behind her and had recaptured her hands and pulled them close to him so that she could not but feel his excitement. Whether for that reason or because the sight of the marriage beds reduced her to defenceless immobility, she went limp under his passionate aggression. And as he tore impatiently at her clothing, and she was afraid that now her underlinen would be damaged, she herself helped him as a criminal might help the hangman, and it filled him almost with horror to note how smoothly things now took their course and in what a matter-of-fact way Mother Hentjen, when they fell on to the bed, laid herself on her back to receive him. And it filled him with a horror still more profound to see her lying rigid and motionless, as if submitting to a familiar duty, as if she were merely recapitulating an old and familiar act of submission, without interest, without enjoyment. Only her round head rolled to and fro on the bedcover as if in persistent negation. He felt the warmth of her body and whipped up his own lust to provoke and overmaster hers. He clutched her head between his hands as if to squeeze out of it the thoughts that were congealed within it, refusing to flow out to him, and his mouth followed the unlovely lines of her heavy cheeks and her low forehead that remained motionless and unresponsive, as unresponsive as the masses for whom Martin had sacrificed himself and who were still unfree. Perhaps Ilona might have the same feeling about Korn's massive insensitivity, and for a moment he was glad to think that his sacrifice was the same as hers, and that it was right, and that it was done for her and for redemption into righteousness. Oh, to release oneself, to strip oneself more and more, to annihilate oneself with all the sin that one had accumulated and bore about, yet to release her too whose mouth one sought for, to annihilate Time that had her in its grip, Time that had embedded itself in these ageing cheeks; oh, the desire he had to annihilate the woman who had lived in Time, to bid her be born again timeless, motionless and perforce at one with him! His seeking mouth had found hers, that was now pressed against his like the muzzle of an animal against a pane of glass, and Esch was enraged because she kept her soul tightly enclosed behind her set teeth so that he should not possess it. And when with a hoarse sound she opened her lips at last, he felt an ecstasy such as he had never yet experienced in a woman's arms, he flowed boundlessly into her, yearning to enter into possession of her who was no longer a woman to him but a re-won heritage wrested from the unknown, the matrix of life, annihilating his ego by transcending its confines till it was featureless and submerged in its own enlargement. For the man who wills Goodness and Righteousness wills thereby the Absolute, and it was revealed to Esch for the first time that the goal is not the appeasement of lust but an absolute oneness exalted far above its immediate, sordid and even trivial occasion, a conjoint transit, itself timeless and so annihilating time; and that the rebirth of man is as still and serene as the universal spirit that yet contracts and closes round man when once his ecstatic will has compelled it, until he attains his sole birthright: deliverance and redemption.

How little it mattered, after all, that one was Mother Hentjen's lover! There are many men who think that life is centred in the existence of some particular woman. Esch had always known how to keep himself free from that prejudice. Especially now, even although Frau Hentjen often strangely usurped his thoughts. Especially now. His life was directed to greater and higher aims.

Near the New Market he came to a standstill in front of a book-shop. His eye fell on a picture of the Statue of Liberty stamped in gilt on green linen; beneath it was the title, *America To-day and To-morrow*. He had bought but few books in his life, and he was surprised at himself for going into the shop. Its smooth counters and the orderliness of its rectangular books reminded him vaguely of a tobacconist's. He would have liked to linger and talk, but since no one encouraged him he merely paid for the book and came out with a package in his hand that he did not know what to do with. A present for Frau Hentjen? She would certainly have not the slightest interest in it, and yet there was some inexplicable connection between her and his purchase. In his perplexity he came again to a standstill in front of the shop. Behind the glass pane on a line hung a bright array of foreign phrase-books, and on their covers waved the flags of their respective nations as if to cheer on aspiring students. Esch betook himself to his midday meal in the restaurant.

One is shy of producing an unsuitable gift, and so Esch carried his into the window-seat; that was where he always read the newspaper after dinner, so he might as well sit there with his book. It didn't take long for Mother Hentjen to call across the empty room: "Well, Herr Esch, of course you can afford to sit down and read books in the middle of the day." "Yes," he answered, "I'll show it you," got up and brought it to her at the buffet. "What's it for?" she said as he held the book out; he indicated by a jerk of the head that she was to look at it; she turned over a page here and there, regarded one or two pictures with closer attention, and simply handed the book back with a "very nice." Esch was disappointed; he had indeed suspected that she wouldn't be interested, for what did a woman like her know of the greater and higher aims of life! None the less he remained standing, expecting something else to happen . . . but all that happened was a remark from Mother Hentjen: "I suppose you're thinking of spending the whole afternoon over that stuff?" Esch retorted: "I'm not thinking of anything," and in a huff carried the book to his own room to read it in peace. And he came to the conclusion that he would emigrate by himself. By himself, all alone. Yet he could not help assuming again and again that his study of the American work was to benefit not only himself but Mother Hentjen.

He read a portion of it every day. At first he had contented himself with the illustrations, and now when he thought of America it seemed to him that the trees there were not green, the meadows not brightly coloured, the sky no longer blue, but that all American life was deployed against a polished and elegant chiaroscuro as in the brownish grey photographs, or against the sharp contours of the delicately limned pen-drawings. Later on, however, he became absorbed in the text. The recurring statistics certainly bored him, but he was too conscientious to skip them and succeeded in learning a good deal by heart. He was deeply interested in the American police system and the law courts, which, the book averred, were organized in the service of democratic freedom, so that any man able to read a book intelligently could gather that in America no cripples were thrown into jail at the bidding of wicked shipping firms; it would be as well therefore for Martin to go with him. Esch turned over the pages at random, and strangely enough the photograph of the giant liner at the landing-stage in New York revealed Mother Hentjen in her brown-silk dress, the light-pink parasol in her hands, leaning over the railing watching the swarm of strangers, while Martin with his crutch sat on a chest, and the air was filled with syllables of the English language.

And thoroughgoing as he was, Esch decided after some hesitation to visit once more the book-shop in which he had felt so much at home. Making light of the fresh expense he purchased the English phrase-book with the inviting Union Jack and forthwith set himself to learn the English words, behind each of which he saw the word " Liberty " in the elegant half-tones of a silky and glossy photograph, as if in this one word all that had ever existed in the past and been expressed in the old language must now be resolved and redeemed. He even made up his mind that they must speak English to each other, and that Mother Hentjen must be instructed in English to that end. But with his healthy contempt for all reverie he did not stop short at merely wishing for freedom: his profits were accumulating, and although the receipts for the last few days of the wrestling had fallen off somewhat, he had in any case a clear surplus of about two hundred marks, which he now definitely set aside as the nucleus of his travelling expenses; hence he could take action, he could escape from his prison, he could begin his new life. He was often drawn nowadays to the Cathedral. When he was on the steps overlooking Cathedral Square, and English-speaking tourists chanced to appear, it was like a breath of freedom invigorating him and caressing his brow as he stood with bared head in the warm summer wind. The very streets of Cologne began to take on another aspect, one might even say a more innocent aspect, and Esch regarded them with kindliness and almost with a hint of malicious triumph. Once he was on the other side, across the sea, they too would have a different look. And if he ever came back he would let the English-speaking guide show him over the Cathedral.—

After the performance he waited for Teltscher; the air was soft and rainy as they walked through the night. Esch stopped suddenly: " Look here, Teltscher, you've always been boasting about an American engagement: it's time you did something about it." Teltscher loved to discuss his grand prospects: " If I've a mind to, I can get as many engagements over there as I want." Esch dissented: " With your knife-throwing stunt . . . h'm, well . . . don't you think wrestling or something of that kind would go better over there? " Teltscher laughed scornfully: " You're surely not thinking of taking our girls over! " " Well, why not? " " You're an idiot, Esch, if you would take over that kind of stuff. In any case . . . over there they expect real sporting turns, but the kind of thing our girls do . . ." He laughed again. Esch suggested: " But couldn't we get a good team together? " " Nonsense, people over there aren't going to wait till we arrive," said Teltscher, " and where could you find trained girls here? " . . . he reflected . . . " if these cows of ours were anything to look at there might possibly be something in it. But only in Mexico or South America." Esch did not grasp his meaning at first, and Teltscher was provoked by his stupidity: " They're always hard up for women out there . . . and if the wrestling wasn't a draw the girls would at least be provided for, and we could keep all the travelling expenses in our pockets." That seemed obvious enough. After all, why not South America or Mexico? And the half-tone photographs in Esch's mind took on a brilliantly coloured Southern luxuriance. Yes, it was a convincing scheme. Teltscher said: " You've hit on a good thing this time, Esch. Make it your job to fit out the circus with new girls worth looking at. I know one or two fellows who could easily arrange a tour for us over there. And then we'll set sail with the whole cargo." Esch knew that the proposal savoured abominably of white slave traffic. But he could ignore that knowledge, for the wrestling matches were not illicit, and even if they gave any cause for suspicion what did it matter? that would only pay off a few scores against a police force that locked up innocent men. A police force that worked in the cause of freedom and accepted no money from shipping firms wouldn't need to be scored off. White slave traffic, of course, wasn't very refined, but after all even Mother Hentjen's business was against her principles. Nor did Lohberg approve of his shop. And in any case it was better to take Teltscher to America with the circus than to leave him here throwing knives. They passed a bored policeman who was patrolling his beat in the rain, and Esch would have liked to assure him that the police would be none the worse off, for he would deliver Nentwig into their hands sooner or later! Esch was a man who upheld law and order and fulfilled his pledges, even though the other parties were swine. "Police swine," he growled. The wet asphalt shone like a photographic film, dark brown in the light of the yellow lamps, and Esch saw before him the Statue of Liberty whose torch consumed and released all the husks of one's past life, delivering into flame all that was dead and gone—and if that was murder, it was a kind of murder beyond the jurisdiction of the police: murder in the cause of redemption. His decision was taken, and when Teltscher advised him on parting: "And don't forget, it's always blonde girls they want out there, nothing but blonde," he accepted the fact that he was to seek out and provide blonde girls. He had only to settle up his old scores, and then they would set sail with their cargo of blondes. From the lofty deck of the ocean liner they would look down on the swarm of smaller craft. They would cry a farewell to the Old World, a final good-bye. Perhaps the blondes on the ship would strike up a farewell song in chorus, and when the ship on its taut tow-rope glided past the river shores perhaps Ilona would be walking on the bank and would wave a hand, herself a blonde, but rescued from all danger, and the level water would broaden between them.

Esch should really have admitted that his mistress stood on the same plane as himself: for if he kept love in a subordinate place Mother Hentjen ignored it. In that she was his match, although moved by other considerations than his. She regarded love as something so profoundly secret that she scarcely ventured to pronounce the word. She forgot again and again the existence of this lover who was now established and whom she could not prevent from stealing in upon her of an afternoon when she was taking her nap or at night when her last customers had departed, and again and again at his approach she was overwhelmed with petrified astonishment, a state of petrifaction that only began gradually to wear away when the dim parlour and the alcove had received them both: then it dissolved into a feeling of detached isolation, and the dark alcove in which she lay looking up at the ceiling began to float away till soon it seemed no longer a part of her familiar house, but was like a soaring chariot hanging somewhere in infinite space and darkness.

Only then did she realize that somebody else was there beside her, occupied with her, and it was no longer Esch, it was no longer even a man she knew, it was a Someone who had strangely and violently thrust himself into her isolation, and yet could not be reproached for his violence since he was a part of that isolation and could be found only within it, a Someone, quiet and yet threatening, demanding assuagement for his violence, and therefore one had to play the game with him that he demanded, and though the game was compulsory it was yet strangely guiltless, since it was engulfed in isolation and even God shut His eyes to it. But he with whom she shared the bed was little likely to suspect the nature of that isolation, and she was sternly on her guard to keep him from impinging upon it. A profound muteness enveloped him, and she would not let that disconcerting silence be assailed, even should he mistake it for insensibility or stupidity. Silence abolished shame, for shame was born only in speech. What she felt was not bodily lust but release from shame: she was so isolated that, as if alone for all eternity, she could no longer be ashamed of a single fibre in her body. He could not understand her muteness, and yet was disheartened by the shameless silence that invited and submitted to him in brutish immobility. She gave him barely a sigh, and he was all agonized expectation and hope that she would finally let her voice go in a cry of satisfied animal lust. Too often he waited in vain, and then he hated the solicitous crook of the arm with which she invited him to lay down his head and sleep on her plump, unmoved shoulder. But when she sent her lover away it was with hard abruptness, as if she suddenly wanted to annihilate both him and the knowledge he shared with her: she pushed him out through the door, and as he stole down the stairs he could feel her hatred at his back. That gave him an inkling that it was a strange, strange land he had been in, and in spite of himself the knowledge always impelled him back to her again with torment and increasing desire. For even in the bliss of losing himself, of sinking tranced and nameless in the shamelessness of sex, the desire to overcome the woman kept stubborn vigil, the desire to force her to acknowledge him, to make the present moment flame up in her like a torch that burned up all else, so that in its glare she should be aware of her mate, and out of the silence of night that enveloped everything should let her voice ring out passionately, and say " du " to him and to him alone, as if he were her child. He no longer knew what she looked like, she was beyond beauty and ugliness, beyond youth and age, she was only a silent problem that he was set to master and to resolve.

Although in many respects Esch could not have wished for a better, and even had to admit that it was a lofty kind of love, surpassing ordinary standards, that had laid its spell upon him, yet it always annoyed him, time and again, that whenever he came into the restaurant Mother Hentjen, anxious lest the other customers should suspect something, was so markedly cold to him that against her will she made him conspicuous. Had it not been that he wanted to avoid further notice and even scandal, and had not his cheap and bountiful dinner been in question, he would simply have stayed away. As it was, he made an effort to be compliant and to strike the happy mean in his visits; but he could not manage it, he could not please Mother Hentjen whatever he did: if he appeared in the restaurant she put on a sulky face and obviously wished him gone, and if he stayed away she asked him spitefully if he had perhaps been off with his negress.

Teltscher thought that they could not decently refuse to give Gernerth a chance to share in the South American project. With that the plan would have acquired a certain solidity in Esch's eyes. But Gernerth declined, giving as an excuse his family, which he wanted to have with him when he took on his new contract in autumn. So the windbag Teltscher remained Esch's sole associate. He was certainly not much to depend on, but the project should not be postponed for all that; Esch began his canvassing at once, and set out on the search for women wrestlers fit for export. Perhaps in its course he might actually run across the negress whom they still wanted; that of course would be an extra piece of luck.

He again made his round of the dens and brothels, and if he sometimes felt a slight twinge of conscience in doing so, it was only because Frau Hentjen, if she should find out, would never believe that he devoted himself to such a task out of mere business considerations. So, as a kind of proof of his erotic indifference, as a moral though quite preposterous alibi, he extended his business researches to include the homosexual resorts, resorts which hitherto he had avoided almost apprehensively. Yet he felt vaguely that there must be another reason for his desire to visit them. What took place in them should have left him quite unmoved, and it was really queer, the horror that overcame him when he saw these men dancing with each other, cheek pressed against cheek. Then he could not help thinking of his first visit to one of those filthy dens when he was a mere lad at a loose end in the world, a lad who could scarcely remember his mother, and how he had felt that he wanted to run away to her the first time that he had caught sight of a male prostitute, tightly laced and in long skirts, singing obscene songs in a falsetto voice. If he forced himself to gaze at such abominations again, considering that the sight of them almost made him vomit, Mother Hentjen would be compelled to realize, in spite of her prudishness, how little pleasure he got out of his job. God knows, he would rather run to her than haunt such places, searching for he knew not what, as if he were looking for his lost innocence. Quite preposterous to think that one might run up against, say, the chairman of a company, for these street boys were certainly beneath the notice of a man like that. All the same, with such a queer lot one had to be prepared for anything. And as in venturous situations one exercises self-control, Esch did not bash in the painted mugs of these little manikins when they spoke to him; on the contrary he was on his best behaviour, treated them to sweet liqueurs, asked how they were getting on and—if they became confidential—inquired also into their source of income and the names of their kind uncles. True, he wondered sometimes why he listened to all their chatter, but he pricked up his ears when the name of Chairman Bertrand was mentioned; then the vague picture that he carried in his mind of that great man, a picture scarcely legible and yet larger than life-size, acquired gradually more colour, took on strangely tender hues, and became at the same time a little smaller as it grew more sharp and definite. Bertrand, it seemed, sailed up and down the Rhine in a motor-yacht, and his crew were very handsome; everything on this dream-boat was white and blue; once he had come to Cologne and little Harry had had the great honour of finding favour in his eyes; they had gone as far as Antwerp in the fairy yacht and in Ostend had lived like gods; but usually he was too grand to pay any attention to the kind of boys that came here. His castle stood in a great park in Badenweiler; deer grazed in the meadows and strange flowers scented the air; he stayed there when he was not in distant lands; nobody had entry to his castle, and his friends were Englishmen and Indians of fabulous wealth; he owned a motor-car, and it was so huge that one could sleep in it at nights. He was richer than the Kaiser.

Esch almost forgot his own work, so powerfully was he possessed by the desire to find Harry Köhler; and when he succeeded, his heart beat so fast and he bore himself so respectfully that one might have imagined he did not know that the small youth was little better than a street boy. He forgot his hatred, forgot that Martin had to suffer so that this lad might lead a fine life; yes, he felt almost jealous because to this boy who was accustomed to fine and well-to-do company he could not offer anything better than a visit to the wrestling performance, which, however, he affably put at Herr Harry's disposal. But the boy, not in the least impressed, simply refused with a disgusted "Pah!" so that Esch felt ashamed of having suggested anything so unseemly; yet as he felt annoyed too, he said rudely: "Well, I haven't a yacht to invite you to." "How? What do you mean by that?" was the suspicious, yet strangely gentle reply. Alfons, the fat, blond musician, who was sitting coatless at the table in a gaudy silk shirt with rolls of fat beneath it that looked like a woman's breasts, laughed, showing his white teeth: "He means—you know what yourself, Harry." Harry looked offended: "I hope you don't intend to insult anyone, my dear sir." God forbid, Esch replied glibly, that was far from his thoughts; he was only sorry because he knew that Herr Harry was used to finer things. With a smile of gentle resignation Harry waved his hand languidly: "That's past." Alfons patted his arm: "Never mind, my boy, there's lots here willing to comfort you." Harry shook his head in gentle melancholy. "One can only love once." This fellow talked like Lohberg, thought Esch, and he said: "That's true." For although the Mannheim idiot wasn't very often right, in this case he seemed to be right, and Esch said again: "Yes, that's true." Harry was obviously pleased to find one who understood him, and looked at Esch gratefully, but Alfons, who did not want to hear such sentiments, became indignant: "And all the friendship we offer you, Harry, means nothing to you?" Harry shook his head: "What does the little scrap of intimacy amount to that you call friendship? As if love had anything to do with friendship and intimacy!" "Well, my boy, you have your own views of love," said Alfons tenderly. Harry spoke as though from memory: "Love is great distance." While Alfons replied: "That's far too deep for a poor devil of a musician, my boy," Esch could not but think of Frau Hentjen's silence. The band was making a great din, and Harry, leaning over the table so as not to have to shout, said mysteriously and in a low voice: "Love is a matter of distance; here are two people, and each is on a separate star, and neither can know anything of the other. And then suddenly distance is annihilated and time is annihilated, and they have flown together, so that they have no separate awareness of each other or of themselves, and feel no need of it. That is love." Esch thought of Badenweiler; of a remote love in that remote castle; something of the kind was perhaps preordained for Ilona. But while he was still brooding over this, a pang of rage and pain darted through him at the thought that never would he be able to discover whether it had been with this noble form of love or another that Herr and Frau Hentjen had loved each other. Harry continued as if he were reciting a verse from the Bible: "Only in a dreadful intensification of strangeness, only when the strangeness has become in a sense infinite, can the miracle happen, the unattainable goal of love: the mystery of oneness . . . yes, that's how it is." "Prosit!" said Alfons glumly, but to Esch it seemed that this boy had been given knowledge of higher things, and the hope awoke in him that that knowledge might also hold the answer to his own questions. And although his thoughts were by no means in harmony with those which Harry had expressed, he said, as he had once said to Lohberg: "But in that case one could not go on living after the other," and he was filled with the half-joyful, half-bitter assurance that the widow Hentjen, seeing that she was still alive, could not have loved her husband. Alfons whispered to Esch: "For Heaven's sake, don't say such things before the boy," but he was too late, for Harry looked at Esch in horror and said tonelessly, just a trace more tonelessly than necessary: "I'm not really living now." Alfons pushed across a double glass of liqueur to him. "Poor fellow, ever since that affair he's talked like this . . . that man completely turned his head." Esch felt himself jerked back into reality; he put on an innocent air: "Who?" Alfons shrugged his shoulders. "Oh, him, the Lord God himself, the angel of purity . . ." "Hold your jaw, or I'll scratch your eyes out," panted Harry, and Esch, who felt sorry for the boy, said imperiously: "Leave him in peace." Suddenly Harry broke out into hysterical sobbing: "I'm not really living now, I'm not . . ." Esch felt rather helpless, for he could not employ here the methods which he was accustomed to use with girls when they cried. So that man had ruined this boy's life too, it seemed; Esch wanted to do something to comfort Harry and said abruptly: "We'll shoot this Bertrand for you." Harry screamed: "You'll do nothing of the kind!" "Why not? You should be pleased; he's earned it." "You shan't, you shan't do it . . ." the boy panted, glaring at him " . . . don't you dare to touch him. . . ." Esch was irritated at the boy for so stupidly misunderstanding his good intentions.

"A swine like that must be put away," he persisted. "He's not a swine," Harry said beseechingly, "he's the noblest, the best, the handsomest man in the world." In a sense the boy was certainly right, one couldn't injure such a man. Esch was on the point of giving his promise. "Hopeless," said Alfons dejectedly, drinking up his liqueur. Harry had leant his head between his hands, and nodding like an image he began to laugh: "Him a swine! Him a swine!" then his laughter suddenly changed into sobs again. When Alfons made to draw him to his fat, silken breast Esch had to interpose to prevent a fight. He told Alfons to clear out, and then turned to Harry: "Let's go. Where do you live?" Quite passive now, the boy obeyed him, and named his address. When they reached the street Esch took his arm as if he were a girl, and the one providing, the other accepting protection, they felt almost happy. A light wind was blowing from the Rhine. Before his door Harry clung to Esch, and seemed about to offer his face to be kissed. Esch pushed him through the door. But Harry slipped out again and whispered: "You won't do anything to him!" and before Esch knew what was happening the boy had embraced him, awkwardly kissed his sleeve, and vanished into the house.

The attendance at the wrestling performances was palpably falling off, and something had to be done in the way of publicity. Without consulting the others, Esch decided on his own responsibility to persuade *The People's Guardian* to insert a report. But before the dingy white door of the editorial office he recognized quite clearly that once more it was something else that had led him here. In itself this visit was quite meaningless and futile; the entire wrestling business had become indifferent to him, for it was not achieving anything even for Ilona, and so something more significant, more decisive, must be done for her, and he saw clearly too that *The People's Guardian* would not insert a report now, if they had omitted to do so hitherto because of some proletarian prejudice or other. Fundamentally the attitude of the Socialist paper was praiseworthy: at least it knew its right hand from its left, and drew a clear-cut distinction between the bourgeois and the proletarian points of view. One should really draw Mother Hentjen's attention to such strength of character: she might no longer disdainfully dismiss these people, who, although ordinary Socialists, yet condemned the wrestling business as much as she did herself, and she might no longer look askance at Martin either for being a Socialist. Esch was brought up with a start when he thought of Martin; the devil alone knew what he, August Esch, was doing here in this place! but it was clear that it had no connection with the wrestling. He was still brooding over this while he entered, and not until he was forced to jog the editor's memory by mentioning the strike—for the editor, most unflatteringly, had failed to recognize him—not until then did it dawn on Esch that he had come here on Martin's account. He said abruptly: "I have an important piece of news for you." "Oh, the strike!" with a wave of the hand the editor reduced that event to triviality, "that's ancient history." "Indeed!" replied Esch angrily, "but Geyring is still in prison." "Well? He got three months, didn't he?" "Something has got to be done," Esch heard himself saying in a louder voice than he had intended. "Well, don't shout at me like that—I didn't lock him up." Esch wasn't a man to be put off by such words. "Something has got to be done," he persisted grimly and impatiently, "I know some of the customers that your fine Herr Bertrand associates with . . . and they're here in Cologne, not in Italy!" he added triumphantly. "We've known that for several years, my dear friend and comrade. Or is that the piece of news you wanted to tell us?" Esch felt stunned. "Well, but why don't you do something, then? He's put himself in your hands." "My dear fellow," said the other, "you seem to have somewhat childish ideas of things. All the same you ought to know that we live in a civilized country." He waited now for Esch to take his leave, but Esch did not move, and so for a while the two men sat opposite each other, not knowing what to make of each other, not understanding each other, and each seeing only the other's naked moral unsightliness. Red spots of anger appeared on Esch's cheeks, and faded again into tan. The editor was once more wearing his light-brown velvet jacket, and his slightly plump face with the brown, drooping moustache was at once soft and strong like the velvet of his jacket. A slight trace of coquetry lay in this correspondence, reminding Esch of the finicking attire of the youths at the homosexual resort. He became aggressive: "So you're shielding that homosexual of yours, are you? And Martin can do time for it, for all you care?" He twisted his mouth into an expression of disgust, showing his strong teeth. The editor became impatient: "Look here, my dear sir, what business is it of yours anyway?" Esch grew red in the face: "You deliberately hinder anything that might get him out . . . you wouldn't print my article; you shield the scoundrel that got him thrown into prison, this Bertrand . . . and you, you give yourself out as a guardian of freedom!" He laughed bitterly. "With you freedom is in safe keeping!" A fool, evidently, thought the editor, and so he replied quietly: "Look here, technically speaking it's quite impossible for us to publish as news something that you bring us weeks and months too late; it's just . . ." Esch jumped up. "You'll get news that you don't like from me yet," he shouted, rushing out and slamming the dingy white door behind him, which, however, did not remain shut, but went on banging.

When he reached the street he stopped aghast. Why had he blazed up like that? Could he alter the fact that these Socialists were swine? Once more Frau Hentjen had proved to be right in scorning the whole crew of them. "The corrupt Press," he kept on saying to himself. And he had gone there with the best intentions too, had wished to give them an opportunity to justify themselves in Frau Hentjen's eyes. Things as they were and things as they ought to be began anew to get entangled in a most exasperating confusion and chaos. Only one thing was certain, that the editor had behaved like a swine, firstly by his general attitude, and secondly because he sought to shield this Bertrand with all the resources of a corrupt Press, yes, a corrupt Press. And this chairman fellow himself was a proper swine, although the boy Harry would not admit it, and there was nothing one could do to put a stop to him. On the other hand what the boy had said about love was quite right. Nothing was simple! at most only one thing had come out clearly: Frau Hentjen could not have loved her husband; she must have been forced into marriage with that swine. And as Esch's thoughts filled with hatred of the world around him, and of the swine who should be done in, as such swine deserved, he began more and more definitely to hate the chairman Bertrand, to hate him for his blasphemies and his crimes. He tried to picture Bertrand sitting in a comfortable chair after dinner in his castle, surrounded by luxury, a fat cigar in his hand, and when that elegant figure at length emerged as from a cloud of tobacco smoke, it was somewhat like that of a dandified snippet of a tailor, strongly resembling the portrait of Herr Hentjen which hung over the mantelpiece in the restaurant.

For Mother Hentjen's birthday, which was duly celebrated every year by the regular customers, Esch had hunted out a small bronze Statue of Liberty, and the gift seemed to him ingenious, not only as hinting at their American future, but also as a happy pendant to the Schiller statue, with which he had scored such a success. At midday he put in an appearance with it.

Unfortunately the present failed of its effect. If he had handed it to her in dead secrecy she might have appreciated the beauty of the sculpture, but the panic fear into which any public familiarity, any sign of intimacy, threw her, so blinded her that she evinced but little delight, nor did she become any warmer in her manner when he apologetically added that the statue would probably go well with the Schiller monument. "Well, if you think so ..." she said non-committally, and that was all. Of course the new present, too, would have served very well to embellish her room; but to show him that he must not flatter himself that he was entitled to claim such a privileged position for everything he brought her, and to prove to him once and for all that she still upheld the inviolateness of her room, she went upstairs and fetched the Schiller monument, and planted it along with the Statue of Liberty on the mantelpiece beside the Eiffel Tower. There were now collected the bard of freedom, the American statue and the French tower, as symbols of an attitude which Frau Hentjen did not share, and the statue stretched its arm upwards, stretched its torch upwards towards Herr Hentjen. Esch felt his gifts desecrated by Herr Hentjen's gaze, and he would have liked to ask that the portrait at least should be removed; yet what help would that have been? this restaurant in which Herr Hentjen had worked would remain the same, and it was almost more to his liking that everything should remain frankly and honestly where it was. Why try dishonestly to conceal something which it was impossible to conceal! And he made the discovery that what drew him here was not merely the excellence of the food dispensed to him under the eyes of Herr Hentjen, but that he also needed Herr Hentjen in some mysterious way as a strange and bitter seasoning to his food; it was the same inescapable bitter dose that he accepted in Mother Hentjen's moroseness, and that made him feel bound inescapably to her when she morosely whispered to him, as now, that he could come that night.

He spent the afternoon in lascivious thoughts of Mother Hentjen's matter-of-fact love rites. And once more he was tortured by that matter-of-factness, which contradicted so blatantly her customary aversion. In whose nightly embraces could she have contracted those habits? A hope in which he himself did not believe faintly dawned, promising that all this would fall away once they were in America, and the comfort of this hope mingled with the excitement which now came over him when he felt her house-door key in his pocket. Esch took out the key, held it in the palm of his hand, and felt the smooth metal of the handle. True, she had refused to learn English, but the wind of the future blew once more through the streets. The key to freedom, he thought. The cathedral rose grey in the late twilight, iron-grey soared the towers, and a breath of the new and the unfamiliar fanned them. Esch counted the hours until night. It was more important to hunt out girls for the South American journey than to go to the Alhambra. Five full hours, then he would be at the house door. Esch saw the alcove, saw her lying on the bed; and the thought of stealing in to her, the thought that at the touch of his aroused body her body would palpitate, made his breathing difficult and his mouth dry. For even last week, as during all the weeks before, she had received him in dull impassivity, and although that brief involuntary palpitation was insignificant in itself, yet it was a point at which the immense dead-weight of habit had been quickened, a tiny point, it was true, and yet a virginal one, and that was a herald of hope and of the future. And to Esch it seemed dishonourable to enter prostitutes' resorts on the evening of Mother Hentjen's birthday, so he betook himself to the Alhambra.

When afterwards he returned to the restaurant he could see from a long way off the yellow radiance on the uneven cobbles outside. The windows with their panes of bull's-eye glass were open, and inside he could see Mother Hentjen sitting, stiff in her silk dress, surrounded by her noisy customers; a bowl of punch stood on the table. Esch remained in the shadow; the thought of entering filled him with loathing. He turned away again, but not to go duteously in search of girls at their resorts; he strode in fury through the streets. On the Rhine Bridge he leant against the iron parapet, gazed down into the black water and across at the sheds on the quay. His knees were trembling, so intense had been his desire to burst the rigid bony construction in which that woman was encased; the whalebones would have cracked in the wild struggle. With an expressionless face he trailed back into the town, mechanically running his hand along the bars of the bridge railing as he went.

The house was dark. Mother Hentjen, a candlestick in her hand, was waiting for him at the top of the stairs. He simply blew out the candle-butt and seized her. But she had already taken off her corsets, nor did she defend herself, but instead gave him a tender kiss. And although this greeting took him quite by surprise, and was perhaps no less novel than that palpitation for which he was waiting so impatiently, yet from this kiss it was terribly and incontrovertibly clear that one of her old habits had been to conclude her birthday celebrations with a tender love rite, and when the longed-for moment now actually arrived, when that blissful palpitation ran through her body, the thought that the touch of Herr Hentjen's body, which in his present position Esch had no wish to picture, had also made her palpitate just like this, became a raging pain; the ghost which he had fancied was laid arose again, more mocking, more inconquerable than ever, and to conquer it and to show this woman that he, he alone was there, he flung himself upon her and sank his teeth into her plump shoulder. It must have hurt her, but she bore it in silence, although she made a wry face as though she had bitten on something sour, and when presently, exhausted, he made to leave her, she clasped him to her as in gratitude,—and yet her heavy awkward arm was like a vice—clasped him so fast that he could scarcely breathe and wrathfully struggled to free himself. She did not give way, but said—it was the first time that she had spoken to him in the alcove—in her usual business voice, in which nevertheless, had he been more sensitive, he might have heard a note almost of fear: "Why were you so late in coming? . . . because another year has been added to my age?" Esch was so stunned by her speaking at all that he did not grasp the meaning of her words; indeed, did not even attempt to grasp it, for the unexpected sound of her voice was to him like the termination of something, was like a sudden illumination after a long and painful process of thought, a sign that things could take on a different aspect. He said: "I'm sick of it, I'm going to finish it off." The blood froze in Frau Hentjen's veins; she had scarcely enough strength left to unclasp her arm from his shoulder; she felt leaden and icy, and her arm fell powerlessly of itself. All that she still knew was that she must not show her dismay before a man, that she must give him his marching orders before he went of his own accord, and summoning all her strength she brought out faintly: "Certainly, for all I care." Esch took no notice of this and went on: "Next week I'll go to Baden." What need had he to tell her this as well? She felt somehow flattered that his resolve to end the affair should shake him so deeply, it seemed, that it was driving him away from Cologne, out into the world. Yet he was pressing his lips again to her shoulder, and that was surely a queer way of showing that he wanted to finish with her. Or did he simply want to indulge his lust up to the very last minute? men were capable of anything! Nevertheless she picked up hope again, and although her voice was still difficult to control she asked: " Why? Is there another girl there like the one in Ober-Wesel? " Esch laughed: " Yes, you might call it that, a girl just like her." Frau Hentjen was indignant at his flippancy on the top of everything else: " It's easy enough to make game of a weak woman." Esch still thought she was referring to the person in Badenweiler: " Oh, the one in Baden isn't so terribly weak as all that." This fed her suspicions anew: " Who is it? " " A secret." She maintained an offended silence, and submitted to his renewed caresses. Presently she asked: " Why should you want another woman? " In spite of himself he could not but secretly admit that this woman with her matter-of fact, almost businesslike and yet so curiously reluctant and chaste surrender, accorded him more intense pleasure and bliss than any other woman could, and that he really wanted nobody else. She said again: " Why should you want another woman? You've only to tell me if I'm not young enough for you." He did not reply, for suddenly the fact that she had spoken at last filled him with excitement and elation; she who hitherto had lain silent in his arms, her head rolling in persistent negation, so unalterably silent that her silence had always seemed to him a legacy from the time of Herr Hentjen. She felt his happiness, and she went on proudly: " You don't need any of those young things; I'm a match for any of them." Nonsense, thought Esch, with a sudden stab of pain, she must be lying. And with a stab of pain he remembered Harry's words and repeated them: " One can only love once," and when Frau Hentjen simply said " Yes," as if she meant to convey by this that he was the man whom she loved, then it was clear what a liar she was; pretended to be disgusted by men and yet sat drinking with them at her table, and let them drink her health; pretended to love him now, and yet was inconquerably matter-of-fact. But perhaps all this was wrong, for she had no children. Once more his desire for the unambiguous, the absolute, was brought up against an unscalable wall. If all this were only past and done with! His journey to Badenweiler appeared to him at that moment as a necessary prelude, an inevitable preliminary to the journey to America. Evidently she guessed at these thoughts of travel, for she asked: " What does she look like? " " Who? " " Why, the Baden girl." Well, what did Bertrand look like? and more clearly than ever he recognized that he could picture Bertrand only by calling up Hentjen's portrait. He replied harshly: " The portrait must be taken away." She did not understand: " What portrait? " " That one below there," he could not bring himself to utter the name, " above the Eiffel Tower." She began to understand, but she rebelled against this attempt of his to mingle in her affairs: " Nobody has ever objected to it." " And that's just why," he persisted, and now it became quite clear to him that it was his affair with Hentjen that he had to settle with Bertrand, and he went on: " and besides, an end must be put to all this." " Well, perhaps . . . " she replied hesitatingly, and her rebellious feelings making her unwilling to understand, she added: " An end to what? " " We must go to America." " Yes," she said, " I know."

Esch had got up. He would have liked to walk up and down, as he was accustomed to do when anything occupied his mind, but there was no room in the alcove, and outside the nuts lay about the floor. So he sat down on the edge of the bed. And although he did his best to repeat Harry's words they changed when he tried to utter them:

" Love is only possible in a strange country. If you want to love really, you must begin a new life and destroy everything in your old one. Only in a new, quite strange life, where everything past is so dead that you don't even need to forget it, can two human beings become so at one that the past and even time itself no longer exist for them."

" I haven't a past," said Mother Hentjen in an offended voice.

" Only then," Esch made an angry grimace which in the darkness Frau Hentjen luckily could not see, " only then will there be no need any longer to deny anything, for then truth will reign, and truth is beyond time."

" I've never denied anything," said Mother Hentjen in defence.

Esch did not let himself be put off: " Truth has nothing to do with the world, nothing to do with Mannheim . . . " he almost shouted, " it has nothing to do with this old world."

Mother Hentjen sighed. Esch gave her a sharp glance:

" There's nothing to sigh over; you must free yourself from the old world, so as to become free yourself. . . ."

Mother Hentjen sighed uneasily: " What's to become of the restaurant? Shall we sell it? "

Esch said with conviction: " Sacrifices must be made . . . that's absolutely certain, for there's no salvation without sacrifice."

"If we go away we'll have to get married," and once more a little apprehensively: " ... I suppose I'm too old for you to marry?"

Sitting on the edge of the bed, Esch regarded her in the light of the flickering candle. With his finger he wrote a " 37 " on the coverlet. He might have given her a cake with thirty-seven candles; no, better as it was, for she made a secret of her age, and would only have been annoyed. He contemplated her heavy, immobile features, and suddenly he would have liked her to be still older, a great deal older than she was. It seemed to him, although he did not know why, that that would have made things surer. If she were suddenly to become young and lie there in the fleeting semblance of youth, it would be all up with the sacrifice. And the sacrifice had to be, had to grow even greater along with his devotion to this ageing woman, so that the world might be put in order and Ilona might be shielded from the daggers, so that all living beings might be reinstated in their first innocence, and no one need any longer languish in prison. Well, one thing could be depended on, Mother Hentjen would soon grow old and ugly. The world seemed to him like a level, smooth, endless corridor, and he said absently:

"We must lay the restaurant with brown linoleum; that would look nice."

Mother Hentjen picked up hope: "Yes, and get it painted too; the whole place is going to ruin ... all these years nothing's been done ... but if you want to go to America ...?"

Esch repeated the words: "All these years...."

Mother Hentjen felt an apology was due: "One has to save, and one postpones a thing from year to year ... and time passes ..." and then she added: " ... and one grows old."

Esch felt irritated: "When there are no children, saving is ridiculous ... nobody ever saved up for me."

But Mother Hentjen was not listening. She merely wanted to find out whether it was worth while having the restaurant painted; she asked: "Are you going to take me to America with you? ... or a young thing?"

Esch replied roughly: "What's all this eternal talk about young and old? ... There will be no young and no old then, and there won't be any time then either ..."

Esch was brought up short. An old woman could not have children. That perhaps was part of the sacrifice. But in a state of innocence nobody had children. Virgins had no children. And as he slipped back into bed he added conclusively: " Then everything will be firm and sure. And what you've left behind you can't do you any more harm."

He tugged the coverlet into position and also drew it carefully over Mother Hentjen's shoulder. Thereupon he put out his hand for the tin extinguisher that hung on the candlestick and that Herr Hentjen too had employed on such occasions, and clapped it on the flickering candle.

Mannheim lies on the way to Baden. And Esch remembered that a man must do his duty by his friends. Something had been bothering him for a long time and now he knew what it was: he could not leave his friends' money in a losing business. They had earned more than fifty per cent. on their investment so far and that was all right, but now these profits must be secured. It was time to quit. His own three hundred marks were on a different footing. Should he lose them it would serve him right. For with a profit of fifty per cent. and two months' expenses over and above that—and not a bad two months either—where did the sacrifice come in which was to redeem Ilona? And to finance his flight to America and liberty out of such ill-gotten gains would be another falsification: it was high time to call off the wrestling matches, profits and all. Mother Hentjen was right enough in her prophecy that he and all his pack of women would end up in disgrace and scandal.

But meanwhile he had to secure the money for Lohberg and Erna. It wasn't easy to buttonhole Gernerth on the matter: in the evenings he kept grumbling about the empty theatre and in the daytime he was hard to catch: he was never in the Alhambra, he never seemed to enter his flat at all, and at Oppenheimer's place there was nothing but two untidy rooms and no sign of anybody. Moreover, if one asked him where he usually took his meals, Gernerth replied: " Oh, I just make do with a sandwich, the father of a family can't spread himself much," which was, of course, hardly true, for one day when the English tourists were crossing the Cathedral square, who should come out of the Cathedral Hotel's marble vestibule but Herr Gernerth himself, looking well-fed and with a fat cigar in his mouth? " Publicity, my dear friend, publicity," he had said, and made himself scarce, as if anybody would have taken it amiss were he to live all the time in the Cathedral Hotel, and his whole family with him. To-day, anyhow, he wouldn't get off: Esch would take care of that!

So in the evening Esch opened the door of the manager's office, locked it behind him, grinning widely, pocketed the key, and with another wide grin presented to the trapped Gernerth a neatly ruled account of the profits to date due to Herr Fritz Lohberg and Fräulein Erna Korn on their invested capital of 2000 marks, amounting to 1123 marks, which with the capital made a sum-total of 3123 marks to be repaid, and under it was written "settled in full in the name of the said parties, August Esch." Besides that he demanded his own money. Gernerth shrieked murder and robbery. In the first place Esch had no legal power to sign a settlement, and in the second place the wrestling matches were still going on, and money couldn't be withdrawn from a going concern. They wrangled for some time, until at length with many lamentations Gernerth agreed to pay out the half of the sum due to Lohberg and Erna, while the other half was to remain invested and share in any further profits that arose. But for himself Esch could extract nothing save an advance of fifty marks for travelling expenses. Perhaps he had been too complaisant. In any case that was enough for the journey to Baden.

Frau Hentjen in her brown silk came to the station and peered round cautiously for any sign of an acquaintance who might see her and gossip about her. For although it was early there were swarms of people. At the other platform there stood a train going in the opposite direction, and several carriages for emigrants, Czechs or Hungarians, were being shunted on to it, and Salvation Army officials were running up and down. Now, Mother Hentjen's presence at the station was but right and proper: it was high time she gave up her stupid affectation of secrecy. All the same, Esch had a bad conscience when he saw the emigrants and the Salvation Army people. "Silly sheep!" he grumbled. He could not tell why he was so provoked. Apparently he had caught the absurd disease of secrecy from Mother Hentjen, for when one of the Salvation girls passed by he looked the other way. Frau Hentjen remarked it: "I suppose you're ashamed of my being here? Perhaps you've got another woman travelling with you?" Esch with some rudeness told her not to be a fool. But that was the last straw: "That's all one gets for compromising oneself . . . one can't touch pitch without being defiled." Once more Esch could not understand what bound him to this woman. As she stood there facing him in the daylight the remembrance of her sexual submission and of the dim alcove, the images that haunted him as soon as he was away from her, sank into oblivion as if they had never existed. With this same train he and she had travelled together to Bacharach; that was the beginning of the affair—perhaps to-day would see its end. Evidently she felt his detachment, for she said suddenly: " If you're unfaithful to me, I'll soon let you see. . . ." He was flattered and wanted her to go on; at the same time he wanted to hurt her: " All right, I'm going to do it this very day . . . what'll I see? " She stiffened and made no answer. That softened him, and he took her hand, which lay heavy and awkward in his. " Well, well, what'll happen then? " She said with a vacant eye: " I'll do you in." It was like a promise and a hope of redemption; yet he forced himself to laugh. She was not to be diverted, however, from her thoughts. " What else could I do? " After a pause: " You're probably going as far as Ober-Wesel? . . . to that woman? " Esch grew impatient: " Nonsense, I've told you a hundred times that I must settle up my affairs with Lohberg in Mannheim . . . aren't we going to America? " Frau Hentjen was not convinced: " Be honest about it." Esch impatiently waited for the signal to be given for the train's departure; he must on no account betray his intention to visit Bertrand: " Haven't I invited you to come with me? " " You didn't really mean it." But now that the signal was just going to be given it seemed to Esch that he really had meant the invitation to be taken seriously, and as he stood holding her plump arm he wanted to give her a kiss; she fended him off: " What, here before all these people! " And at that moment he had to climb into the train.

He had really intended to go straight through to Badenweiler, and it was only when he saw the name of Saint-Goar station that he definitely decided to get off at Mannheim. Yes, and from Mannheim he would write to her; that would soothe her down—and Esch smiled tenderly as he thought of her desire to kill him; he might really give her the chance. In any case his visit to Badenweiler was a bit of a venture, a risk that might lose him everything, and it was only decent to hand over other people's money first. The sentence " Human life isn't to be lightly taken " occurred to him, and wove itself into the rhythm of the rolling wheels. He saw Mother Hentjen lifting a dainty revolver, and then he heard Harry saying again: " You're not to do anything to him." Then Lohberg too, and Ilona and Fräulein Erna and Balthasar Korn appeared in a row before him, and he was amazed to think he had not seen them for so long; perhaps they hadn't been alive at all in the interval. They raised their arms in rhythmical measure to greet him, and it was as if an invisible and elegant showman were jerking them like marionettes on wires that suddenly revealed themselves. A third-class compartment is like a prison-cell, and up on the stage, high up on the left side where that tooth was missing, a grey screen from the side-wings suddenly came forward, a pasteboard screen behind which there was nothing save the dusty grey wall of the stage. But on the screen the word " Prison " appeared clearly, and although he knew that there was nothing behind it he knew all the same that there was Somebody in that prison, Somebody who did not exist and yet was the chief character in the play. But the stage, on which the pasteboard prison projected like a tooth, was cut off by an enormous back-drop on which a beautiful park was painted. Deer were grazing beneath mighty trees, and a girl dressed in shimmering spangles was plucking flowers. The gardener, in a wide-brimmed straw hat, his shining shears in his hand and a little dog beside him, was standing beside a dark lake whose fountain sent a crystal jet into the air like a glittering whip and spread coolness around. Far in the distance could be seen the lights and the ornamental outline of a magnificent castle with a black-white-and-red banner waving from the battlements. And that brought back all the uncertainty.

Now that Esch was approaching Mannheim it came into his head that Erna had certainly been sleeping with Lohberg, that pure Joseph. There was really no question about it, it was to be taken for granted and was hardly worth thinking over, it was to be taken for granted as much as the nose on one's face or the feet one walked on. Nothing and nobody could have shaken Esch's conviction that this was so; what else could the couple have found to do together? And yet he was mistaken. For even though life does not offer much variety, and though very little is necessary to bring two people of opposite sexes to an understanding, there are many things that are less to be taken for granted than one would think. A man like Esch who is still entangled in the earthly life of day after day, or has risen only a very little way above it, can easily forget that there is a Kingdom of Heaven whose stability throws all that is earthly into uncertainty, so that it can suddenly become doubtful whether one does actually walk on one's feet. In this case the fact was that Lohberg was restrained from crossing the boundary of idealistic and noble friendship partly by his shyness and partly by his unsleeping mistrust of the female sex, especially since sordid experience had taught him to dread the poison of sordid disease, and since he could not help remembering that Erna had been exposed to the attentions of a professed rake, living cheek by jowl with her. Lohberg was that kind of man. He merely went walking with Fräulein Erna Korn, drank coffee with her, and regarded his acquaintance with her as a time of probation and penance that would find its consummation only when a sign from on high was given him, the sign, so to speak, of true redeeming grace.

Esch, of course, knew that the idiot was virtuous, but was incapable of conceiving the extent of his virtue, and even more incapable of realizing that he himself was still a cause of disquietude to Fräulein Erna, that he still disturbed her blood, if not her heart, and that it was probably on his account that she was in no hurry to give Lohberg the sign of redeeming grace, nay, even deliberately delayed it, regarding such delay as a proper preparation for the married state. These things Esch was incapable of divining, and still less that the pair of them found much pleasure in discovering grave defects in his character, and with their usual enthusiasm even believed that their common interest in his failings was a good foundation for a life-partnership.

Innocent of these developments, Esch had reckoned on a ceremonious and joyous welcome. Instead of that, Fräulein Erna actually shrank when he appeared in the doorway. Oh, she said, quickly pulling herself together, it was indeed kind of Herr Esch to let his friends see him again, oh, it was really kind of Herr Esch to condescend to remember them after not having even taken the trouble to send them a line. And then she said: "Who pays the piper calls the tune," with many other scathing remarks, so that Esch didn't even get as far as the lobby. Korn, however, who had heard their voices, came out of the living-room in his shirt-sleeves, and since he was of coarser fibre than his sister and had never bestowed a thought on Esch for the past two months, and thus was not offended by his silence, but would rather have been blankly astonished had it ever occurred to Esch to write to him, Korn was quite overjoyed to see him, for not only did he remain attached to all that he had once known, he also saw in the newly arrived Esch a source of entertainment and a welcome provider of money for the use of the empty room. And Korn shook his guest's hand with exclamations of delight, and was inviting him simply to walk into his old room again, which was waiting exclusively for him, when Fräulein Erna detained him and half turning to her brother said: she didn't know if that arrangement would do. This roused Korn's anger: " Why shouldn't it do as it did before? If I say it does, it does." Undoubtedly Esch, as a tactful man, should then have taken his leave with expressions of regret, but even if he had been tactful, which he was not, he was too intimate with the family to prevent curiosity from getting the upper hand of tact; what had been happening in his absence? And he simply stood rooted in astonishment. Meanwhile Fräulein Erna, who was also accustomed to plain speaking, satisfied his curiosity very quickly, for she hissed at her brother that a woman who was about to make a respectable marriage couldn't be expected to take a strange man under her roof; as it was, she had enough disgrace to put up with in that house, and if her future husband wasn't so magnanimous he would have made himself scarce already. Korn, in his vulgar way, retorted: " Papperlapap, shut your mouth. Esch is going to stay." But Fräulein Erna's hints drove all else out of Esch's head, and he cried: " Well, what a surprise; my heartiest congratulations, Fräulein Erna, who's the lucky man? " Fräulein Erna could do no less than accept his congratulations and intimate that she was on the point of coming to an agreement with Herr Lohberg. She took Esch's arm and led him into the living-room. Yes, and her fiancé, too, would be with them in a moment or so. And as they stood talking of Lohberg Korn had the brilliant idea of hiding Esch in a dark corner so that the unsuspecting Lohberg might get a shock when Esch suddenly took part in the conversation like a ghost.

When the bell rang in the lobby and Erna went to open the door, Esch obediently betook himself into a dark corner of the room. Korn, who remained sitting at the table, made imperious signs that he was to tuck himself still further in. For Korn was a man who set great store by technical perfection and was apt to grow angry if a hitch occurred in his arrangements. But it was not a fear of Korn's anger that made Esch hold himself so still in his corner, no, he was not at all the man to be scared into a corner, nor was it a place of humiliation and punishment for him; of his own free will he flattened himself closer to the wall, heeding little whether his sleeve grazed the distemper or not, for in that shadowy retreat he became strangely and unexpectedly aware of a desire to increase the distance between himself and the others at the table. The few minutes that elapsed before Lohberg entered did not suffice for him to think it out clearly, but it came into his head that he was slipping once more into that curious isolation which was somehow connected with Mannheim, and which forbade him to make common cause with the others, an insistent isolation that was, however, so pleasant to him that it could not be too solitary, and if he could only have got far enough into his corner, would have made him a redeemed and noble hermit withdrawn from the world, a spirit commanding the company at the table, who were bound to the flesh. It was a state that could not have lasted long, for such reflections are indulged in only when time does not allow of their being thought out to a conclusion, not to say acted upon, and Esch had already forgotten them by the time that Lohberg came in according to programme and was so thoroughly confounded that he was even glad to see the newcomer. Esch certainly did not quite belong to the company, no more than Ilona did, but when they were all sitting round the table they were as one family and cross-questioned each other about many things. And since these questions soon reached money matters, Esch proudly drew out his note-case and laid 1561 marks and 50 pfennigs on the table. Fräulein Erna stretched out her hand delightedly to gather in, as she thought, her investment plus the profits, but when Esch explained that she would get as much in the end, but meanwhile had to share that sum with Lohberg since half of her money was still invested, she cried that that was a loss instead of a profit. And even when he tried to make it clear to her, she would not listen to reason, but swore she was not to be taken in, she could count as well as anybody: if you please—she got out paper and pencil—219 marks, 25 pfennigs, she made it, there it was in black and white, and raging, she thrust the paper under Esch's troubled nose. Lohberg kept his mouth shut, although as a business man he must have understood the situation well enough. Unwilling to get into trouble with his ladylove, the cowardly idiot. Esch said rudely: " I have my own sense of decency—apparently more than can be said of some people that are holding their tongues." And he grabbed Erna's arm, but not out of love; it was with most unloving anger and force that he banged her arm, paper and all, back on the table. Perhaps she had really understood the matter all along, or it might have been the firmness of Esch's grip; in short Fräulein Erna fell silent. Korn, hitherto a detached spectator, merely remarked that Teltscher, the Jew, must be a rogue. Well, then, retorted Esch, he should tell that to the police, for every rogue should be reported instead of having innocent men locked up. And since Lohberg's cowardly

THE ANARCHIST 123

and disingenuous behaviour required punishment, he humiliated the fellow with the words: "As for innocent men, they're forgotten. Has Herr Lohberg, for instance, ever paid a visit to poor Martin?" Erna, who was still cowed but filled with healthy resentment, replied that she knew of other people who forgot their friends, yes, even ruined them, and that it was Herr Esch's business to bother about Martin. "That's what I've come here for," said Esch. "Aha," said Fräulein Erna, "if it hadn't been for that we should never have seen you again," and hesitatingly, almost timidly, as if only because she was bound not to abandon a good quarrel, she added: "nor our money either." Korn, however, who was a slow thinker, said: "You must have the Jew locked up."

That was, indeed, a remarkable solution of the problem, and although Esch had himself suggested it, he yearned to retort that it was merely a second-rate and partial solution compared with the much better, more radical, and as it were spiritual solution he now had an inkling of. What good would it do to lock up Teltscher for a month or two when Ilona would be exposed once more to knife-throwing? It struck him for the first time that Ilona wasn't present, although she really ought to have been there; almost as if it were intended that she should not see him until his task was accomplished. Anyhow, task or no task—here he was, promising to pay up profits in full, even while he was thinking of the great sacrifice he was to make! If the balance was ever to be truly struck the wrestling matches simply would have to be a dead loss. And since that implied that the wrathful Erna's money would be thrown away after all, he had a sense of guilt that was at bottom not at all unpleasant; but since it was no business of theirs he began to hector the others: so that was all the thanks he got, he was sorry he had ever troubled to bring the money, since that was how he was welcomed, but in any case he would write to Gernerth about the balance. He could do as he pleased, said Fräulein Erna spitefully. Then she would be good enough to write about it herself, for he had expressly disclaimed all responsibility. She certainly would not. Very well, then he would do it, for he was an honest man. "Indeed?" remarked Fräulein Erna. And so Esch demanded pen and paper and departed to his room without another look at those present.

In his room he strode up and down as was his habit when agitated. Then he began to whistle, so that the others might not think he was annoyed, and perhaps also because he was feeling lonely. Soon he heard Erna and Lohberg coming into the lobby. They were very subdued;

obviously Lohberg, coward that he was, was still trembling and rolling his pale eyes helplessly from side to side. As so often, Lohberg's image called up Mother Hentjen's. She, too, was helpless now, and had to submit to everything, poor woman. He listened to hear if Lohberg and Erna were abusing him. A fine predicament Mother Hentjen had landed him in with her silly jealousy; he needn't have been here, he might have been in Badenweiler hours ago. But in the lobby all was quiet. Lohberg must have gone; and Esch sat down and wrote in his clerkly hand: " To Herr Alfred Gernerth, Theatre Manager, Alhambra Theatre, Cologne. Kindly remit my capital of 780.75 marks, in return for which I shall send you a final quittance. Respectfully yours." With the letter in one hand and the inkpot and pen in the other he went straight across into Erna's room.

Erna, shuffling about in felt slippers, was just making down her bed, and Esch was amazed that she had managed to change her shoes so quickly. She was beginning to object to his intrusion when she remarked his equipment: " What are you doing with that rubbish?" He ordered her: " Sign here." " I'll sign no more for you. . . ." But meanwhile she had run her eye over the letter and went to the table with it: " All right," with a shrug; it wouldn't be of any use, the money was gone, thrown away, wasted, one would just have to put up with that; a man like Herr Esch, of course, didn't give a straw. Her abuse of him once more roused his curious feeling of guilt towards her; oh, what about it, he would help her to get her money, and he seized her hand to show her where to sign. When she tried to snatch it from him he was again annoyed; he grasped her hand more firmly with most unloving force, and for the second time it happened that Fräulein Erna grew silent and defenceless. At first he did not notice this, but merely guided her hand for the signature, then, however, her oblique lizard-like glance as she looked up at him struck him as an invitation. And when he embraced her she laid her cheek close to his breast. The fact that she did so did not trouble him at all; he was little disposed to ask whether it was merely the echo of her old fancy for him, or whether she wanted to revenge herself for Lohberg's lack of manliness, or—and that would have seemed most probable to Esch—whether she simply submitted because he happened to be there, because it was fated to happen, because they no longer had to wrangle over marriage. The situation had been cleared up: Erna had an admirer and he himself was going to America with Mother Hentjen; even his anger against Lohberg was allayed, and he almost felt a kind of tenderness for the idiot who was like Mother Hentjen in so many respects, and since Fräulein Erna must have taken over many of her wooer's qualities, being so intimate with him, to embrace Erna was in a way, although in a far-off way, like embracing a piece of Mother Hentjen, and couldn't be called unfaithfulness. Yet the recollection of their old quarrels was not yet quite banished, they still hesitated, there was a flash, as it were, of hostile chastity, and Esch was within an ace of returning to his own room, as of yore, without achieving anything. But of a sudden she said: "Hush!" and drew away from him: the main door outside had creaked, and Esch realized that Ilona had come in. They stood motionless. But when the footsteps outside died away and the door into the living-room, behind which Korn's bedroom lay, was locked, they too were locked in each other's arms.

As he crept later into his own bedroom he could not help thinking of Mother Hentjen, and that he had got off at Mannheim only to allay her jealous suspicions. That was all she got from her silly jealousy. Of course it had been only in joke, his threat to be unfaithful to her that very day. Yet it had turned out to be true, and it wasn't his fault. Besides, it wasn't really unfaithfulness; one could not so easily be unfaithful to a woman like that. All the same, it was a dirty thing to do. And why? Because he should have made a clean sweep of things and gone straight to the point, because in all decency he should have gone to Badenweiler instead of pandering to a woman's silly jealousy. That was what he got for it. A fine predicament, but it couldn't be helped now. Esch turned his face to the wall.

He opened his eyes and recognized his old room; the bright morning sun was streaming through the curtains, and like a lance the fear transfixed him: wasn't he late for the warehouse? but he remembered then that he was quit of the Central Rhine Shipping Company, that he was free and on holiday. Nobody had the power to waken him for judgment. He went on lying in bed, although it rather bored him, simply because he could lie as long as he chose. It was very likely, too, that Mother Hentjen would do him in, for she would never understand that he had been true to her after all; she would want to kill him, in any case, and that alone brought a comforting assurance of freedom. The man who is about to die is free, and he who is redeemed into freedom has taken death upon him. He could see the battlements of a castle on which a black flag drooped quietly, yet it might have been the Eiffel

Tower, for who can distinguish the future from the past? In the park was a grave, the grave of a girl, the grave of a girl transfixed by a knife. In the face of death all things are permissible, free, gratis, so to speak, and strangely inconsequent. A man might make up to any woman in the street and ask her to sleep with him, and it would have the same pleasant inconsequence as sleeping with Erna, whom he would leave behind to-day or to-morrow when he journeyed into the darkness. He could hear her bustling about in the flat, the bony little creature, and he lay waiting for her to come in as she used to, for one must make hay while the sun shines. That the freedom to be unfaithful had first to be paid for by an act of unfaithfulness, and that all the same one desired to be killed for it, was certainly more than Mother Hentjen would ever understand; what did she know of such complicated balancing? Or how could she ever trace the falsifications that are so cunningly insinuated into the world, that only a skilled accountant could dare to die a redeemer's death? For the slightest error if overlooked could make the whole structure of freedom totter. At that point he heard Fräulein Erna's voice from the kitchen: " May I bring my lord his coffee now? " " No," shouted Esch, " I'll be there in a minute," sprang out of his bed, had his clothes on in a twinkling, drank his coffee and was down at the tramway stop in no time, himself astounded at the speed with which he had moved. The tram bound towards the prison had not yet arrived, and it was only because he had to wait that Esch wondered whether it was merely the thought of his visit to Martin that had driven him out of bed so quickly, or whether it was Erna's voice that was responsible. It wasn't a pleasant voice, especially when she was scolding, as on the previous evening. But Esch wasn't the man to be spurred by a sharp tongue. So it couldn't have been her voice, or else he would have been driven out of the flat long ago, as on that occasion, for instance, when she had called him into the kitchen to look at the sleeping Ilona. As for Ilona, he had no need to set eyes on her again, neither here nor anywhere else. And it would be best to keep these things at a distance, to refuse to admit that he had probably fled from Erna and her evil lusts, from that inconsequent lust in which he was to be involved henceforward, but which could not face the daylight, since night alone was the time for freedom.

At the jail he discovered that visitors were allowed only three times weekly; he must apply again next day. What was he to do? Go on to

Badenweiler without further delay? He began to swear at this interference with the freedom of his movements. At length, however, he said: "Oh well, a reprieve," and the word "reprieve" stuck to him, haunting his mind, and gave him even a proud and comforting sense of brotherhood with a man so powerful as Bertrand, for the reprieve concerned both of them. He could not go off into the darkness without having seen Martin first, and it would have been ridiculous, even degrading, to let his visit to Mannheim mean nothing but a night with Erna. When a man takes a long journey he should leave no loose ends behind him, he should rather greet all his friends and say good-bye. So he went first down to the docks to look up his acquaintances in the warehouses and in the canteen. He felt almost like a long-lost relative returning from America, a little shy in case people should not know him again. For instance, it was quite possible that the watchman wouldn't even let him through the gates. But his reception was very amiable, perhaps because all those he met probably felt they no longer had a hold on him; the customs men at the gate welcomed him at once with light friendliness, and he had a short talk with them. Yes, they said, laughing, now that he wasn't with the Shipping Company he had no business there, and Esch said, he would soon let them see whether he had no business there, and they did not make the slightest attempt to prevent him from coming in. Nobody hindered him from looking at all the sheds and cranes, warehouses and goods trucks, to his heart's content, and when he shouted in at the warehouse doors, the storekeepers and stevedores came out and stood like brothers before him. Yet he did not regret leaving it all, he merely impressed it with great clearness on his memory, sometimes caressing a goods wagon and sometimes a gangway, so that the feeling of dry wood clung to his hard palm. Only in the canteen was he disappointed; he looked for Korn but Korn was not there; Korn was stupid and kept out of the way, and Esch had to laugh, for he was no longer jealous of Ilona; Ilona would be spirited out of Korn's clutches into an inaccessible castle. So he merely drank a brandy with the policeman and betook himself along the accustomed street, no longer accustomed and yet more familiar than ever, till he came to a corner where the tobacco-shop regarded him expectantly, as if Lohberg had been waiting within for him with great impatience, waiting to have a chat.

Lohberg was really there behind his till with the large cigar-cutter in his hand, and as Esch came in he amiably laid the instrument down, for he had much to beg Esch's pardon for, and yet neither of them mentioned it, for Esch was ready to forgive and did not want Lohberg to burst into tears. Perhaps it was against the spirit of this agreement that Lohberg began to speak of Erna, but it was such a paltry infringement that Esch barely noticed it. Who could waken him until he chose? He was free! "She's a fine comrade," said Lohberg, "and we have many interests in common." And since Esch was free to say what he chose, he said: "Yes, she would never do you in." And he looked up at Lohberg's worried face that Mother Hentjen could have squashed merely with her thumb, and he was sorry for Erna because she wasn't big enough even to do that. Lohberg, however, smiled timidly, he was a little scared by the grisly jest, and under the eyes of his grim visitor he shrank and diminished. No, he was no fit opponent for a man like Esch; it is only the dead that are strong, though in life they may have looked like miserable snippets. Esch stalked about the shop like a ghost, sniffing the air, opening first one drawer and then another, and sliding the palm of his hand over the polished counter. He said: "When you're dead you'll be stronger than I am . . . but you're not the kind to be done in," he added contemptuously, for it struck him that even a dead Lohberg would be negligible; he knew the fellow too well, he would always be an idiot, and it was only those one didn't know, those who had never existed, who were omnipotent. Lohberg, however, still suspicious where women were concerned, said: "What do you mean? Do you mean would my widow be provided for? I've insured my life." That would certainly be a good reason for poisoning him off, said Esch, and could not help laughing so loudly that the laughter somehow stuck in his throat and hurt him. Mother Hentjen, now, that was a woman. She would have no truck with poison, she would simply spit a man like Lohberg on a pin as if he were a beetle. She was a woman to be regarded with consideration and respect, and it amazed Esch that he had ever thought of comparing her with Lohberg. And he was a little touched, because for all that she put on an air of weakness, and was probably quite right in doing so. Lohberg's skin prickled, and he rolled his pale eyes: "Poison?" he said, as if it were the first time he had ever heard the word, though it was always on his tongue, or at least as if it were the first time he had actually understood it. Esch's laughter became condescending and somewhat scornful: "Oh, she won't poison you, Erna's not that kind of woman." "No," said Lohberg, "she has a heart of gold; she wouldn't hurt a fly...." "Or spit a beetle on a pin," said Esch. "I'm sure she wouldn't," said Lohberg. "But if you're ever unfaithful to her she'll do you in all the same," threatened Esch. "I'll never be unfaithful to my wife," announced the idiot. And suddenly Esch realized, and it was a pleasant and illuminating realization, why he had thought of comparing Lohberg and Mother Hentjen: Lohberg was merely a woman, after all, a kind of natural freak, and that was why it didn't matter if he slept with Erna: even Ilona had slept in Erna's bed. Esch rose to his feet, stood firmly and robustly on his legs, and stretched his arms like a man newly awakened from sleep or nailed to a cross. He felt strong, steadfast and well endowed, a man whom it would be worth while to kill. "Either him or me," he said, and felt that the world was at his feet. "Either him or me," he repeated, striding about the shop. "What do you mean?" asked Lohberg. "I don't mean you," replied Esch, showing his strong white teeth: "As for you, you're going to marry Erna," for that seemed right and proper: the fellow had a fine and highly polished shop, complete with life-insurance policy, and should marry little Erna and go on living in peace; he himself, on the other hand, had wakened up and accepted the task laid upon him. And since Lohberg went on singing Erna's praises, Esch said what was expected of him, and what the other had long been waiting for as a sign from on high: "Oh, you and your Salvation Army twaddle ... if you hum and haw much longer she'll slip through your fingers. It's high time you took hold of her, you milksop." "Yes," said Lohberg, "yes, I think the time of probation is now fulfilled." The shop looked bright and friendly in the light of that dull summer day; its yellow-oak fittings made a solid and enduring impression, and beside the patent till lay a ledger with neatly added columns. Esch sat down at Lohberg's desk and wrote to Mother Hentjen that he had arrived safely and was well on the way to settle all his business.

His second night in Erna's bed he regarded as a formality that a free man was entitled to comply with. They had had a friendly talk about her marriage to Lohberg, and made love to each other almost tenderly and sentimentally, as if they had never fought tooth and nail. And after that long and wakeful night he rose with the pleasant feeling of having helped Erna and Lohberg to their joint happiness. For every man has many potentialities in him, and according to the chain of logic he throws round them he can convince himself that they are good or bad.

Immediately after breakfast he started for the prison. In Lohberg's shop he bought some cigarettes for Martin; nothing else occurred to him. The heat was sweltering, and Esch could not help thinking of that afternoon in Goarshausen on which he had pitied Martin because of the heat. In the prison he was shown into the visiting-room, which had barred windows giving on the bare prison yard, across which the yellow-washed buildings threw sharply cut shadows. The yard looked as if the executioner's block might well be set up in the middle of it, that block by which the criminal had to kneel and wait for the keen edge of the axe that was to sever his head. When Esch had come to this conclusion he did not want to look at the yard any longer, and turned away from the window. He examined the room. In the middle stood a yellow-painted table with splashes of ink on it that told of previous use in an office; there were also one or two chairs. The room was like an oven although it was in the shadow, for the early morning sun had streamed into it and the windows were shut. Esch became drowsy; he was alone and he sat down; he was left to wait.

Then he heard footsteps in the paved corridor and the clacking of Martin's crutches. Esch rose to his feet as if to greet a superior. But Martin came in exactly as if he were coming into Mother Hentjen's. If an orchestrion had been at hand he would have hobbled over to it and set it going. He looked round the room and seemed pleased that Esch was alone, went up to him and shook his hand. " 'Morning, Esch, good of you to come and see me." He leaned his crutches against the table, just as he always did in Mother Hentjen's, and sat down. " Come on, Esch, sit down too." The warder who had escorted him was reminiscent of Korn in his uniform; he had remained standing by the door according to regulations. " Will you not take a seat too, Herr Warder? There's nobody coming and I certainly won't try to escape." The man muttered something about the service regulations, but he came up to the table and laid down his huge bunch of keys. " So," said Martin, " now we're all comfortable," and then they were silent all three, sitting round the table staring at the notches in it. Martin was rather yellower than usual; Esch did not dare to ask how his health was. But Martin could not help laughing at the embarrassed silence and said: " Well,

August, tell me all the news from Cologne, how's Mother Hentjen, and everybody else?"

In spite of his burning cheeks Esch felt himself redden, for suddenly it struck him that he had exploited the prisoner's absence to steal his friends from him. Nor did he know whether he should give them away before the warder. After all, few people care to be mentioned in connection with a criminal in the visiting-room of a prison. He said: "They're all getting on well."

Probably Martin had understood his constraint, for he did not insist on a more exhaustive answer, but asked: "And you yourself?"

"I'm on my way to Badenweiler."

"To take the waters?"

Esch felt that Martin had no need to make fun of him. He answered dryly: "To see Bertrand."

"Upon my soul, you're getting on! He's a fine chap, Bertrand."

Esch was not certain if Martin was still joking or being somehow ironical. A fine sodomite was what Bertrand was, that was the truth. But he couldn't say that in front of the warder. He muttered: "If he was really a fine chap you wouldn't be sitting here."

Martin looked a question.

"Well, you're innocent, aren't you?"

"I? I have it in black and white, and sworn to in a court of law, that I've already lost my innocence several times."

"Oh, stop making silly jokes! If Bertrand's such a fine chap he need only be told exactly what has happened to you. Then he'll see to it that you're let out."

"Is it you that's going to enlighten him? Is that why you're making for Badenweiler?" Martin laughed and stretched his hand out over the table to Esch: "My dear August, what an idea! It's a good thing you won't find him there. . . ."

Esch said quickly: "Where is he?"

"Oh, he's still on his travels, in America or somewhere."

Esch was dumbfounded: so Bertrand was in America! Had got there first, was basking before him in the light of freedom. And although Esch had always suspected that the greatness and liberty of that far country had a very significant though not fully comprehensible connection with the greatness and freedom of the man he could never reach, he felt now as if Bertrand's journey to America had annulled for ever his own plan of emigration. And because of this, and because everything was so remote and inaccessible, he fell into a rage with Martin: " A chairman of a company can get easily enough to America . . . but Italy would do him just as well."

Martin said peaceably: " Well, Italy, then, for all I care."

Esch reflected whether he should ask in the inquiry office of the Central Shipping where Bertrand was to be found. But suddenly that seemed to him superfluous, and he said: " No, he's in Badenweiler."

Martin laughed: " Well, you may be right, but even so they won't let you in . . . is there some girl or other behind all this, what? "

" I'll soon find ways and means of getting in," said Esch threateningly.

Martin scented trouble: " Don't do anything silly, August, don't worry the man; he's a decent chap and should be respected."

Obviously he has no idea of all that's hidden behind Bertrand, thought Esch, but he did not dare to mention it and merely said: " They're all decent enough; even Nentwig," and after some consideration he added: " All dead men are decent too, but one can only find out what that decency was worth by looking at the legacies they leave behind them."

" What do you mean? "

Esch shrugged his shoulders: " Nothing, I was just saying . . . yes, that it doesn't matter in the long run whether a man's decent or not; he's always decent on one side; and that doesn't come into question; the question is what did he do? " And he added angrily: " That's the only way to keep yourself from being at sixes and sevens."

Martin shook his head in amusement mingled with sorrow: " Look here, August, you have a friend here in Mannheim who's always prating about poison. Seems to me he must have poisoned you. . . ."

But Esch continued undismayed: " For we don't know black from white any longer. Everything's topsy-turvy. You don't even know what's past from what's still going on. . . ."

Martin laughed again: " And I know even less what's going to happen."

" Do be serious for once. You're sacrificing yourself for the future; that's what you told me yourself . . . that's the only thing left to do, to sacrifice oneself for the future and atone for all that is past; a decent man must sacrifice himself or else there's no order in the world."

The prison warder's suspicions were aroused: " You mustn't make revolutionary speeches here."

Martin said: " This man's no revolutionary, Herr Warder. You're more likely to be one yourself."

Esch was astounded that his remarks could be so construed. So he had turned into a Social Democrat, had he? Well, so be it! And obstinately he went on: " Let them be revolutionary, for all I care. Anyhow, you yourself have always preached that it doesn't matter whether a capitalist is a decent fellow or not, for it's as a capitalist he has to be opposed and not as a man."

Martin said: " Look at that, Herr Warder, do you think we should be allowed visitors? This man will poison me through and through with his heresies, and me just newly regenerated." And he turned to Esch: " You're the same old muddlehead, my dear August."

The warder said: " Duty's duty," and since he was in any case too hot, he looked at his watch and announced that their time was up.

Martin took his crutches: " All right, lead on." He gave Esch his hand. " And let me tell you again, August, don't do anything silly. And many thanks for everything."

Esch was not prepared for such a sudden break-up. He kept Martin's hand in his own and hesitated about shaking hands with the hostile warder. Then he offered the man his hand after all, because they had been sitting at the same table, and Martin nodded his approval. Then Martin departed, and Esch was again amazed because he went exactly as if he were only leaving Mother Hentjen's, and yet he was going into a prison cell! It seemed indeed as if nothing that happened in the world mattered at all. Yet there was nothing that wasn't significant: one had only to force it to be so.

Outside the prison gate Esch drew a deep breath; he dusted himself as if to convince himself of his own existence, discovered the cigarettes he had intended for Martin, and once more felt that inexplicable and terrible rage against him, and once more his mouth was filled with curses. He even called Martin a ridiculous tub-thumper, a demagogue, as they said, although there was really nothing he could reproach the man with except, at the very most, that he had carried himself as though he were the chief figure in the drama, while there were much more important characters. . . . But that was what demagogues were like.

Esch took a tram back to the town, was irritated by the sight of the conductor's uniform, and collected his things from Fräulein Erna's flat. She received him with every mark of affection. And in his rage at the confusion of the world he treated her overtures with scorn. Thereupon he took a brief farewell and hurried to the station to catch the night train for Müllheim.

When desires and aims meet and merge, when dreams begin to foreshadow the great moments and crises of life, the road narrows then into darker gorges, and the prophetic dream of death enshrouds the man who has hitherto walked dreaming in sleep: all that has been, all aims, all desires, flit past him once more as they do before the eyes of a dying man, and one can well-nigh call it chance if that road does not end in death.

The man who from afar off yearns for his wife or merely for the home of his childhood has begun his sleepwalking.

Many preparations, it may be, have already been made, only he has not yet noticed them. As, for instance, when it strikes him on the way to the station that houses are composed of regular rows of bricks, that doors are made of sawn planks and windows of rectangular panes of glass. Or when he remembers the editor and the demagogue, both of whom pretend to know the difference between right and left, although that is known only to women, and by no means to all women. But a man cannot always be thinking of such matters, and so he quietly drinks a glass of beer in the station.

Yet when he sees the train for Müllheim come roaring in, that great, long serpent darting so surely towards its goal, he is again struck down, suddenly struck by doubt of the engine's reliability, for it might take the wrong road; struck by the fear that he, with evident and important duties to fulfil on earth, might be diverted from these duties and cast adrift perhaps even as far as America.

In his perplexity he would gladly approach some uniformed official, as unpractised travellers do, and ask a question, but the platform is so extended, so immeasurably long and bare, that he can scarcely race along it, and must think himself lucky, breathless maybe but still lucky, to reach the train at all, whatever its destination. Of course he strives to make out the names of the towns posted on the carriages, but soon realizes that it is a useless effort, for the names are mere words. And the traveller hesitates a little uncertainly before his carriage.

Uncertainty and breathlessness are quite enough to make a hasty-tempered man swear, still more when, startled by the signal for departure, he has to scramble up the inconvenient steps at a breakneck pace into the carriage, and barks his shin on one of them. He swears, he swears at the steps and their awkward construction, he swears at fate. Yet behind this rudeness there lurks a more relevant and even more maddening recognition, which the man could formulate if his mind were awake: mere human contrivances all these things are, these steps fitted to the bending and stretching of the human leg, that immeasurably long platform, these signboards with words upon them, and the locomotive's whistle, and the glittering steel rails—no end to the human contrivances, and all of them engendered in barrenness.

Vaguely the traveller feels that by such reflections he lifts himself above the trivial daily round, and he would like to stamp them on his mind for the rest of his life. For though reflections of that sort might be deemed general to the human race, yet they are more accessible to travellers, especially to hasty-tempered travellers, than to stay-at-homes who think of nothing, not even if they climb up and down their stairs ever so often daily. The stay-at-home does not observe that he is surrounded by things of human manufacture, and that his thoughts are merely manufactured in the same way. He sends his thoughts out, as if they were trusty and capable commercial travellers, on a journey round the world, and he fancies that thus he brings the world back into his harbour and into his own transactions.

But the man who sends himself out instead of his thoughts has lost this premature sense of security: his temper rises against everything that is of human manufacture, against the engineers who have designed the steps precisely to those measurements and not to others, against the demagogues who prate of justice, order and liberty as if they could rearrange the world according to their theories, against all dogmatists who claim to know better than others his anger rises, now that there is dawning within him the knowledge of ignorance.

He is painfully aware of a liberty allowing things to be otherwise. Imperceptibly the words with which things are labelled have lapsed into uncertainty: it is as if all words were orphan strays. Uncertainly the traveller walks up the long corridor of the carriage, a little bewildered to see glass windows like those in houses, and with his hand he touches their cool surfaces. The man who takes a journey can thus fall easily into a state of detached irresponsibility. And since the train goes roaring on at full speed, apparently darting towards a goal, apparently rushing into irresponsibility, and can be stopped in its career by nothing less than the emergency brake, and since beneath his very feet it is hurrying him off with great dispatch, the traveller who has not yet lost his conscience in the painful liberty of the open day makes an attempt to turn and walk in the opposite direction. But he arrives nowhere, for here there is nothing but the future.

Iron wheels roll between him and the good firm earth, and the traveller in the corridor thinks of ships with long passages in which cabin is ranged beside cabin, floating on top of a mountain of water high over the sea-bottom that is the earth. Sweet, never-to-be-fulfilled hope! what boots it to crawl into the belly of a ship when nothing but murder can bring liberty?—never, ah, never will the ship anchor beside the castle in which one's loved one dwells. The traveller in the corridor gives up his perambulations, and while he pretends to be looking at the landscape and the distant mountains he presses his nose flat against the window-pane as he used to do when he was a child.

Murder and Liberty, as closely akin as Birth and Death! And the man who is pitched headlong into liberty is as orphaned as the murderer who cries for his mother as he is led to the scaffold. In the rushing train only the future is real, for every moment is given to a different place, and the people in the carriages are as content as if they knew that they were being snatched from expiation. Those who are left behind on the station platform have made a last effort, by waving handkerchiefs and uttering cries, to rouse the conscience of their departing friends and summon them back to their duties, but the travellers cling to their irresponsibility, shut the windows on the pretext that the draught might give them stiff necks, and unpack the eatables which they need not now share with anyone.

Some of them have stuck their tickets in their hat-bands so that their innocence may be visible from afar, but the majority hunt with feverish haste for their tickets when the voice of conscience is heard and the uniformed official appears. The man who is thinking of murder is soon detected, and it avails him little that like a child he is gorging himself on a chaotic mixture of food and sweetmeats; it remains a meal in the shadow of the block.

They are sitting on benches which the designers, with shameless and perhaps premature knowingness, have made to fit the twice-curved form of the seated body, they are sitting eight in a row, packed tight in a wooden cage, they roll their heads and hear the creaking of wood and the light squeak of rods above the rolling, pounding wheels. Those facing the engine despise the others who are looking back into the past; they are afraid of the draught, and when the door is thrown open they fear that someone might come in and make them look over their shoulders. For the man whose head is turned the wrong way can no longer judge between guilt and atonement, he doubts that two and two make four, doubts that he is his own mother's child and not a changeling. So even their toes are carefully pointed forward in the direction of the business affairs that are to occupy them. For the occupations they follow bind them together in a community,—a community that has no power but is full of uncertainty and malice.

The mother alone can assure her child that he is no changeling. Travellers, however, and stray orphans, all those who have burned their bridges behind them, are no longer certain how they stand. Pitched headlong into freedom they must build up a new order and justice for themselves; they will no longer listen to the sophistries of engineers and demagogues, they hate the human factor in all political and technical constructions, but they do not dare to rebel against the stupidities of a thousand years and to invoke that terrible revolution of knowledge in which two and two will no longer be capable of addition. For there is no one present to assure them of their once lost and now recovered innocence, no one on whose bosom they may lay their heads, fleeing away into forgetfulness from the freedom of the open day.

Anger sharpens the wits. The travellers have carefully arranged their luggage on the rack, and now they plunge into angry and critical discussion of the political institutions of the Empire, of public order and the nature of law; they cavil at existing things and institutions with nice precision, although in words of whose reliability they are no longer sure. And in the bad conscience of their new liberty they are afraid lest they may hear the terrible crash of a railway accident, which might spit them bodily on the iron rods of the carriage. One is always reading about that kind of thing in the newspapers.

Yet they are like people who have been roused too soon from sleep into freedom, roused to catch the train in time. So their words become more and more uncertain and drowsy, and soon all conversation dies away in an indistinguishable muttering. One or the other remarks, indeed, that he would rather shut his eyes than go on staring at the racing landscape, but his fellow-travellers, escaping into their dreams, decline to listen. They doze into slumber with their fists clenched and their coats drawn over their faces, and their dreams are filled with rage against engineers and demagogues who, strong in the knowledge of infamy, call things by names that are false, so shamelessly false that the angry dreamer must give new and tentative names to everything, yet wistfully yearns that his mother could tell him the true names, and so make the world as secure as a settled home.

Everything is too remote and too near, as it is in childhood, and the traveller who has committed himself to the train and from afar off yearns for his wife, or merely for the home of his childhood, is like one whose sight is beginning to fail him, and feels stirring within him the terror of blindness. Many things around him are clouded, at least he thinks that they are as soon as he has covered his face with his coat, and yet a new knowledge burgeons within him, a knowledge that may have lain unnoticed for some time. He has begun his sleepwalking. He still follows the road laid down by the engineers, but he walks only on the extreme verge of it, so that one cannot but fear that he will be precipitated headlong. He still hears the voice of the demagogue, but it comes as a mere unmeaning murmur. He stretches his arms sideways and forwards like a poor tight-rope dancer who, high above solid earth, knows of a better support. Tranced and compelled his captive soul presses on, and the sleeper soars upwards to where the pinions of the loved one are ruffled by his breath like the down that is laid on a dead man's lips, and he desires to be asked, like a child, what his name is, so that in the arms of his woman, breathing deeply of home, he may sink into dreamlessness. He is not yet at a great height, but he is already on the first pinnacle of aspiration, for he knows no longer what his name may be.

> *The desire that someone should come to pay the debt of sacrificial death and redeem the world to a new innocence: this eternal dream of mankind may rise to murder, this eternal dream may rise to clairvoyance. All knowledge wavers between the dreamt wish and the foreshadowing dream, all knowledge of the redeeming sacrifice and the kingdom of salvation.*

Esch spent the night in Müllheim. When he climbed into the little local train to Badenweiler the vaporous light of morning still lay on the green hills of the Black Forest. The world looked clear and near like a dangerous toy. The engine was so short of breath that one felt one wanted to let out a few hooks at its throat; but whether it was pulling the train rapidly or slowly it was impossible to tell. In spite of this Esch trusted himself to it unthinkingly. When it stopped the trees greeted him with a greater friendliness than ever before, and caressed by soft and fragrant airs a kiosk arose beside the railway buildings offering a large assortment of pretty picture postcards. Any of them would have looked effective in Mother Hentjen's collection, and Esch chose one, a lovely card showing the Schlossberg, stuck it in his pocket, and sought a shadowy seat that he might write in peace. But he did not write. He remained calmly sitting, like one who has nothing more to trouble about, and his hands rested placidly on his knees. He sat like this for a long time, gazing through half-closed lids at the green leaves of the trees, sat so long that when at last he walked through the untroubled streets and saw human beings going to and fro, in his astonishment he could not tell how he came to be there. Before a house stood a sinister motor-car, and Esch regarded it closely to see whether it was big enough to sleep in. He looked round lazily at everything, for he felt the security and relaxation of the horseman who has reached his goal, and, turning in his saddle, sees the others still a long way behind; all his tension fell from him, and quite at his ease, almost hesitatingly, he addressed himself to the last stretch, ardently longing, indeed, for some unexpectedly high and difficult obstacle to rise before him ere his goal was reached and he could grasp his obscure triumph. So it was almost a matter for grief to him—and propitious as the day was, it was unpropitious to grief—that he should be making towards Bertrand's house with such certainty: without knowing the place and without asking, he knew all the turns to take. He climbed the gently winding avenue; the breath of the woods met him, caressed his brow, caressed his skin beneath his collar and shirt-cuffs, and to receive the coolness he took his hat in his hand and opened the buttons of his waistcoat. Now he went in through a park gate, almost unaffected by the discovery that the estate did not in the least resemble the grandiose vision that had floated before him in his dream pictures. And although in none of the high windows was Ilona to be seen in shimmering spangles, the more lovely foil to this lovely scene, already at her goal and languidly resting there, yet, though this was a deep disappointment, the dream picture remained unscathed, and it was as though what he saw palpably before him now were only a symbolical representation erected for a momentary and practical purpose, a dream within a dream. At the top of the sloping deep green sward, which lay in the morning shadow, stood the house, a villa executed in a severe and solid style, and as though the wayward and evanescent coolness of the morning, as though the symbolism of the scene wished once more to duplicate itself, at the end of the slope rose an almost soundless fountain, and its waters were like a crystalline draught which one longed to drink simply because they were so limpid. Out of the lodge covered with honey-suckle which stood behind the gate appeared a man in grey who asked what Esch wanted. The silver buttons on his coat were not the appurtenances of a livery or uniform, for they glittered softly and coolly, as though they had been sewed on expressly for this shimmering morning, and if yesterday Esch had still felt for a moment his self-confidence sinking, and doubted whether after all he would manage to penetrate to the Chairman, now all his doubts vanished, and he felt he might almost claim to belong to those who could go out and in here without hindrance. The behaviour of the lodge-keeper, who made no attempt to enter his name and business in a duplicate block, did not even surprise Esch, nor did it occur to him that perhaps it would have been more fitting for him to wait at the door; falling in step with the man he walked on by his side, and the man silently allowed it. They entered a cool and shadowy ante-room, and while the other vanished through one of the many white varnished doors, which softly opened before and softly closed behind him, Esch felt the soft yielding carpet under his feet and waited for the messenger, who presently returned and led him through several apartments, until they came to another door, at which with a bow his conductor left him. And although he had now no more need of a guide, it seemed to him that it would have been more fitting, and even more desirable, had the flight of rooms extended for a long distance still, perhaps into eternity, into an unattainable eternity guarding the inner shrine, guarding the presence chamber so to speak; and he almost imagined that in some miraculous and unseemly and clandestine way he had indeed traversed an endless flight of endless rooms when he now found himself in the presence of this man who held out his hand to him. And although Esch knew that it was Bertrand, and that there could be no doubt about it, now or at any time, yet it seemed to him that this man was only the visible symbol of another, the reflected image of someone more essential and perhaps greater who remained in concealment, so simply and smoothly, so effortlessly did everything go. And now he was looking at this man, who was clean-shaven like an actor and yet was not an actor; the man's face was youthful, and his wavy hair was white. There were a great many books in the room, and Esch sat down beside the writing-table as if he were in a doctor's consulting-room. He heard the man's voice, and it was sympathetic like that of a doctor: " What brings you to me? "

And the dreamer heard his own voice saying softly: " I'm going to hand you over to the police."

" Oh! What a pity! " the reply came so quietly that Esch too did not dare after this to raise his voice. Almost as if speaking to himself he repeated:

" To the police."

" Why, do you hate me? "

" Yes," Esch lied, and was ashamed of the lie.

" That isn't true, my friend, you like me very well."

" An innocent man is sitting in prison in your place."

Esch felt that the other was smiling, and he saw Martin before him, smiling as he sometimes did in speaking. And the same smile was now in Bertrand's voice:

" But, my dear boy, in that case you should have given me in charge long ago."

One could make nothing of this man. Esch said defiantly: " I'm not a murderer."

Then Bertrand actually laughed, softly and inaudibly, and because the morning was so lovely, yes because the morning itself seemed so lovely, Esch could not summon up the annoyance natural in a man who is laughed at; he forgot that he had just spoken of murder, and had it not been unseemly in the circumstances he would have liked also to join in Bertrand's soft laughter. And although the two ideas he now had in his head did not really go together, or if they did, then only in some relation difficult to grasp, he summoned up all his seriousness and went on:

" No, I'm no murderer; you must set Martin free."

But Bertrand, who evidently understood everything, seemed to understand this too, though his voice, more serious now, still kept its tone of reassuring and light gaiety: " But Esch, how can anybody be so cowardly? Does one need a pretext for a murder? "

Now the word had been uttered again, even if it had only flitted by like a silent, dark-hued butterfly. And Esch thought that there was really no need for Bertrand to die now, seeing that Hentjen was already dead in any case. But then like a soft and clear illumination came the thought that a human being might die twice. And Esch said, marvelling that this thought had not come to him before: " You're at liberty to fly, of course," and he added temptingly, " to America."

It was as though Bertrand were not speaking to him: " You know, my dear fellow, that I shan't fly. I've waited too long already for this moment."

And now Esch felt a rush of love for this man who stood so much higher than himself and yet talked to him of death as though to a friend, to him, an obscure employee in his business and an orphan to boot. Esch was glad that he had kept the firm's books so well and rendered faithful and honest service. And he felt afraid to say that he understood how things stood with Bertrand, or to beg Bertrand to do him in: he simply nodded his head understandingly; Bertrand said: " No one stands so high that he dare judge his fellows, and no one is so depraved that his eternal soul can lose its claim to reverence."

Then Esch saw everything more clearly than ever before, saw too that he had deceived himself and others, for it was as though the knowledge that Bertrand possessed about him now flowed back to him: no, never had he believed that this man would set Martin free. But Bertrand, both judge and judged, said with a slightly disdainful wave of the hand: " And if I were to fulfil your craven hope and your unfulfillable condition, Esch, wouldn't we both feel ashamed of ourselves? You, who in that case would be only an ordinary little blackmailer, and I, for delivering myself into the hands of such a blackmailer? "

And although nothing escaped Esch, the overwakeful dreamer, neither the somewhat contemptuous gesture of the hand, nor the ironical curl that could now be seen on Bertrand's smiling lips, yet the hope refused to leave him that in spite of everything Bertrand would fulfil the condition or at least fly: Esch clung to this hope, for suddenly the fear had arisen in him that with Herr Hentjen's second death his desire for Mother Hentjen might die too. But that was his private affair, and to make Bertrand's fate dependent on it seemed to him as despicable as to extort money from Bertrand, and besides it did not accord with the purity of the morning. So he said: " There's no other way out—I must give you in charge."

And Bertrand replied: " Everyone must fulfil his dream, whether it be unhallowed or holy. Otherwise he will never partake of freedom."

Esch did not wholly understand this, and to reassure himself he said: " I must give you in charge. Otherwise things will get worse and worse."

" Yes, my dear chap, otherwise things will get worse and worse, and we must try to prevent that. Of us two I have certainly the easier part; I need only go away. The stranger never suffers, he is released from everything,—it is the one who remains behind in the coils that suffers."

Esch thought he could see again the ironical curl on Bertrand's lips: fatally entangled in the coils of that cold remoteness Harry Köhler could not but perish miserably, yet Esch could not feel angry with the man who brought such ruin on others. Indeed he too would have liked to dismiss the matter with a disdainful wave of the hand, and it was almost like a corroboration of Bertrand's words when he said: " If there was no expiation, there would be no past, present, or future."

" Oh, Esch, you make my heart heavy. You hope for too much. Time has never been reckoned yet from the day of death: it has always begun with the day of birth."

Esch, too, had a heavy heart. He was waiting for this man to give the command for the black flag to be hoisted on the battlements, and he thought: " He must make way for the other who will begin the new dispensation of Time."

But Bertrand did not seem to be saddened by the thought, for he said casually, as though in parenthesis: " Many must die, many must be sacrificed, so that a path may be prepared for the loving redeemer and judge. And only through his sacrificial death can the world be redeemed to a new innocence. But first the Antichrist must come—the mad and dreamless Antichrist. First the world must become quite empty, must be emptied of everything in it as by a vacuum cleaner—nothingness."

That was illuminating, like everything that Bertrand said, so illuminating and frank that the challenge to imitate his ironical tone became almost an obligation, almost a token of acknowledgment: " Yes, order must be established, so that one can begin at the beginning."

Yet even while he said this Esch felt ashamed, ashamed of the sarcastic inflection of his voice; he was afraid lest Bertrand should laugh at him again, for he felt naked in front of him, and he was grateful when Bertrand merely corrected him in a mild voice: " Your order, Esch, is only murder and counter-murder—the order of the machine."

Esch thought: " If he were to keep me here with him there would be order: everything would be forgotten, and cloudlessly the days would flow by in peace and clarity; but he will cast me out." And of course he would have to go, if Ilona were here. So he said: " Martin sacrificed himself, and yet he redeemed nobody."

Bertrand made a slight, somewhat contemptuous, hopeless gesture with his hand: " No one can see another in the darkness, Esch, and that cloudless clarity of yours is only a dream. You know that I cannot keep you beside me, much as you fear your loneliness. We are a lost generation. I too can only go about my business."

It was only natural that Esch should feel deeply stricken, and he said: " Nailed to the cross."

Now Bertrand smiled again, and because he had been repulsed, Esch could almost have wished Bertrand to die at that moment if the smile had not been so friendly, friendly and subdued, like Bertrand's words which divined everything: " Yes, Esch,—nailed to the cross. And in the hour of final loneliness pierced by the spear and anointed with vinegar. And only then can that darkness break in under cover of which the world must fall into dissolution so that it may become again clear and innocent, that darkness in which no man's path can meet another's —and where, even if we walk side by side, we will not hear each other, but will forget each other, as you too, my last dear friend, will forget what I say to you now, forget it like a dream."

He pressed a button and gave orders. Then they went into the garden which stretched away illimitably behind the house, and Bertrand showed Esch his flowers and his horses. Dark butterflies flitted silently from flower to flower, and the horses made no sound. Bertrand had a buoyant step as he walked through his property, and yet it sometimes seemed to Esch as though this light-footed man should be walking on crutches, for the heavens were in eclipse. Then they sat down together and ate; silver and wine and fruit decked the table, and they were like two friends who knew all about each other. When they had eaten Esch knew that the hour of parting was near, for the evening might unexpectedly overtake them. Bertrand accompanied him to the steps which led to the garden, and there the great red motor-car with the smooth red-leather seats, which were still hot with the rays of the midday sun, was already waiting. And now that their fingers touched in farewell, Esch felt an overwhelming desire to bow over Bertrand's hand and kiss it. But the driver of the car sounded his horn loudly, so that the guest had hastily to climb in. Hardly was the car in motion before a powerful, yet warm wind arose, so that house and garden seemed to be whirled away, and this wind did not subside until they reached Müllheim, where a lighted train with its engine snorting awaited the traveller. It was Esch's first drive in a motor-car, and it was very beautiful.

> *Great is the fear of him who awakens. He returns with less certainty to his waking life, and he fears the puissance of his dream, which though it may not have borne fruit in action has yet grown into a new knowledge. An exile from dream, he wanders in dream. And even if he carries in his pocket a picture postcard which he can gaze at, it does not avail him: before the Judgment he stands condemned a false witness.*

Often it may happen that a human being never notices that the lineaments of his desire have altered in the course of a few hours. The change may consist merely in certain fine distinctions, nuances of light and shade which our average traveller is totally unaware of, yet his longing for home has unexpectedly been transformed into a longing for the promised land, and even if his heart is full of a vague dread, a dread of the darkness of his quiescent, waiting home, yet his eyes are already filled with an invisible radiance which has appeared from somewhere, invisible as yet, although one can divine that it is the radiance beyond the ocean, where the dark mists thin away: but if the mists should rise, then the radiant outspread rows of fields over there come into sight, and the gently sloping lawns, a land in which eternal morning is so embedded that the fearful traveller begins to forget women. The land is uninhabited, and the few colonists are strangers. They hold no intercourse with one another; every man lives alone in his stronghold. They go about their business and till the fields, sow and weed. The arm of justice cannot reach them, for they have neither rights nor laws. In their motor-cars they drive over the prairies and the virgin land, which has never yet been traversed by roads, and all that drives them on is their insatiable longing. Even when the colonists have made a home there they still feel strangers; for their longing is a longing for things afar off, and is directed towards far distances of an ever greater, never attainable radiance. And that is the strange thing about them, for they are a western people, that is to say a people whose gaze is turned towards the evening as though they awaited there not the night but the gates of dawn. Whether they seek this radiance because they wish to think clearly and definitely, or simply because they are afraid of the dark, remains disputable. All that is known is that they either settle where the forests are sparse, or clear the trees to make a spacious park; for though they love the coolness of the grove, they tell each other that they must protect their children from its uncanny gloom. Now whether this be true or not, it shows in any case that the ways of colonists are not so rude as those of colonists and pioneers are generally supposed to be, but resemble rather the ways of women, as their longing resembles the longing of women, which though ostensibly a longing for the man they love, is in reality a longing for the promised land into which he shall lead them out of their darkness. Yet one must be cautious in expressing such generalizations: for the colonists easily take offence, and then they withdraw into a still more impenetrable solitude. In the prairies, however, in the grass-lands which they love, rich in hills and veined with cooling streams, they are a cheerful race, although they are too shamefast to sing. Such is the life of the colonists, remote from care, and they seek it beyond the ocean. They die lightly and still young, even should their hair be already grey, for their longing is a perpetual rehearsal of farewell. They are as proud as Moses when he beheld the promised land, he alone in his divine longing, and he alone forbidden to enter. And often one may see among them the same somewhat hopeless and somewhat contemptuous gesture of the hand as in Moses on the mount. For irrevocably behind them lies the home of their race, and inaccessibly before them stretches the distance, and the man whose longing has been transformed without his knowledge sometimes feels like one whose sufferings have been merely deadened, and who can never fully forget them. Vain hope! For who can tell whether he is pressing towards the blessed fields, or straying like a lost orphan? Even though one's grief for the irretrievable becomes less and less the farther one presses into the promised land, even if many things thin away into vapour in the deepening radiance, and one's grief too becomes lighter, more and more transparent, perhaps even invisible, yet it does not vanish any more than the longing of the man in whose sleep-wandering the world passes away, dissolving into a memory of the darkness of woman, desirous and maternal, where at last it is only a painful echo of what had once been. Vain hope, and often groundless arrogance. A lost generation. And so many of the colonists, even when they appear cheerful and untroubled, suffer remorse of conscience, and are more prone to repentance than many who lead more sinful lives. Indeed it is possible that there may be some who can no longer endure the peace and clarity to which they have surrendered themselves, and although one may assume that their insatiable longing for far-off things has grown so great that of necessity it had to swing round to its opposite, to what may have been its original starting-point, yet it is none the less credible that colonists have been observed sobbing with their hands over their faces as though they were yearning for home.

And so, the nearer he approached Mannheim in the dimly breaking dawn, the more painfully was Esch overcome by dread, and he scarcely knew whether the train might not be carrying him straight to the restaurant in Cologne, or whether Mother Hentjen might not be waiting at Mannheim to conceive a child by him. He was disappointed when all that awaited him was the letter on which in any case he had reckoned, and he felt disinclined to read it at all. Especially as he could see from the confounded letter that it had been written under Herr Hentjen's portrait. Perhaps for that reason, but perhaps too out of mere dread, Esch's hand trembled when, in spite of everything, he reached for the letter.

He gave Erna hardly a glance, ignored her reproachful looks, and went at once into the town, for he had a report to hand in at the police headquarters. Strangely enough, however, he landed first in Lohberg's shop, where he passed the time of day, and then he considered whether he should pay a visit to the docks. But he had already lost all desire even for that, and he would have liked best to take a tram out to the prison, although he knew quite well that there was no admittance before the afternoon. Loneliness threatened him, although it was still far off, and at last he stood before the Schiller monument, and would have been quite happy had he found the Eiffel Tower and the Statue of Liberty beside it. Perhaps it was merely the difference in the dimensions, but the life-size monument suggested nothing to him, and he found that he was no longer able even to picture Mother Hentjen's restaurant. Thus he frittered away the morning and wrestled with his memories; yes, he must hand in a report to the police, yet he was unable to formulate to himself the contents of that report. With a feeling of immense relief he gave up the plan at last when it dawned upon him that the Mannheim police, who had imprisoned Martin, were unworthy of receiving such a charge, and that he still remained under an obligation to provide the Cologne police with a substitute, as it were, for Nentwig. He felt irritated at himself: that might surely have occurred to him before, but now everything was in order, and he lunched in Lohberg's company with a good appetite.

Then he took a tram to the prison. Again it was a scorching day, again he found himself sitting in the visiting-room—had he ever left it? for everything had remained as it was, and nothing seemed to lie between that visit and this—again Martin entered with the warder, again Esch felt that agonizing feeling of emptiness in his head, again it was incomprehensible to him why he should be sitting in this official chamber, incomprehensible although it was happening for a definite end and after long premeditation. Fortunately he could feel the cigarettes in his pocket which he would take care this time to hand over to Martin, so that at least the visit might wipe off his former omission. But that was a pretext, yes a pretext, thought Esch, and then: a man's legs must work if his head won't. Everything exasperated him, and as they sat all three at the table again, this time it was Martin's ironically friendly air that exasperated him particularly—it reminded him of something that he did not want to admit to himself.

" So, back from your rest cure, August? You're looking first-rate, too. Have you run up against all your friends? "

Esch was not lying when he replied: " I've run up against nobody."

" Aha! So you weren't at Badenweiler after all? "

Esch could not answer.

" Esch, have you been playing the fool? "

Esch still remained silent, and Martin became serious: " If you've been up to any mischief I'm finished with you."

Esch said: " Things are too queer. What mischief could I be up to? "

Martin replied: " Have you a good conscience? Something isn't as it should be! "

" I have a good conscience."

Martin still regarded him searchingly, and Esch could not but think of the day when Martin had followed him in the street as though to strike him from behind with his crutch. But Martin was now quite friendly again and asked: " And what are you doing here in Mannheim still? "

" Lohberg is going to marry Erna Korn."

" Lohberg . . . oh, I remember now, the tobacconist fellow. And you're staying on because of that? " Martin's eyes had become suspicious again.

"I'm leaving to-day in any case . . . to-morrow at latest."

"And what's to happen to you after that?"

Esch wished he were somewhere else. He said: "I'm thinking of going to America."

Martin's aged boy's face smiled: "Well, well, you've wanted to do that for a long time . . . or have you some particular reason for wanting to leave the country now?"

No, Esch replied; he simply fancied that there were good prospects over there at present.

"Well, Esch, I hope I'll see you again before you leave. Better to be going because you have prospects than because you're running away from something . . . but if it shouldn't be so, you won't see my face again, Esch!" That sounded almost like a threat, and silence once more sank on the three men sitting at the ink-spotted table in the hot, airless room. Esch got up and said that he must hurry if he was still to catch the train that day, and as Martin once more regarded him questioningly and suspiciously, he pushed the cigarettes into Martin's hand, while the uniformed warder behaved as though he did not see anything, or maybe he had not really seen anything. Then Martin was led away.

On the way back to the town Martin's threat rang in Esch's ears, and perhaps indeed it had already come true, for all at once he could no longer picture Martin to himself, neither his hobbling walk, nor his smile, nor even that the cripple would ever enter the restaurant again. Martin had become strange to him. Esch marched on with long, awkward strides as though he had to increase as quickly as possible the distance between him and the prison, the distance between him and all that lay behind him. No, that man would never run after him again, so as to strike him from behind with his crutch; no man could really run after another, nor could the other send him away, for each was condemned to go his own lonely path, a stranger to all companionship: what mattered was to free oneself from the coil of the past, so that one might not suffer. One had simply to walk fast enough. Martin's threat had had singularly little effect, as if it were a clumsy work-a-day copy of a higher reality with which one had been already familiar for a long time. And if one left Martin behind, if one so to speak sacrificed him, that too was merely a work-a-day version of a higher sacrifice; but it was necessary if the past was to be finally destroyed. True, the streets of Mannheim were still familiar, yet he was making his way into a strange land, into freedom;

he walked as on a higher plane, and when next day he arrived at Cologne he would no longer feel abashed before the city and the scenes it presented, he would find them submissive and humble, submissively ready for transformation. Esch made a disdainful gesture with his swinging hands, and even achieved an ironical grimace.

He was so deeply sunk in thought that he passed Korn's door without noticing it; only when he was on the top floor did he realize that he must descend one flight again. And when Fräulein Erna opened the door he started back. He had forgotten her, and there she was looking at him now through the slit of the partly opened door, showing her yellowish teeth and making her demands upon him. It was the demon of the past itself barring the gate of longing, the grimacing mask of the work-a-day world, more invulnerable and mocking than ever, demanding that one should for ever descend anew into the coils of dead-and-gone things. And here a good conscience could not avail him, here it could not avail him that at any moment he was at liberty to leave this place for Cologne or America,—for a breathspace it seemed to him that Martin had caught him up after all, and as though it were Martin's vengeance that was pushing him down, down to Erna. But Fräulein Erna seemed to know that there was no escape for him, for like Martin she smiled all-knowingly and as in secret intelligence of a still obscure obligation binding him to her world, an obligation that was inescapable and threatening and yet of supreme importance. He gazed searchingly into Fräulein Erna's face; it was the face of a withered Antichrist and gave no answer. "When is Lohberg coming?" Esch asked the question abruptly and as though in the vague hope that the answer would solve his problem; and when Fräulein Erna slyly hinted that she had intentionally refrained from inviting her fiancé, it was undoubtedly a flattering mark of preference, and yet it made him furious. Without regarding her offended looks he ran from the house to invite Lohberg for a visit that evening.

And indeed Esch felt comforted when he found the fool, so deeply comforted that he at once begged for his company and purchased all sorts of eatables and even two bouquets, one of which he stuck in Lohberg's hand. Small wonder that at the sight of them Fräulein Erna should clasp her hands and cry: "Why, here's two real cavaliers!" Esch replied proudly: "A farewell celebration," and while she was setting out the table he sat with his friend Lohberg on the sofa and sang: *Must I then, must I then, leave my native Town*, which won him disapproving and melancholy glances from Fräulein Erna. Yes, perhaps it was really a farewell celebration, a celebration of release from this work-a-day community, and he would have liked to forbid her to lay a place for Ilona. For Ilona too must be released by now and already at the goal. And this wish was so strong that in all seriousness Esch hoped that Ilona would stay away, stay away for ever. And incidentally he felt a little elated at the thought of Korn's disappointment.

Well, Korn really gave signs of being disappointed; though to be sure his disappointment expressed itself in coarse abuse of that Hungarian female, and in rabid impatience for immediate nourishment. Meanwhile he moved his broad bulk with astonishing agility through the room; addressed himself to the liqueur bottles, then to the table from which with his blunt fingers he lifted a few slices of sausage, and when Erna refused to allow this he turned upon Lohberg and with upraised hands shooed him from the sofa, which he claimed for himself by prescriptive right. The noise which the man Korn raised while doing this was extraordinary, his body and voice filled the room more and more, filled it from wall to wall; all that was earthly and fleshly in Korn's ravenously hungry being swelled beyond the confines of the room, threatening mightily to fill the whole world, and with it the unalterable past swelled up, crushing everything else out and stifling all hope; the uplifted and luminous stage darkened, and perhaps indeed it no longer existed. "Well, Lohberg, where's your kingdom of redemption now?" shouted Esch, as though he were seeking to deafen his own terrors, shouted it in fury, because neither Lohberg nor anybody else was capable of giving an answer to the question: why must Ilona descend into contact with the earthly and the dead? Korn sat there on his broad hindquarters and ordered brutally: "Bring in the food!" "No!" shouted Esch, "not till Ilona comes!" For though he was almost afraid of seeing Ilona again, everything was at hazard now, and suddenly Esch was full of impatience for Ilona to appear—as it were to be the touchstone of truth.

Ilona entered. She scarcely noticed the company, simply obeyed the signal of the silently chewing Korn and sat down beside him on the sofa, and in obedience to his equally silent command slung her soft arm languidly round his neck. But for the rest all that she saw was the good things on the table. Erna, who observed all this, said: "If I were you, Ilona, I would keep my hands off Balthasar while I was eating, at least." True, she was merely talking in the air, for Ilona obviously still did not understand a word of German, indeed must not understand it, just as she must not know of the sacrifices that had been made for her. Ignorant of their speech, she could hardly be regarded any longer as a guest at the table of the flesh-bound, but rather as a mere visitor to the prison of the work-a-day world, or as a voluntary captive. And Erna, who to-night seemed to know many things, made no further mention of earthly matters, and it was like an admission of a more subtle understanding when she lifted the bouquet from the table and held it under Ilona's nose: " There, smell that, Ilona," she said, and Ilona replied: " Yes, thank you," and it rang as from a distance which the munching Korn would never reach, rang as from a higher plane ready to receive her if only one did not grow weary in sacrifice. Esch felt light-hearted. Everyone must fulfil his dream, whether it be evil or holy, and then he will partake of freedom. And great pity as it was that the ninny should get Erna, and little as Ilona would ever guess that now the final line had been drawn under an account, it was a settlement and a turning-point, a testimony and the act of a new consciousness when Esch got up, drank to the company, and having briefly and heartily congratulated the betrothed couple, proposed a toast to their health, so that everybody, with the exception of Ilona for whose sake it was really done, looked quite dumbfounded. But as it expressed their secret wishes, their next emotion was gratitude, and Lohberg with moist eyes shook Esch's hand again and again. Then at Esch's request the happy couple gave each other the betrothal kiss.

Nevertheless what had been done did not yet appear to him final, and when the party was breaking up, and Korn had already retired with Ilona, and Fräulein Erna was preparing to put on her hat so as to keep Esch company in escorting her newly betrothed to his home, then Esch objected; no, he did not regard it as seemly that he, a bachelor, should spend the night in the house of Lohberg's fiancée, he would be very happy to seek a lodging for the night in Herr Lohberg's house or to exchange rooms with him; they should think it over again, for after their betrothal they must have a great many things to talk about; and thereupon he pushed the two of them into Erna's room and betook himself to his own.

In this way ended the first day of his release, and the first night of unaccustomed and unpleasant renunciation broke in.

The sleepless man who with moistened finger-tip has quenched the quiet candle beside his bed, and in the now cooler room awaits the coolness of sleep, with every beat of his heart approaches death without knowing it; for strangely as the cool room has expanded round him, just as stiflingly hot and hurried has time grown within his head, so stifling that beginning and end, birth and death, past and future, crumble to dust in the unique and isolated present, filling it to the brim, indeed almost bursting it.

Esch had considered for a moment whether Lohberg might not after all decide to go home and want his company. But with an ironical grimace he concluded that he might safely go to bed, and still grinning he began to take off his clothes. By the light of the candle he read again Mother Hentjen's letter; the copious items of news about the restaurant were boring; on the other hand there was one passage which pleased him: "And do not forget, dear August, that you are my only love in all the world and will always be, and that I cannot live without you, and would not rest in the cold grave without you, dear August." Yes, that pleased him, and now on Mother Hentjen's account too he was glad that he had sent Lohberg in to Erna. Then he moistened his finger-tip, put out the candle, and stretched himself on the bed.

A sleepless night begins with banal thoughts, somewhat as a juggler displays at first banal and easy feats of skill, before proceeding to the more difficult and thrilling ones. In the darkness Esch could not help grinning still at the thought of Lohberg slipping under the blankets to the coyly tittering Erna, and he was glad that he had no need to be jealous of the ninny. In truth his desire for Erna had now completely gone, but that was all to the good and as it should be. And in reality he only dwelt on the happenings in the other room to demonstrate how indifferent they left him, how indifferent it was to him that Erna was now caressing with her hands the meagre body of the idiot, and suffering such a misbegotten monstrosity beside her, and how totally indifferent what impressions, what phallic images—he employed a different term—she carried in her memory. So easy was it for him to picture all this that it seemed without importance, and besides with that pure Joseph one was not even certain that things would take such a course. Life would be an easy business if things of that kind left him just as indifferent in Mother Hentjen's case,— but the mere impact of the thought was so painful that he started violently, not entirely unlike Mother Hentjen at certain moments. He would gladly have sought refuge with Erna for himself and his thoughts, had not something barred the way, something invisible, of which he only knew that it was the threatening and inescapable presence of that afternoon. So he turned his thoughts to Ilona; all that was needed to establish order there was that the hurtling knives should be erased from her memory. As a preliminary rehearsal, so to speak, for more difficult feats, he tried to think of her, but he was unsuccessful. Yet when at last he managed to picture to himself, with rage and loathing, that at that moment she was languidly and submissively enduring the presence of Korn, that dead lump of flesh, regardless of herself, just as she had stood smiling in the midst of the daggers, waiting for one of them to strike her to the heart— oh, then he suddenly saw the end of his task; for it was self-murder that she was committing in such a curiously complicated and feminine fashion, self-murder that dragged her down into contact with earthly things. That was what she must be rescued from! His task was defined, but it had become a new task! Indeed, if it were not for that threatening something barring the way, he would simply dismiss Ilona from his mind, walk over to Erna's room, seize Lohberg by the collar, and curtly order him to take himself off. After that one would be able to sleep quietly and dreamlessly.

Yet just when he was on the point of picturing to himself how peaceful the world would be then, and already felt within himself the unequivocal desire for a woman, the sleepless Esch was pulled up by an idea which was at once a little comical and a little shocking: he dared not return to Erna, for then it would no longer be possible to tell who was the father of her child. So that was the inexplicable obligation, that was the threat which had made him start back when he saw Erna that afternoon! Yes, it all seemed to fit in; for there was one who had stepped aside to make place for another from whose advent the new dispensation of time was to begin, and it seemed right, too, that a messiah's father should be a pure Joseph. Esch tried again to summon his ironical grimace, but he was unsuccessful this time; his eyelids were too tightly shut, and no one can laugh in the dark. For night is the time of freedom, and laughter is the revenge of those who are not free. Oh, it was just and right that he should be lying here sleepless and wide awake, in a cold and strange excitement which was no longer the excitement of desire, lying in a semblance of death as in a vault, since the unborn was lying motionless and undreaming likewise. Yet how could one believe that Bertrand had been sacrificed, so that out of the paltry earthly vessel that was called Fräulein Erna new life should spring? Esch cursed to himself, as the sleepless sometimes are accustomed to do, but while he cursed he suddenly realized that after all it did not fit in, inasmuch as the magical hour of death should be the hour of procreation too. One could not be at the selfsame time in Badenweiler and Mannheim; so the conclusion he had drawn was a premature one, and everything was perhaps more complex and more noble.

The darkness of the room was cool. Esch, a man of impetuous temperament, lay motionless in his bed, his heart hammered time down to a thin dust of nothingness, and no reason could any longer be found why one should postpone death into a future which was in any case already the present. To the man who is awake such ideas may seem illogical, but he forgets that he himself exists for the most part in a kind of twilight state, and that only the sleepless man in his overwakefulness thinks with really logical severity. The sleepless man keeps his eyes closed, as though not to see the cold tomblike darkness in which he lies, not to see it, yet fearing that his sleeplessness may topple over into mere ordinary awakeness at the sight of the curtains which hang like woman's skirts before the window, and all the objects which may detach themselves from the darkness if he were to open his eyes. For he wants to be sleepless and not awake, otherwise he could not lie here with Mother Hentjen cut off from the world and safe in his tomb, full of a desire which is lust no longer; yes, he was robbed of desire now, and that too was good. United in death, thought Esch, lying in his semblance of death, yes, united in death, and in truth that would have been comforting, if he could but have refrained from thinking of Erna and Lohberg, who were also in a way united now in death. But in what a way! Well, the sleepless man has no inclination left for cynical witticisms, he wants, as it were, to let the metaphysical content of experience work upon him, and to estimate justly the extraordinary distance that separates his couch from the other rooms in the house, wishes in all seriousness to meditate on the attainable final communion, on the fulfilment of his dream which will lead him to consummation; and as he cannot grasp all these things he becomes morose and aggrieved, becomes enraged and meditates now only on the question: how the dead can possibly give birth to the living. The sleepless man runs his hand over his closely cropped hair, a cool and prickling sensation remains in the palm of his hand; it is like a dangerous experiment which he will not repeat again.

And when by such means he has advanced to more difficult and remarkable feats, his rage waxes, and perhaps it is only the rage of impotent joyless desire. Ilona was committing self-murder in a peculiarly complicated and feminine fashion, suffering night after night the presence of a dead lump of flesh, so that her face was already puffy as though it had been touched by corruption. And every night that that image of obscene lust was imprinted on her the corruption must increase. So that was the reason why he had feared to see Ilona that afternoon! The knowledge of the sleepless man grows into a clairvoyant foreshadowing dream of death, and he recognizes that Mother Hentjen is already dead, that she, the dead woman, can have no child by him, that for this reason alone she has written him a letter instead of coming to Mannheim, written it under the portrait of the man from whose hands she accepted death, just as now Ilona is accepting death from that animal Korn. Mother Hentjen's cheeks too were puffy, time and death were embedded in her face, and the raptures of her nights were dead, dead as the automatic musical instrument which ground out its tune mechanically, one had only to press a lever. And Esch became furious.

The sleepless man does not know that his bed is standing in a certain position in a house in a certain street, and he refuses to be reminded of it. It is notorious that the sleepless are easily moved to anger; the rolling of a solitary tramcar through the night streets is enough to arouse them to fury. And how much stronger then must be their rage over a contradiction so colossal and so terrible that it cannot even be put down to a book-keeping error? In panic haste the sleepless man sets his thoughts flying to discover the meaning of the question which, coming from somewhere or other, from afar off, perhaps from America, now presses on him. He feels that there is a region in his head that is America, a region that is none other than the site of the future in his head, and yet that cannot exist so long as the past keeps breaking in so boundlessly into the future, the wrecked and annihilated overwhelming the new. In this storm that breaks in he himself is carried away, yet not only he, but everyone around him is swept away by the icy hurricane, all of them following the pioneer who has first flung himself into the storm, to be whirled away so that time may once more become time. Now there was no more time left, only an extraordinary amount of space; the sleepless man in his overwakefulness listens and knows that all the others are dead, and even if he shuts his eyelids ever so tightly so as not to see it, he knows that death is always murder.

So the word had appeared again, yet not flitting silently like a butter-fly; but with the rattling clangour of a tramcar in the night streets the word murder had reappeared, and was shouting at him. The dead handed death on. There must be no surviving. As though death were a child, Mother Hentjen had conceived it by the dead tailor fellow, and Korn was imparting it to Ilona. Perhaps Korn too was dead; he was as fat as Mother Hentjen, and of redemption he knew nothing. Or if he were not dead already, he would die—faint comforting hope— would die like the snippet of a tailor, after he had consummated his murder. Murder and counter-murder, shock on shock, the past and the future broke upon each other, broke in the very moment of death which was the present. That must be thought out very vigilantly and very seriously, for only too easily might another book-keeping error slip in. And already how immeasurably difficult it was to distinguish sacrifice and murder from each other! Must all be destroyed ere the world could be redeemed to a state of innocence? Must the deluge break in, was it not enough for one man to sacrifice himself, for one to step aside? Esch still lived, although like all the sleepless he was dead to all appearance, Ilona still lived, although death had already touched her, and only one man was bearing the burden of sacrifice for the new life and the creation of a world in which daggers might no longer be flung. That sacrifice could never be undone now. And as all abstract and universally valid generalizations are to be found in the state of sleepless overwakefulness, Esch arrived at the conclusion: the dead are murderers of women. But he was not dead, and on him lay the obligation to rescue Ilona.

Again arose in him the desire, the impatient desire, to receive death from Mother Hentjen's hand, and the doubt whether it had not already happened. If he submitted himself to that death which came from the dead, he might propitiate the dead, and they might rest content with the one sacrifice. A comforting thought! And as the sleepless man can be more violently overcome with rage than the awake in their twilight state, so his happiness may be far more ecstatic, and he may experience it, one might almost say, with a sort of wild lightness of heart. Yes, that light and liberated feeling of happiness may become so bright that the very darkness behind the closed eyelids catches its radiance. For now it was absolutely certain that Esch, who was alive, a living man by whom women might conceive, if he resigned himself to Mother Hentjen and her body of death, must by this unprecedented measure not only consummate Ilona's redemption, must not only put her for ever beyond the reach of the daggers, must not only retrieve her beauty for her and cancel from her flesh all trace of mortality, cancel it so completely that she would regain a new virginity, but that by doing this he must also of necessity rescue Mother Hentjen from death, vivify again her loins, so that she might bear the one whose task it would be to renew Time.

Then it seemed to him as though his bed were returning with him from a great distance, until at last it rested again in a certain position in a certain alcove, and Esch, reborn in newly awakened longing, knew that he was at his goal, not, it was true, that final goal in which symbol and prototype return to their identity, yet none the less at that temporary goal with which earthly mortals must rest content, the goal that he termed love and that stood as the last attainable point on that coast beyond which lay the unattainable. And, as it were, in antithesis to the symbol and the prototype, women seemed curiously united and yet divided; Mother Hentjen might be sitting in Cologne waiting for him, Ilona might have receded into the unattainable and the invisible, and he knew that he would never see her again—but out there on that horizon where the visible and the invisible, the attainable and the unattainable became one, their ways crossed and their two silhouettes dissolved and merged into each other, and even if they were to separate, they would still remain united in a hope never to be fulfilled: the hope that, embracing Mother Hentjen in perfect love, bearing her life as his own, quickening and redeeming her from death in his arms, embracing in love this woman growing old, he might lift from Ilona the burden of approaching age and of memory, might create as a setting for Ilona's new and virginal beauty the higher plane of his desire; yes, widely separated as the two women were, they yet became one, the reflected image of one, of that invisible entity to which he could never turn back, and which yet was home.

The sleepless Esch was at his goal. In his overwakefulness indeed he had already foreknown the outcome, and he saw that he had merely been spinning a logical chain round it, and had remained wakeful merely because the chain had grown longer and longer; but now he permitted himself to forge the last link, and it was like a complicated book-keeping task which he had solved at last, indeed even more than a book-keeping task; it was the real task of love in all its absoluteness that he had taken upon him in submitting his earthly life to Mother Hentjen. He would gladly have made this conclusion known to Ilona, but in view of her imperfect mastery of the German language he would have to abstain.

Esch opened his eyes, recognized his room, and then went contentedly to sleep.

He had decided for Mother Hentjen. Finally. Esch did not look out through the carriage window. And when he turned his thoughts to this perfect and absolute love of his it was like a daring experiment; acquaintances and customers would be drinking in the brightly lit restaurant; he would enter, and regardless of all those eyewitnesses, Mother Hentjen would run to him and fling herself on his breast. But when he arrived in Cologne the picture seemed to have altered strangely; for this city was no longer a city that he knew, and his way through the evening streets seemed to stretch for miles and was strange to him. Incredible that he had been away for only six days. Time had stopped, and the house that awaited his entry was quite indefinite, the restaurant quite indefinite in shape and size. Esch stood in the doorway and looked across at Mother Hentjen. She sat enthroned behind the buffet. Above the mirror a light burned under a red shade, silence hung in the air, not a customer was to be seen in the forlorn room. Nothing happened. Why had he come here? Nothing happened; Mother Hentjen remained behind the buffet and said at last in her usual phlegmatic way: "Good-evening." And she glanced nervously round the room. Rage rose up in him, and all at once he could not understand why he had decided for this woman. So he too merely said, "Good-evening," for although he somehow approved of her proud coldness, and knew also that he had no right to repay her in the same coin, yet he felt angry; a man who had decided in his heart for unconditional love was entitled at any rate to be met on an equal footing,—he rapped out: "Thanks for your letter." She looked round the empty restaurant and said furiously: "What if anyone were to hear you?" and Esch, fully roused, replied with particular distinctness: "And what if they did . . . let this stupid mystery-mongering stop now, for heaven's sake!" said it without point or object, for the restaurant was empty, and he himself did not know why he was there. Mother Hentjen became silent with terror, and mechanically put up her hand to her coiffure. Since she had accompanied him to the train she had keenly regretted being so forward, giving herself away so completely, and after sending that imprudent letter to Mannheim she had actually fallen into a genuine panic; she would have been grateful to Esch now for not mentioning it. But now that with a set, implacable face he openly exploited his advantage, she felt herself again defencelessly caught in a grip of iron. Esch said: " I can go, of course, if you like," and now she would really have issued from behind her counter if the first customers had not at that moment entered. So the two of them remained standing where they were in silence; then Mother Hentjen whispered in a contemptuous tone which was intended to show that she merely wished to carry their quarrel to a finish: " Come back to-night." Esch made no reply, but sat down at his table before a glass of wine. He felt an orphan. His calculations yesterday, which had seemed so clear, had now become incomprehensible to him; how could his deciding for this woman help Ilona? he gazed round the restaurant and still felt it strange; it meant nothing to him now, he had left all those things too far behind. What was he doing in Cologne at all? he should have been in America long ago. But then his glance caught Herr Hentjen's portrait, hanging above the insignia of liberty, and it was as though it suddenly reminded him of something; he asked for paper and ink, and in his most beautiful clerkly script wrote: " I beg to bring to the notice of the Chief Commissioner of Police that Herr Eduard von Bertrand, resident in Badenweiler, Chairman of the Central Rhine Shipping Company Limited in Mannheim, is guilty of illicit practices with persons of the male sex, and I am prepared to appear as a witness and furnish proof of my accusation."

When he was about to append his signature he stopped suddenly, for he had been on the point of adding: " In the name of his bereaved relatives and friends," and although he could not help smiling at this, he was startled. Finally, however, he added his name and address to the communication, and having carefully folded it, deposited it in his pocket-book. Until to-morrow, he told himself, a last respite. The picture postcard from Badenweiler was also sticking in his pocket-book. He considered whether he could present it to Mother Hentjen that night, and felt forlorn. But then he saw before him the alcove, saw her again in her painfully submissive readiness to receive him, and as he passed the buffet he said, and his voice was hoarse: " Well then, to-night." She sat stiffly in her chair and seemed to have heard nothing, so that filled with new rage, a different rage however from the first, he turned back again, and raising his voice recklessly, said: " Be so good as to remove that portrait over there." She still sat immobile, and he slammed the door behind him.

When later he returned and made to open the house door he found it barred from inside. Without considering whether the maid might hear him, he rang the bell, and as nobody answered he went on ringing furiously. That did the trick; he heard footsteps; he almost hoped that it might be the little maid; he would tell her that he had forgotten something in the restaurant, but apart from that the maid would not disdain him, and that would be a lesson for Mother Hentjen. But it was not the maid, it was Frau Hentjen in person; she was still fully dressed and she was crying. Both circumstances increased his rage. They climbed the stairs in silence, and up in her room he fell upon her at once. When she submitted, and her kisses became tender, he asked threateningly: " Is that portrait going to be removed? " She did not know at first of what he was speaking, and when she did she did not quite understand for a moment: " The portrait? . . . oh, the portrait? why? don't you like it? " In despair before her inability to understand he said: " No, I don't like it . . . and there's a lot of things besides that I don't like." She replied complaisantly and politely: " If you don't like it I can easily hang it up somewhere else." She was so unutterably stupid that it would probably take a thrashing to make her understand. However, Esch restrained himself: " The portrait must be burned." " Burned? " " Yes, burned. And if you pretend to be so stupid much longer, I'll set fire to the whole place." She recoiled from him in terror, and, pleased with the effect of his threat, he said: " You should be glad; it isn't as if you had any great love for the place." She made no reply, and even if her mind was probably blank, and she only saw the flames rising from her roof-top, yet it was as though she were trying to conceal something. He said sternly: " Why don't you speak? " His harsh tone completely paralysed her. Could this woman not be driven by any means to drop her mask? Esch had risen and now stood threateningly at the entrance to the alcove as though to prevent her from escaping. One would have to call things by their real names, otherwise one would never make anything out of this lump of flesh. But when he asked: " Why did you marry him? " his voice was hoarse and strangled, for with the question so many wild and hopeless emotions surged up in him that in thought he had to fly to Erna for comfort. He had left her, though she did not torment him and it had been completely immaterial to him what phallic images she carried in her memory. And it had been equally immaterial to him whether she had children, or prevented them by artificial devices.

He dreaded Mother Hentjen's answer, did not want to hear it, yet he shouted: "Well?" And Mother Hentjen, her fear that she had given herself away too much reawakened, perhaps also dreading that the nimbus surrounding her, on whose account she imagined Esch loved her, might be in danger of vanishing, gathered herself together: "It's so long ago . . . you don't need to let that worry you." Esch pushed forward his under jaw and bared his strong teeth: "It shan't worry me . . . it shan't worry me . . ." he shouted, "it doesn't worry me in the least. . . . I don't give a hang for it." So this was how she requited his absolute and untiring devotion and his torments. She was stupid and callous; he, who had taken her fate upon him, he, who wanted to take upon him her life although it had been aged and defiled by death, he, August Esch, who was prepared to make the decision and give himself absolutely to her, who longed that all his strangeness might be merged in her, so that all her strangeness and all her thoughts, no matter how painful to him, might become his as it were by way of exchange: it needn't worry him! Oh, she was stupid and callous, and being so he had to beat her; he went up to the bed and hit out at her and struck her on the fat immobile cheek, as though by doing so he might reach the immobility of her spirit. She did not defend herself, but remained lying rigid, and even if he had flung knives at her, even then she would not have moved. Her cheek was red where he had struck her, and when a tear trickled down over it his anger was softened. He sat down on the bed, and she moved to the side to make room for him. Then he said imperiously: "We must get married." She simply answered, "Yes," and Esch was on the point of flying into a new rage, because she did not say that she was glad at last to be rid of the hated name. But the only reply she could think of was to put her arm round him and draw him to her. He was tired, and submitted; perhaps it was all right, perhaps it did not matter, for where the kingdom of salvation was concerned everything was uncertain, every hour uncertain, every figure and every reckoning. Yet he felt embittered again; what did she know about the kingdom of salvation? And did she even want to know about it? probably as little as Korn! it would certainly take some time to hammer it into her head. But meanwhile one must simply allow for that, must wait until she could understand it, must let her carry on her life as she was doing. In the land of justice, in America, it would be different; there the past would fall away like tinder. And when she asked him constrainedly whether he had stopped at Ober-Wesel, he was not annoyed, but shook his head seriously and growled: "Of course not." And so they celebrated their marriage night, and agreed to sell the business, and Mother Hentjen was grateful to him for not setting fire to anything. In a month's time they might be on the high seas. To-morrow he would see Teltscher and set the American project going again.

He remained longer than usual. Nor did they descend the stairs on tiptoe this time. And when she let him out there were already people in the streets. That filled him with pride.

Next morning he betook himself to the Alhambra. Of course nobody was there. He rummaged among the correspondence on Gernerth's desk, found an unopened envelope which bore his own handwriting, and was so taken aback for a moment that he did not recognize it: it was Erna's letter that he had himself written in Mannheim. Well, she would raise another fine outcry if she had received no reply all this time. And really not without justification. A careless lot, those theatre people.

At last Teltscher came wandering in. Esch was almost glad to see him again. Teltscher was in a gracious mood: "Well, high time for you to be back,—everybody disappears on private business and Teltscher is left to do all the measly work." Where was Gernerth? "Oh, in Munich with his precious family—grave illness in the family, they've got colds in the head or something." He would soon be back, Esch supposed. "He'll have to come back soon, the Herr Manager; last night there were scarcely fifty people in the theatre. We'll have to talk it over with Oppenheimer." "Right," said Esch, "let's go and see Oppenheimer."

They agreed with Oppenheimer that they would have to announce the end of the show. "Have I warned you, or haven't I?" said Oppenheimer. "Wrestling is all right, but nothing but wrestling! who would come to see that?" The decision suited Esch very well; all that he need do was to have his share paid to him when Gernerth returned, and the sooner the end came, the sooner they would get to America.

This time he asked Teltscher of his own accord to lunch with him, for now it was a matter of setting about the American project. Hardly were they on the pavement before Esch drew the list from his pocket and ticked off the girls whom he had earmarked for the journey. " Yes, I've got a few too," said Teltscher, " but first Gernerth must pay me back my money." Esch was surprised, for Teltscher should surely have been satisfied with Lohberg's and Erna's contributions. Teltscher said in exasperation: " And whose money have we been financing the wrestling matches with, do you think? Gernerth's money is tied up, don't you know that? He gave me the stage properties in pledge, but what can I do with them in America?" All this was somewhat surprising, but all the same when the business was liquidated Gernerth's money would be released, and then Teltscher could go to America. " Ilona must come too," decided Teltscher. That's where you make your mistake, my dear fellow, thought Esch, Ilona won't be mixed up with these things again; for though she might still be attached to Korn, that would not last much longer; soon she would be living in a distant, inaccessible castle, in whose grounds the deer grazed. He said that he must visit the police headquarters, and they made the necessary detour. In a stationer's shop Esch bought several newspapers and an envelope; he stuck the papers in his pocket, and with many flourishes addressed the envelope on the spot. Then he took out of his pocket-book the carefully folded sheet of paper, stuck it into the envelope and went over to the police buildings. As soon as he emerged again he continued his conversation; there was no need for Ilona to go with them. " Don't talk stuff," replied Teltscher, " in the first place, think of the splendid engagements we could get over there, and secondly, if the American idea should come to nothing, we must set to work here. She's idled long enough; besides, I've written to her already." " Nonsense," replied Esch rudely, " if you're dealing in young girls you can't take a woman with you." Teltscher laughed: " Well, if you think I shouldn't, you'll have to indemnify me for the damage to my prospects. You're a big capitalist now . . . and one generally brings back money from a business excursion, doesn't one? " Esch was alarmed; it seemed to him that Teltscher had glanced knowingly across at the police buildings—what could that mean? What did the Jewish conjurer know? he himself knew nothing of this business excursion; he turned on Teltscher: " Go to the devil! I haven't brought back any money." " No harm intended, Herr Esch, don't take it in that way, I didn't mean anything."

They turned into Mother Hentjen's restaurant, and to Esch it seemed again as though Teltscher possessed some secret knowledge, and might suddenly turn on him and say, "Murderer." He was afraid to look round the room. At last he raised his eyes and beheld a white patch, edged with cobwebs, where Hentjen's portrait had hung. He glanced across at Teltscher, but Teltscher said nothing, for he obviously had not noticed anything, had not noticed anything at all! Esch felt almost exultant; partly out of high spirits, partly to distract Teltscher's attention from the disappearance of the portrait, he went up to the orchestrion and set it noisily going; in response to the din Mother Hentjen appeared, and Esch felt a strong temptation to greet her with affectionate and tempestuous ardour; he would have liked to introduce her as Frau Esch, and if he refrained from this tender jest, it was not only because he felt grateful to her and prepared to respect her shyness, but also because Herr Teltscher-Teltini was quite unworthy of such a mark of intimacy. On the other hand Esch did not feel in the least bound to push discretion too far, and when after lunch Teltscher prepared to leave he did not accompany him as usual, to return afterwards by circuitous ways, no, he said quite openly that he would stay for a little and read his papers. He pulled the newspapers out of his pocket, put them back again, and remained sitting with his hands resting peacefully on his knees. He did not want to read. He contemplated the white patch on the wall. And when everything was quiet he went up the stairs. He felt grateful to Mother Hentjen and they had a pleasant afternoon. They spoke again of selling the business, and Esch thought that perhaps Oppenheimer might find a purchaser. And they tenderly discussed their marriage. There was a spot on the ceiling of the alcove that looked like a dark butterfly, but it was only dirt.

In the evening he dutifully set out on his search for girls. On his way it struck him that he should first look in to see what that lad Harry was doing. His search was in vain and he was about to leave the wretched place when Alfons entered. Fat Alfons presented a comical picture; his greasy dishevelled hair was sticking to his skull, his silk shirt was open, showing his white hairless breast, and one was reminded somehow of rumpled pillows. Esch could not help laughing. Alfons sat down beside a table near the door and groaned. Esch went up to him still laughing, yet in doing so it was as though he were trying to stifle something: "Hullo, Alfons, what's the matter?" The fat musician gazed at him with dull and hostile eyes. "Have a drink, and tell me what's wrong." Alfons drank a glass of brandy and remained silent. Finally he said: "Good God

... it's past belief ... he's to blame for it himself, and he asks what's wrong!" "Don't talk nonsense. What is wrong?" "Good God! Why, he's dead!" Alfons put his hands under his chin and gazed in front of him; Esch sat down at the table. "Well, who is dead?" Alfons stammered: "He loved him too much." Now it sounded funny again. "Who loved whom?" Alfons's voice suddenly broke: "Don't talk like that; Harry's dead. . . ." So, Harry was dead. Esch could not really take it in and gazed somewhat blankly at the fat musician, down whose cheeks tears were running: "You put him quite beyond himself with your silly talk last time ... he loved him too much ... when he read it in the papers he locked himself in ... this afternoon ... and now they've found him ... veronal." So, Harry was dead; in some way that fitted in, it was bound to come. Only Esch could not see how it fitted in. He said, "Poor chap," and suddenly he saw it and was filled with relief and joy because that forenoon he had handed in his letter at the police headquarters; here murder and counter-murder, debit and credit cancelled each other, here was for once an account that balanced itself perfectly. Funny to think that in spite of this he himself seemed to be in some way to blame. He said again: "Poor chap ... why did he do it?" Alfons glared at him in blank astonishment: "But he saw it in the newspapers. . . ." "Saw what?" "There," Alfons pointed to the bunch of newspapers peeping from Esch's coat-pocket. Esch shrugged his shoulders—he had forgotten the newspapers. He pulled them out; there it was, in large letters, and with many circumlocutions, on the black-bordered last page, for all the firms with which he was connected, and his staff officials, and his workers, had insisted on the melancholy privilege of divulging the sad news that Herr Eduard von Bertrand, Chairman of the Board of Directors, a knight of various distinguished orders, etc., after a short serious illness had passed away. On the front page, however, along with a highly eulogistic obituary notice, was the information that, it was supposed in a sudden fit of mental aberration, the deceased had put an end to his life with a revolver shot. Esch read all this, but it did not very much interest him. It merely proved to him how right it was that the portrait had been removed that day. Funny that a man like this musician, who was not implicated at all, could make such a song about it. With a faint ironical grimace he clapped the fat musician benevolently and comfortingly on the flabby shoulder, paid for the brandy, and went back to Frau Hentjen. Stepping out complacently with long strides, he thought of Martin and reflected that now the cripple would no longer pursue him and menace him with his hard crutches. And that too was good.

Alone, Alfons put his head between his hands and stared in front of him. Esch seemed to him a bad man, like all men who sought women in order to possess them. He had learned by experience that all men of that type sowed evil. They seemed to him like savages running amok, raging through the world so that at their approach all one could do was to step aside. He scorned those men who rushed about in such a stupid fury, greedy not for life, which they obviously did not see, but for something which lay outside it, and to gain which they destroyed it in the name of this love of theirs. The musician was too dejected to think this out clearly; but he knew that although those men spoke with great ardour of their love, all that they meant by it was possession, or what is usually understood by that term. Of course he himself did not count, for at best he was a thoughtless chap, a poor devil of an orchestra player; but he knew that one did not attain the absolute by a long way when one decided for some woman. And he forgave the malignant rage of men, for he saw quite well that it sprang from fear and disappointment, saw that these passionate and evil men hid themselves behind a remnant of eternity to shield themselves from the fear that was always at their backs, telling them they must die. A stupid and thoughtless orchestra player he might be, but he could play sonatas from memory, and, versed in all kinds of knowledge, in spite of his sadness he could smile at the fact that human beings in their thirst for the absolute yearn for eternal love, imagining that then their lives can never come to an end, but will endure for ever. They might despise him because he had to play potpourris and polkas; nevertheless he knew that these hunted creatures, seeking the imperishable and the absolute in earthly things, would always find no more than a symbol and a substitute for the thing which they sought, and whose name they did not know: for they could watch others dying without regret or sorrow, so completely were they mastered by the thought of their own death; they furiously strove for the possession of some woman that they might in turn be possessed by her, for in her they hoped to find something steadfast and unchangeable which would own and guard them, and they hated the woman whom in their blindness they had chosen, hated her because she was only a symbol which they longed to destroy in their anger when they found themselves once more delivered over to fear and death. The musician felt pity for women; for although they wished for nothing better, yet they were not subject to that destructive and stupid passion for possession, they were less goaded by fear, and were thrilled more deeply when music was played to them, and stood in a more intimate and trustful relation to death: and in that women were like musicians, and even if one were oneself only a fat homosexual orchestra player, yet one could feel akin to them, could acknowledge that they had a faint divination that death was a sad and beautiful thing; for when they wept it was not because they had lost a possession, but simply because something that they had touched and seen had been good and gentle. Oh, those whose hearts thirsted for possession did not know the rapturous chaos of life, and the others knew little more of it; yet music divined it, music the melodious symbol of all that could be thought, music that annulled time so that it might be preserved in rhythm, that annulled death so that it might rise anew in sound. One who divined this, like the women and the musicians, might accept the disgrace of being thoughtless and stupid, and the musician Alfons ran his fingers over the rolls of fat on his body as though they were a good soft covering through which he could feel the presence of something precious and worthy of love; people could despise him and jeer at his effeminacy, well, he was only a poor devil, but nevertheless he was capable of surrendering himself more blissfully and passively and submissively to all the diverse manifestations of the eternal than those who jeered at him and yet made out of a tiny scrap of mortality the symbol and goal of their wretched striving. It was he who should despise the others. He was sorry even for Esch, and he could not help thinking of the heroic battle-music to whose strains the gladiators entered the arena, that the warrior, his courage stimulated, might forget that death stood at his back. He considered whether he should watch by Harry's bed, but he shuddered at the thought of the waxen face, and he decided instead to get drunk and watch the waiters and the customers, who moved about and yet bore on their faces the stamp of death.—

At the same hour that night Ilona rose from her bed and by the light of the tiny red lamp under the image of the Virgin regarded the sleeping form of Balthasar Korn. He was snoring, and when the sound ceased it was like the cessation of the music in the theatre before her act; and presently in the whistling of his breath the thin whizzing of the hurtling knives could be heard. Really she was not thinking of this at all, although she had received Teltscher's letter calling her back. She regarded Korn and tried to picture how he would have looked as a little boy and without his black moustache. She did not know clearly why she was doing this, but it seemed to her that then the Mother of God gazing from the wall would be readier to forgive her sin. For sin it was to have employed him for her unholy lust under the holy eyes of the Virgin, and if she had not been infected with disease as a young girl she too might have had children. That she had to forsake Korn left her indifferent, for she knew that someone else would succeed him; and that she had to return to Teltscher also left her indifferent; it did not give her a moment's thought that he was waiting for her in Cologne and counting on her; she simply knew that he needed her so that he might have someone at whom to throw his daggers. Also the fact that she was to go to America left her indifferent. She had travelled about too much already, and America was a place like any other place. She was without hope and without fear. She had learned to leave men, but for to-night she felt that she still belonged to Korn. She bore a scar on her neck, and she felt that the man to whom she had been unfaithful that time had been justified in trying to kill her. If Korn had been unfaithful to her, however, she would not have killed him, but merely thrown vitriol at him. Yes, in matters of jealousy such an apportionment of punishment seemed to her fitting, for if one possessed another one would want to destroy, but if one merely employed another one could content oneself with making the object unfit for use. That held good for everybody, even for a queen. For all human beings were the same, and no one could do any good to another. When she stood on the stage it was light, and when she lay with a man it was dark. One lived to eat, and ate to live. Once a man had killed himself because of her; it had not touched her very deeply, but she liked to remember it. Everything else sank into shadow, and in the shadow human forms moved like darker shadows which melted into one another and struggled to detach themselves again. Everybody did nothing but evil, it was as though they could not help punishing themselves for seeking enjoyment in one another. She was a little proud that she too had brought fatality, and when that man killed himself it had been like an act of expiation and a compensation from God for her barrenness. Many things were incomprehensible, indeed all. One could not brood over the meaning of happenings; but when children came into the world the shadows seemed to thicken and become corporeal, and then it was as though a sweet music filled the world of shadows from end to end. That too perhaps was why Mary bore the Christ-Child up there above the red lamp. Erna would marry and have children: why had Lohberg not taken her, instead of that skinny sallow little thing? She contemplated Korn and found in his face nothing of what she sought; his hairy hands lay on the sheet and had never been tender and young. She shuddered at the sight of his red-lit fleshy face with the black moustache, and went softly on her bare feet across to Erna's room, slipped gently and insinuatingly in beside her, tenderly pressed herself against that angular body, and in this posture fell asleep.

Esch now comported himself already almost as a prospective husband, or, more correctly, a protector, for though they had not yet let fall any hint of their engagement, Esch knew what was due to a weak woman, and she allowed him to guard her interests. He was empowered to deal not only with the man who brought the mineral water and ice, but also with Oppenheimer, who at his suggestion had been entrusted with the disposal of the business. For in addition to his theatrical work the enterprising Oppenheimer undertook, whenever he got the chance, the disposal of real estate, and acted for various kinds of agencies, and he was of course delighted to devote all his attention to this matter. For the moment, it was true, his mind was distracted by other cares. He came to look over the house, but half way up the stairs he remained standing and said: " Quite inexplicable, this business of Gernerth; I hope to God nothing has happened to him . . . well, why should I bother, it isn't my business." And although he repeated this again and again as though to quiet his mind, he returned just as often to the fact that Gernerth had now been away for eight days, now, at the very moment when they were about to wind up the wrestling business and would need the money for the salaries and the rent, which was in arrears. That Gernerth, such a scrupulous fellow, should have allowed the rent to get into arrears, he could never have believed it. And when they had done so splendidly until recently, yes, quite splendidly. At present, of course, they weren't even covering their expenses. Well, high time that it was wound up. " And that ass Teltscher has let him go away without even leaving the desk key, and can't do anything. And Gernerth has all his money in the Darmstadt Bank! . . . too lofty and artistic, of course, Herr Teltscher, to bother his head about such matters."

Esch had listened indifferently until now, especially as it seemed quite understandable to him that Teltscher should be more interested in the American project than in the wrestling, which was coming to an end. But now he pricked up his ears: money in the Darmstadt Bank? He flew at Oppenheimer: " My friends' investments are in that money in the Darmstadt Bank; it must be handed over! " Oppenheimer wagged his head: " Really it isn't any concern of mine," he said, " but to make sure I'll send a telegram to Gernerth in Munich. He must come and put things in order. You're right, there's no use in beating about the bush." Esch approved of the idea, and the telegram was sent off; they got no reply. Anxious now, they sent two days later a telegram to Frau Gernerth, reply prepaid, and learned that Gernerth had not returned to Munich at all. That was suspicious. And at the end of the week they must settle up all the accounts! There was nothing for it but to notify the police; the police discovered that three weeks before all the money that remained in the Darmstadt Bank had been lifted by Gernerth, and now no more doubt remained; Gernerth had absconded with the money! Teltscher, who had stuck up for Gernerth to the last moment, and now called himself the stupidest Jew in the world for being diddled again by a rotter, Teltscher was suspected of having played into Gernerth's hands. In view of the theatre properties which Gernerth had left him in pledge, it took him all his time to prove his innocence; but that he succeeded in doing so really helped him very little—he had hardly enough money left to tide him over the next few days. Helpless as a child, he blamed himself and the world at large, kept on repeating tiresomely that Ilona would have to come, and several times a day pestered Oppenheimer with requests for an immediate engagement. Oppenheimer took the blow more philosophically, for it was not his money that had been lost; he comforted Teltscher: things weren't so bad after all, as owner of the theatre properties a man with the name of Teltscher-Teltini would make a splendid theatre manager; if he could only get hold of some working capital everything would be all right again, and he would have many dealings yet with old Oppenheimer. Teltscher saw the idea at once, and recovered his old vigour so quickly and so completely that in a jiffy he had hatched out a new plan and straightway run with it to Esch.

But by the last turn of events Esch had been more than annoyed. Although he had always divined, yes even known, that the American journey would never come to anything, and although simply perhaps because of this he had been so lax and casual in securing girls for it, and although finally he actually felt a certain satisfaction at the fact that his inner convictions had been justified: nevertheless his whole life had been directed towards this American plan, and he felt now shaken to the depths, for it seemed to him that the foundations of his connection with Mother Hentjen had been undermined. Where was he to go with her? and how did he stand in relation to this woman now? He had wanted her to see him as the lord and master of a whole troupe of artists, and now the whole lot had left him stranded in this measly fashion! He felt ashamed to face Mother Hentjen.

It was while he was in this mood that Teltscher burst in upon him with his plan: "Look here, Esch, you're a capitalist now, you could come in as my partner." Esch stared at him as though he had gone out of his wits: "A partner? Have you gone off your head? You know as well as I do that it's all up with the American plan." "One can earn a living in Europe," said Teltscher, "and if you want to invest your money profitably . . ." "Money? What money?" shouted Esch. Well, there wasn't any need to shout: he had heard casually that someone had come in for a legacy, said Teltscher, and it made Esch quite furious: "You've surely gone quite off your head," he shouted, "what is all this drivel? Isn't it enough that I've been swindled once by you . . . ?" "If that scoundrel Gernerth clears out, you can't hold me responsible for it," said Teltscher in an offended voice, "I've lost more than you, and because I'm down and out you needn't insult me when I bring you an honourable proposal." Esch growled: "It's not a matter of my losses, but the losses of my friends. . . ." "I offer you the chance of winning the money back again." That was a hope, of course, and Esch asked what Teltscher's proposals were. Why, with the theatre properties they could start something, Oppenheimer thought that too, and Esch had seen for himself that money could be made once one set about it with any degree of skill. "And if I refuse?" Then of course there was nothing for it but to store the theatre properties and secure an engagement somewhere with Ilona. Esch became reflective; so Teltscher would have to get an engagement with Ilona? . . . throw knives? . . . hm . . . he would think it over.

Next day he made inquiries of Oppenheimer, for with Teltscher the greatest caution was imperative. Oppenheimer confirmed Teltscher's statements. "I see . . . then he'll have to get an engagement again with

Ilona...." "He can count on me, I'll soon get an engagement for him," said Oppenheimer, "what else is there left for him to do?" Esch nodded: "And if he were to rent a theatre himself, he would need money...?" "I don't suppose you have the few thousands needed?" said Oppenheimer. No, he hadn't. Oppenheimer wagged his head to and fro: it couldn't be done without money; perhaps they could interest somebody else in the matter... how about Frau Hentjen, for example, who wanted to sell her business and would have a lot of ready money at her disposal? He had no influence there, said Esch, but he would put the proposal to Frau Hentjen.

He did not like doing it, it was a new task, but there was no getting round it. Esch felt the victim of a most insidious attack. Quite possible that in spite of everything Oppenheimer and Teltscher were in league; the two Jews! Why should nothing remain for a bounder like that but to throw knives? as though there weren't honest and decent work to be had! And what was that he had drivelled about a death and a legacy? They had driven him into a cul-de-sac, it was as though they knew that nothing once done could be undone; that Ilona must be shielded from the knives and the world saved from injustice, that Bertrand's sacrifice must not have been in vain, any more than the removal of Herr Hentjen's portrait! No, nothing could be undone, nothing must be undone, for justice and freedom were involved, freedom, whose safety one dared no longer leave to the demagogues and the Socialists and the venal hirelings who wrote for the Press. That was his task. And that he had to retrieve Lohberg's and Erna's money seemed to him a part and a symbol of this higher task. And besides, if Teltscher could not rent a theatre, then the money would be lost for ever! There was no escape. Esch set the accounts against each other, made his calculations, and the sum gave the clear answer: he must induce Mother Hentjen to yoke herself like him to the task.

When he saw this clearly his uncertainty and anger faded. He mounted his bicycle, rode home, and sent Lohberg a detailed account of Herr Gernerth's incredible and revolting crime, adding that he had at once taken reliable measures to protect the investors, and begging the esteemed Fräulein Erna not to be disturbed.

So it was all up with America. Now he would have to stay in Cologne. The door of the cage had slammed to. He was imprisoned. The torch of liberty was quenched. Strangely enough he could not feel angry with Gernerth. For the real blame lay with a greater than Gernerth, with one who in spite of all temptation and inducement had politely declined to fly to America. Yes, that seemed to be the law, though it was not justice; whoever sacrificed himself must give up his liberty first of all. Nevertheless his position remained an incredible one. Esch repeated: " Imprisoned," as though he had to convince himself of it. And almost with a quiet mind, disturbed only by the merest twinge of conscience, he told Mother Hentjen that they would have to postpone the American journey for the present, for Gernerth had sailed in advance to make arrangements for them over there.

Really one could tell Mother Hentjen whatever one liked; she had never shown the slightest interest either in the wrestling or in Herr Gernerth, and besides in what happened around her she saw only what it suited her to see. So now all that she saw was that the dreaded journey to a strange and adventurous land was abandoned, and the knowledge was like a warm and comforting bath into which her soul had been unexpectedly dipped, and which she had to enjoy in silence for a little before she said: " To-morrow I'll have in the painters, or winter will be on us and then the walls won't dry properly," Esch was taken aback: " The painters? But you want to sell the place! " Mother Hentjen put her hands on her hips: " Oh well, it will be a good time yet before we go,—I'll have the place painted, it must be kept in order." Esch shrugged his shoulders and gave in: " Perhaps it will pay us, might get it back in the price." " That's so," said Mother Hentjen. Nevertheless she could not shake off a faint residue of uncertainty—who knew? perhaps the American ghost had not been really laid—and she found it altogether right and proper that she should pay something for her stability and security. So Esch and Oppenheimer were very pleasantly surprised when they found little trouble in persuading Frau Hentjen that the theatrical business must be financed during Gernerth's absence; and she agreed just as readily to a mortgage on the house, which Oppenheimer with great foresight had brought with him. The transaction was concluded, and Oppenheimer pocketed a commission of one per cent.

In this way did Mother Hentjen become a partner in Teltscher's new theatrical venture; thanks to Oppenheimer's agency a theatre was rented in the bustling town of Duisburg, and Mother Hentjen could justly hope that she would share in really ample profits. Esch had insisted on three conditions: first that he should retain the right to inspect the books, secondly that before the liquidation of the affair the remainder of Lohberg's and Erna's capital investment should be repaid (that was only just and reasonable, even if Mother Hentjen had no need to know anything about it), and thirdly he forced Herr Teltscher and Herr Oppenheimer by a clause in the contract to strike out the favourite knife-throwing act from any conjuring performance that might take place. " Off his jump! " said the two gentlemen; but Esch held to his point.

Thus far things had gone smoothly and in irreproachable order. The sacrifice which Mother Hentjen had made had now bound him to her for ever and rendered his decision irrevocable. True, the hated business was not yet sold, but the mortgage was in a way a first step towards the annihilation of the past. And in Mother Hentjen's bearing too there were things that might be read as signs of the beginning of a new life. She contested his marriage plans as little as she had contested the mortgage, and she was filled with a gentleness such as no one had seen in her hitherto. The autumn had come, premature and cold, and she wore again the grey dimity blouse, and was often without her corsets. Even her stiff coiffure seemed to have loosened; no doubt about it, she devoted no longer the old, cunning solicitude to her outward appearance, and in that too one could see the difference between the present and the past. Esch stamped through the house. If one were imprisoned and without anything to do, at least one should get something out of it. All the same, this couldn't be called a new life. At breakfast he sat in the restaurant, and at supper-time he was still sitting there. Mother Hentjen made sundry remarks about wastrels and ne'er-do-wells who liked to give themselves airs, but she fed him willingly. Esch put up with everything. He studied his newspaper, and sometimes examined the picture postcards sticking in the mirror frame, glad that among them there was none with his own handwriting. And he supervised the house-painters and whitewashers in case they should damage anything. It was easy for Mother Hentjen to talk. A fine lot she cared for the new life! With women it was a simple business anyway—Esch had to laugh—they could carry the new life about with them anywhere, under their hearts, that was to say. That of course was why they had no desire to go out into the new world, they had everything already within their four walls and thought that they had only to remain sitting in their cage to be innocent!

There they scrubbed and polished and fancied that by satisfying their petty mechanical instinct for order they had done the trick! The new life in a cage? as if it was as simple as all that!

No, with petty devices, with petty modifications, the new life, the state of innocence, was not to be brought about in captivity. The unchangeable, the already done, the earthly work-a-day world, was not so easy to circumvent. The house stood there unchanged, and no mark of that measly mortgage was to be seen on it. The streets, the towers, round which the autumn wind whistled, were unchanged, and of the breath of the future there was no longer any trace. And really to rouse from sleep Mother Hentjen's memories and Mother Hentjen's past life, one would need to set fire to the four corners of Cologne and raze it to the ground, until not one stone remained on another. For what good did it do him that Mother Hentjen now wore her hair a little less stiffly brushed back? she still strutted unchanged through the streets, and people lifted their hats to her, and everybody knew what name she bore. God knows, he had not thought it would be like this when, for the sake of the sacrifice, he had taken upon him her advancing years and her fading charms. Even if her hair were to grow grey overnight, if all at once she were to become a quite old woman who no longer could remember anything about her life, irrecognizable to all who had known her, a stranger attached by no bond to her accustomed surroundings,— even that might be the new life! And Esch could not keep back the thought that every fresh child aged the mother, and that childless women did not grow old: they were changeless and dead, with no hold on time. But when women were awaiting a new life, then they were filled with the hope that time would begin again for them, and it was as though the thing that aged them re-won for them a new virginity; it was to them a hope that all living beings might attain the state of innocence, a prophetic dream of death and yet new life, the coming of the kingdom of salvation in this ageworn world. Sweet, never-to-be-fulfilled hope.

Frankly, such thoughts would hardly have been to Mother Hentjen's taste. Anarchistic ideas, she would have called them. Perhaps even with justice. For one had revolutionary thoughts and made revolutionary speeches when one found oneself in prison. And did not even know that one was doing it. Esch clattered up and down the stairs, cursed the house, cursed the steps, cursed the workers. A fine appearance this new life of his had! The clean patch on the wall where the portrait had hung was now painted over, so that one might almost imagine that the portrait had been removed merely that the patch might be effaced. For no other reason. Esch stared up at the wall. No, this was no new life at all that he had begun; on the contrary, to all appearances Time had been put back to where it was before. This woman seemed literally resolved to cancel and undo everything. And one day after cleaning and dusting she came down into the restaurant, sweating and blown and yet pleased with herself: " Ouf, you wouldn't believe how much the place was needing a doing up." Esch asked absently: " When was it done up last? " but suddenly it dawned on him that it must have been on the occasion of her marriage; he brought down his fist on the table so that the plates rattled, and shouted: " Of course the cage only needs to be painted each time a new bird is put in it! " A little more, and he would have thrashed her out there in the restaurant. He was tired of being forced to turn his head the wrong way, always having to look back into the past. And on the top of that she expected him to pay court to her; for she seemed in no hurry with the marriage. On every side, unconquerable, the accustomed rose up again. And the substantial strand of settled habit was palpable enough in all her new warmth and softness, and everything went to show that not only did she contemplate taking up her old life again and continuing it for all eternity, but it looked also as though she wished to reduce love and lover alike to the rank of an ornamental accessory, to a sort of painted wall decoration in the house of her life. And even that semi-official intimacy which she had granted him as in a manner of speaking a security for their bond, she was trying now to curtail again. When he went off to Duisburg to supervise Teltscher's accounts, not a word of appreciation did she vouchsafe him, and when he suggested that she might perhaps go there with him some time, she talked of impudence and retorted that he should stay there; that was the sort of company that suited him.

And Mother Hentjen was right! Yes, even in that! She was right to show him that in her house he was no more than a merely tolerated homeless orphan, one with whom nobody could have any real companionship. And yet she was not right! And that perhaps was the worst of all. For behind her apparently justified coldness, behind her apparently righteous condemnation, the old senseless fear peeped out again and again that he too—he, August Esch!—might simply have had his eyes on her money in wanting to marry her. That became quite clear when the deeds of mortgage arrived; Mother Hentjen pried about in the papers for a while with an offended expression and at last said reproachfully: " Why, I never thought the stamp duty would be so high! ... I could easily have paid it out of my savings-bank account if I had known," by which it became clear as the day that she possessed secret reserves and preferred to conceal them, yes, preferred to accept a mortgage on her house rather than let him know anything about them. Not to speak of putting them under his skilled supervision. Yes, that was what this woman was like. She had learned nothing, knew nothing about the kingdom of salvation, and desired to know nothing about it. And the new life was a dead letter to her. She was striving again to return to that commercial and conventional kind of love to which he had submitted and yet could no longer endure: it was a vicious circle from which there was no escape. What had been was inescapable and unalterable. Unassailable. And even if one were to annihilate the whole city—the dead would still remain the mightier force.

And now Lohberg next made his appearance. He showed that his suspicions were aroused because only the capital was to be repaid without his and Erna's promised share of the profits. That was surely the last straw. But when the fool hinted a little awkwardly and yet with a certain pride that every penny would be a godsend to him, for Erna was now well on the way, and they must seriously think of getting married, it sounded to Esch like a voice from the beyond, and he knew that his sacrifice was not yet complete. The faint and shabby hope that this child, for which he disclaimed all responsibility, might after all be Lohberg's, was swallowed up in the unearthly knowledge that for the perfect love he had chosen an atonement must be made, atonement for a blasphemy in which the menacing reverberation of murder could be heard, so that his love was cursed with barrenness, while the child conceived in sin and without love would irrevocably come to birth. And although he was full of anger at Mother Hentjen, who knew nothing of this and thought only of getting her house painted instead of sharing his terrors, he longed for such an atonement, and the wish that Mother Hentjen might raise her arm to kill him again became strong. Yet in spite of this he had to congratulate Lohberg, and shaking him by the hand he said: " Your winnings will be paid if I can do it ... as a christening gift." What else remained to be done? He passed his hand over his stiff closely cropped hair, and a cool prickling sensation remained in the palm of his hand. From Lohberg he learned also that Ilona was going to depart for Duisburg shortly. And he decided that beginning from the first of next month he must have Teltscher's books posted monthly to him in Cologne for supervision.

Yes, what else remained to be done? For it was all as it should be. Erna would have a child born in wedlock, and he would marry Mother Hentjen, and the restaurant would be freshly painted and laid with brown linoleum. And nobody guessed all that lay concealed behind the fine smooth surface, nobody knew by whom the child had been begotten who would now bear Lohberg's name, or that the perfect love in which he had sought salvation was nothing but a cheat and a lie, a blatant swindle to gloss over the fact that he was merely one among an indeterminate number of the snippety tailor's successors, he who had dreamt of flight and the joys of freedom, and yet now was condemned to rattle the bars of his cage. It was growing darker and darker, and the mists beyond the ocean would never thin away.

He began to avoid the house; it had become cramped and unfamiliar. He wandered along the banks of the Rhine, studied the rows of sheds, and gazed after the ships as they slowly floated down the river. He came to the Rhine Bridge, strolled on past the police headquarters to the Opera House, and reached the people's park. To stand on a seat and sing, with girls beating tambourines in front of one, yes, perhaps there was something in that, after all; to sing of the captive soul which could be set free through the power of redeeming love. Probably they were right, these Salvation Army idiots, in saying that first of all one must find one's way to this true and perfect love. Even the torch of liberty could not light one to redemption, for Bertrand, in spite of all his American and Italian journeys, had not been saved. It was simply no use trying to cheat oneself, one remained orphaned, one remained standing shivering in the snow, waiting for the redeeming grace of love gently to descend. Then, yes, then at last the miracle might descend, the miracle of perfect fulfilment. The home-return of the orphan child. The miracle of an ingemination of the world and of individual fate— and the child for whose sake Bertrand had stepped aside would not be a child of Erna's, but of another who in spite of everything would yet bring forth new life! Soon the snow would be coming, soft feathery snow. And the captive soul would be redeemed, hallelujah, would stand up on the bench, higher than he had stood who was accustomed to stand so high. And in his spirit Esch for the first time named that other who was to bear him the child by her Christian name: Gertrud.

Every time he came home he looked in her face. Her face was friendly, and her mouth conscientiously enumerated all the things that she had cooked that morning. And if August Esch had not any great hunger he turned away. It horrified him to think, and the knowledge was inescapable, that her womb was killed, or worse still that only a misbegotten monstrosity was to be expected from it. Only too well did he know the curse, only too well the murderous fury that was wreaked, and would continue to be wreaked, by the dead on women. Again the question tortured him so deeply that he did not dare to pose it . . . had children been denied to her, or had he and his predecessors only served her lust? His covetous rage against Mother Hentjen mounted, and once more he was in no state of mind to call her by the name by which the dead man called her, and he vowed that that name would not cross his lips until she had understood all that was involved. She did not understand, however. She received him submissively and matter-of-factly, and left him alone in his isolation. He tried to submit to fate; it was not perhaps a question of the child so much as of her readiness to have one, and he waited for some signs of that. But there too she failed him, and when, to prompt her, he dropped a hint that after their marriage they would want to have children, she merely returned a dry and matter-of-fact "Yes," but she did not give him the sign he was waiting for, and in their nights she did not cry that he must give her a child. He beat her, but she did not understand, and remained silent. Until he reached the knowledge that even that would not have availed; for even then the doubt would have remained, the ineluctable doubt whether she might not have begged Herr Hentjen too for a child, and the child whose father he longed to be might just as well have been one from Hentjen's loins as from his. No woman can hope to help a man caught in the despairing agonies of the unprovable. And deeply as he tormented himself, she could only look on in incomprehension; nevertheless it was only an unavailing gesture now, it was only, so to speak, a symbol and an intimation, when he beat her. His resistance was broken.

For he recognized that in the actual world fulfilment could never be achieved, recognized ever more clearly that even the farthest away places lay in the actual world, that all flight thither was senseless, as well as all hope of seeking there sanctuary from death, and fulfilment and freedom—and that the child itself, even if it came alive out of its mother's body, signified nothing more than the fortuitous cry of pleasure with which it was conceived, a dying and long since vanished cry which was of no significance for the existence of the lover who evoked it. The child would be a stranger, strange as that long past cry, strange as the past, strange as the dead and as death, wooden and empty. For unchangeable was the earthly though it might appear to change, and even were the whole world born anew, in spite of the Redeemer's death it would never attain a state of innocence in this life until the end of Time.

True, this knowledge was not very clear, but it sufficed to move Esch to organize his earthly life in Cologne, to seek a decent job and go about his business. Thanks to the excellent credentials which he possessed, he secured a prouder and more responsible position than he had yet occupied, and now once more earned all the pride and admiration which Mother Hentjen kept ready to expend on him. She had the restaurant laid with brown linoleum, and now that the danger of emigration seemed finally to be banished, she herself began to speak of their American castles in the air. He entered into her mood, partly because he felt that she was talking in this way to please him, and partly out of a sense of duty; for though he could hardly hope to see America now, he was resolved never to forsake the way that led towards it, never to turn back in spite of the invisible presence that followed him with the spear ready to strike, and an inward knowledge, hovering between dream and divination, told him that his way was now only a symbol and an intimation of a higher way which one had to walk in reality and in truth, and of which this one was only the earthly reflection, wavering and uncertain as a reflection in a dark pool. All this was not completely clear to him, indeed even the words of holy men, in which fulfilment and the absolute might be sought, did not help him. But he recognized that it was mere chance if the addition of the columns balanced, and so after all he could contemplate the earthly as from a higher coign of vantage, as from an airy castle rising from the plain, shut off from the world and yet open like a mirror to it; and often it seemed to him as though all that had been done or spoken or had come about was no more than a procession on a dimly lit stage, a representation which was soon forgotten and never palpably present, a thing already past which no one could lay hold on without increasing earthly suffering. For fulfilment always failed one in the actual world, but the way of longing and of freedom was endless and could never be fully trod, was narrow and remote like that of the sleepwalker, though it was also the way which led into the open arms and the living breast of home. So Esch was strange in his love and yet more at home in the earthly world than formerly, so that it made no difference and everything still remained in the super-earthly, even if for the sake of justice much still remained to be done for Ilona in the sphere of the earthly. He talked to Mother Hentjen of America, the land of freedom, and of the sale of the business, and of their marriage, as to a child whom one wants to please, and sometimes he could call her Gertrud again, even if she remained nameless to him in the nights when he lay with her. They went hand in hand, although each walked a different and endless road. When presently they got married, and the business was knocked down for an absurdly low price, these were stations on their symbolical road, yet at the same time stations on the road leading them nearer to the lofty and the eternal, which, if Esch had not been a Freethinker, he might even have called the divine. But he knew nevertheless that here on earth we have all to go our ways on crutches.

IV

When the theatre in Duisburg went bankrupt and both Teltscher and Ilona were once more left destitute, Esch and his wife put almost the whole of what remained of their means into the theatrical business, and soon they had finally lost their money. Yet Esch now secured a post as head book-keeper in a large industrial concern in his Luxemburg home, and for this his wife admired him more than ever. They went their way hand in hand and loved each other. He still sometimes beat her, but less and less, and finally not at all.

Biographical Note

Hermann Broch was born on 1 November 1886 of Jewish parents from the textile quarter of Vienna. The family background – his father was a wholesale textile merchant from Moravia, his mother the daughter of a Viennese wholesale leather dealer – singled him out, as the first of two sons, for a career in the family firm. Between 1904 and 1906 he studied at the city's Technical College for Textile Manufacture and at the Spinning and Weaving College at Mühlhausen (Mulhouse, Alsace) in preparation for running the Brochs' textile concern at Teesdorf near Vienna. The following year he went on a fact-finding mission to the USA to study methods of cotton production and patented a cotton-mixing machine of which he was co-inventor. Volunteering in 1909 for service in the Austro-Hungarian Imperial Army, he was obliged to discontinue his training with the artillery in Zagreb because of ill health. Later the same year he joined the board of directors of the family spinning works. Having been declared unfit for military service during the First World War, he acted as director of a Red Cross convalescent home for soldiers within the grounds of the Teesdorf factory, while continuing to manage the family business. Broch once self-deprecatingly referred to himself as a 'captain of industry', yet his organizational skills and the constructive paternalism with which the Teesdorf plant treated its work-force had come to the attention of the Austrian business establishment and he was invited to serve in the Arbitration Section of the Austrian Trades Court and the State Anti-Unemployment Bureau.

By the age of forty, Broch had established a reputation not just as a successful industrialist, but also as a formidable autodidact with growing interests in modernist literature and philosophy. Even before the outbreak of the First World War he had begun publishing essays in the prestigious Viennese journal *Der Brenner*; his first work of fiction, the 'Methodological Novella' (later to become part of his 1950 novel *The*

Guiltless), had appeared in Franz Blei's *Summa* (1918); and he had a string of literary, philosophical and cultural essays and reviews to his credit by the mid 1920s. These, together with the fact that he began moving in Viennese *Kaffeehaus* circles, brought him to the attention of Stefan Zweig, Karl Kraus and Robert Musil. Between 1925 and 1930, he enrolled for courses in philosophy, mathematics and psychology at the University of Vienna. His decision to sell the family firm in 1927 and devote himself to intellectual pursuits came as a shock to his family. Broch was no doubt primarily responding to the economic warning signals of the time, but the coincidence of this radical *volte-face* with his intensive work on the first draft of *The Sleepwalkers* suggests that what he called the 'terrible strain' of his 'double existence' had also been instrumental in bringing about the biggest change of direction in his entire life.

The next decisive event in his life was not to be of Broch's own making. In 1938 Hitler's forces invaded Austria and Broch found himself on a Gestapo list. Whether this was because of his Jewishness or his politics remains unclear. His postman is rumoured to have denounced him on account of a subscription to the Moscow journal *Das Wort*, but Broch's voluminous international correspondence with leading pacifists and socialists on behalf of his proposed 'League of Nations Resolution' would have been equally incriminating. Broch spent three weeks in 'protective custody' before being released and instructed to report to the Viennese authorities. He was astute enough to evade further Gestapo attention before successfully fleeing to Scotland where, thanks to the good offices of his English translators Willa and Edwin Muir, he eventually obtained a US visa. Broch arrived in New York in October 1938 and was destined to stay in the United States until he died of a heart attack in May 1951.

'One thing at least I have in common with Kafka and Musil', Broch once remarked, is that 'none of us has an actual biography; we lived and wrote, nothing more.' Certainly, by the time Broch arrived in the United States he was inclined to identify his life exclusively with his writing. He had successfully completed the transition from man of industry to internationally acclaimed writer, mentioned alongside Joyce, Gide, Musil, Huxley and Thomas Mann. *The Sleepwalkers* had enjoyed instant recognition in the early 1930s, although an unfortunate combination of adverse economic circumstances and National Socialist pressures meant that the novel would now be more helpful to him in his new host country than in Europe. Although he had written a number of other works since the appearance of the *Sleepwalkers* trilogy in 1931-2 – including *The Unknown Quantity* (1933), a complex of stories that would become the core of *The Guiltless* (1950), as well as drafts of *The Spell* and *The Death of Virgil* – his principal calling-card was still his first novel; MGM and Paramount were interested in film rights to it, people of the stature of Albert Einstein, Thornton Wilder, Aldous Huxley and T. S. Eliot thought highly of the trilogy, and its theoretical sections on the disintegration of values would, it was hoped, help Broch gain a post at one of the Ivy League universities. However, like many exiles of his generation, he was to remain on the margins of academe. A number of awards (from the Bollingen, Guggenheim and Rockefeller Foundations) enabled him complete his *magnum opus*, the novel *The Death of Virgil*, as well as a long cultural essay on *Hugo von Hofmannsthal and His Times* and, most important of all, to continue working on his Theory of Mass Hysteria, the major project of his final years. While the parallel German and English publication of *The Death of Virgil* in 1945 had benefited from a highly favourable reception, for the following six years Broch was to resume his intolerable 'double existence': having to devote himself – now reluctantly – once more to literary work (above all, his two incomplete novels *The Guiltless* and *The Spell*) in order to placate his publishers and re-establish himself in Europe, while struggling against the passage of time and various illnesses to complete his project on mass hysteria. Broch died, in the eyes of the outside world as the author of two literary masterpieces, but in his own view as someone whose main sociological, political and humanitarian work remained unfinished.

John White